Short Stories with a Twist

Short Stories with A Twist

Kevan Eveleigh

Evan Design Media Ltd.

Short Stories With A Twist

Copyright © 2024 Kevan Eveleigh

The moral right of the author has been asserted.

All rights reserved.
No part of this publication may be reproduced, stored in a retrieval system, or transmitted, in any form or by any means, without the prior permission in writing of the publisher, nor be otherwise circulated in any form of binding or cover other than that in which it is published and without a similar condition including this condition being imposed on the subsequent purchaser.

Published by Evan Design Media Ltd.

ISBN Number: 9798868313639

This is a work of fiction. Names, characters, businesses, places, events, locales, and incidents are either the products of the author's imagination or used in a fictitious manner. Any resemblance to actual persons, living or dead, or actual events is purely coincidental.

Foreword

Make a difference..................

Dear Reader,

I do hope you enjoy this book **Short Stories With A Twist**

Reviews on Amazon etc are hugely important to authors.

If you enjoy these tales I would be extremely grateful if you would take a few moments to leave me a review.

As a self-publisher I like to keep in contact with my readers. Please subscribe to my newsletter at www.kevaneveleigh.co.uk

I will keep you updated from time to time with information about my latest book projects and stories, as well as offering the occasional giveaway e.g. a signed copy of one of the books.

Thank you for your time - I appreciate it.

Kevan Eveleigh

A prophet is not without honour

except in his own country amongst his own kind

Preface

In my head, I began writing this book of short stories almost twenty-five years ago but life intervened and prevented me from fully putting pen to paper.
Writing is difficult, and as a lifelong writer and consumer of literature I know this from experience, but scripting a book is incredibly hard work. It is certainly not for the faint-hearted and I truly meant no pun there as you will see in a few pages from now.
Not only does it take time to write a book, but it also takes original thought and it's easy to copy or criticize other people's efforts.
I did not write this book to impress anyone. I'm too old for the vanity of being published. I only care that people have the chance to read and hopefully enjoy it. That will be rewarding enough for me.
The writing process is a road full of obstacles, the biggest of which is self-doubt. The author's mind plays tricks and tries to tempt him into writing perfect page after perfect page, but one day the penny drops and he realizes it is an impossible task, for there is no such thing as the perfect
book.
The most important thing is always the reader, and it is often too sadly overlooked. Grammar is secondary, and months of productive work may be lost in its minutiae.
Above all people, it is you as the reader, who is the least interested in being sidetracked with a full stop in the wrong place. You are the true King or Queen in the book writing equation and I never forget it. It is for you I write.
Please note that I have used artistic license in this book so that some

of the facts will vary from reality, but as the late, great actor David Niven once said, "Never let the truth get in the way of a good story!"

Twenty years or so ago there was a news story in the South Wales Echo accompanied by a large joyous photograph of a member of staff who was retiring after over forty years in the same school.

I wrote this book of short stories to fulfill a personal silent promise to myself and to one of my early junior school teachers, the lady in that article, a fabulous influence by the name of Miss Colson, who sadly is no longer with us.

Without a second thought, that same week I went to Cwrt-yr-Ala junior school and with the agreement of the Headmaster, I walked across the small hallway, descending a flight of six or seven stairs before knock-ing and entering the classroom on the right.

Decades had passed since I was a seven-year-old in her charge and back in the sixties she would have been quite a young woman but her support, nurturing and encouragement have stuck with me always.

She did not recognize me of course but with one or two quick clues she knew exactly who I was and tears came to her eyes on her penultimate day of teaching.

After some initial chit-chat, she put her hand to her mouth and a worried
look came over her face, followed by an abject apology.

She pointed to the staff cupboard and explained that for nearly forty years she had kept my multiple schoolboy stories and that of a girl class-mate
safely stored, for she had always thought they were too good to simply throw away. It was overwhelming when she said that of all the thousands of pupils she had taught it was only our work that had been retained.

Tears streamed down her cheeks and she confirmed that at the beginning of that final week, those "great works" of junior school literature had finally met their end in the school dustbin as she reluctantly cleaned out her Aladdin's cave.

The other girl pupil wrote amazing stories, quite different to my own, and I always listened attentively for her imagination was unrivalled both then and possibly in any literature that I have ever read. She captivated her childhood audience in a way that Enid Blyton would be proud of, in a descriptive language that kept the listener hooked.

That girl's name I keep private, for I was to learn years later, she died young, the victim of a motorbike accident. She was less than twenty years old and a born storyteller was lost that day.

On leaving that junior classroom for the last time I promised that one day I would complete my book, so please go kindly out of respect for June Colson, a marvelous, self-sacrificing person, who gave her life to that noblest of professions, teaching.

I truly hope that you enjoy my efforts. All I ask is that you keep an open mind, put any prejudices behind you, and enjoy it if you can, but please remember "if you can't say anything good, be a real grown-up and say nothing at all".

Kevan Eveleigh
March 1st, 2024
E: info@kevaneveleigh.co.uk
W: www.kevaneveleigh.co.uk

Epigraph

To my parents

"Good night God bless"

Contents

1	Cliff Hanger	1
2	The Hand That Rocks the Cradle	5
3	Naked and Afraid	39
4	Faint Heart	45
5	The Mighty Caribou	79
6	King of New York	107
7	A Good Suit	173
8	The Graduate	213
9	White Knight	235
10	I Wish I Could Fly	253

Chapter 1

Cliff Hanger

It was life or death.

Fate had brought him to this wild, inhospitable place.

His survival rested on one decision, to jump or not to jump.

This was a critical moment, for he could live, or he could die.

Jump and he might survive, but to do nothing and remain here, meant certain death.

Across the valley floor, moving away from him in the distance, he noticed an irregular column of ant-like orange figures, slowly ascending the spine of a steep, rocky outcrop.

It was a mountain rescue team accompanied by a bright yellow helicopter.

In vain he tried to cry out for help, but his weakened voice was drowned by the swirling wind as the weather closed in around him.

They were as oblivious to his ordeal, as he was to theirs.

He stood at the edge of the perpendicular cliff face, some four hundred feet from the top.

Below him, was another eight hundred feet of sheer blind terror, a vertical wall of limestone, punctuated by the occasional dwarf sapling of equally condemned, occasional vegetation.

Eight feet away, to the right-hand side, across a bottomless void, lay the end of an impossibly dangerous scree slope.

This ran right over the cliff edge, like a jagged, frozen waterfall, down to oblivion.

The slippery, stony incline, was part of a steep gully, galloping up to the freedom of the mountain ridge above.

"Focus!"

"Aim for the scree slope and you will be safe."

Trembling, he balanced on the very edge of the precipice.

His heart rate increased dramatically, uncontrollably, until he could hear it pounding inside his ears.

Involuntarily, his head and whole body vibrated and began to shake.

Panic gave way to fear, and in turn, to horror, as he summoned the courage to look down.

His mind was now racing; everything had been going so well.

He asked himself, "How has it come to this?"

Yesterday there had been two of them trapped in this place, but now he stood alone.

At the bottom of the cliff lay the dead body of his older brother.

The certainty of salvation had lain there for the taking.

All he had to do was to get it right, but he failed.

For several hours he lay dying until his battered, bruised, and crumpled body was consumed by the darkest night when death became his friend.

Once again, he looked out at the bright orange coats in the far distance, now much smaller than before, huddling together, against the oncoming storm as the weather worsened.

He made his decision.

Composing himself, he looked up, and then down.

To maximise his opportunity, he tried to stand up to his full height against the fierce, sapping wind.

His heart rate immediately exploded, faster, faster, faster until he started to lean forward, to let gravity take over. He flexed his legs; he took a huge breath of air ……………now!!!!!!!!!!!!!

* * *

Self-doubt is the most powerful of enemies.

Stepping back, he stopped himself just in time.

He couldn't do it.

Fear welled up inside him, the distress encouraging his emotions to run primitively wild.

Confusion had overtaken sanity.

Now he had lost track of how long he had been there.

He was cold, hungry, thirsty, and bereaved.

Logic kicked in; there were only three possible outcomes.

If he jumped and failed, he would die.

If he stayed here, he would surely perish.

If he jumped and got it right, his life was saved, and his future certain.

***

His mind was made up in an instant. There was only one real choice.

Jump.

Once again, he moved to the edge of the ledge; a stiff westerly breeze hit him straight in the face, and he wobbled a bit, but there was no stopping him this time.

He had to be positive, he had to be bold.

Call it brave, call it survival instinct, but with one last dramatic inch forward he looked resolutely down into the abyss below.

Then he analysed the distance to the scree slope.

"Do it!"

He stood up to his full height, surveyed all around him for the last time, and with all his might he kicked himself off, and away from his rocky prison.

Then nothing.

He began to fall, past the scree slope into the open space, plummeting towards the valley floor, losing height quickly, and all at once the ground started to rise towards him.

Falling, falling, falling, when suddenly an unexpected, unscripted, almighty battle, began to take place.

This was an age-old, colossal contest between evolution and gravity.

Luckily for him, evolution emerged as the victor, as he spread his juvenile wings and soared through the air to join his parents in the distance.

One day, every eagle must take its first flight.

Chapter 2

THE HAND THAT ROCKS THE CRADLE

New-born babies are God's ultimate blank canvas, for we all arrive in this world physically and mentally naked.

Two such infant princes were on a collision course that would be thirty-six years in the making, but only one would emerge as king.

The contrasting paths of a poor Irish labourer, and a rich, titled Englishman, were set.

It was the duty of their parents to prepare them for the conflict.

Fathers and mothers have much to answer for, but of men and women, we know this.

The hand that rocks the cradle rules the world.

* * *

Even if they are loathed to admit it, all males know that motherhood means being a goddess amongst the mere mortals that are men, for maternity is something they can never share.

Mothers are a breed apart behaving in a way that no man can logically understand.

There is no failing here on behalf of man or woman; they are simply different beings. Their brains, actions, thoughts, and deeds are influenced by primaeval factors which evolved long ago.

The man is traditionally perceived by society as the hunter, the defender of the cave, while the female is the nursemaid who brings up the children, yet also the cook and the cleaner, or so we are often led to believe.

It is the female who naturally spends the most time with the infant, forming that amazing bond, that connection, the invisible umbilical cord between mother and child which can never be truly cut.

There are many old sayings that mothers impart to their offspring when raising children. Little sentences and favourite sayings are subtly introduced, to influence, indoctrinate, and teach their little ones to be better people. One such pearl of wisdom endures to this day.

"Manners maketh man."

* * *

"Every cloud has a silver lining," was another favourite saying of Ma O'Reilly's, which she used with all nine of her brood to create hope for the future, even in the darkest days when there was not enough food on the table for all.

Nine children, four girls and five boys, all the product of a big Irish Dublin labourer and his pint-sized seamstress wife, were indeed a handful, especially at the turn of the century when there was scarcely enough nourishment for the mice.

Brendan, the oldest child and first prince of the O'Reilly's, had been born a healthy bouncing boy, whose uneducated mother and father, with hardly a penny between them, had been blessed with good parents before them, good health, and nothing else.

Joseph O'Reilly was the patriarch, and he would take any work he could find, however low-paid, to feed his family.

His diminutive wife was small, wiry, and undernourished, but mentally and physically as strong as an ox, despite her worn-out appearance.

Woe betides the man or woman who picked on the O'Reilly's when Mary Ellen was about.

"She may be seven stones soaking wet but pound for pound she's the best fighter in all of Ireland!" Joseph would often tell their friends.

While Joseph worked long hours digging ditches and labouring, Mary Ellen chaperoned the little ones, took in washing, ironing, and mending, and all the while kept a tiny home immaculately clean.

Everyone contributed to the family fortune, whether it was stirring a cooking pot, running errands, or working with their father.

Despite the everyday poverty of sleeping three to a bed in shifts, eating thin stew for days on end, where gristle was considered meat or the shame of wearing rude clothing often mended several times over, Mary Ellen taught them all the difference between right and wrong, as her mother had taught her.

In the O'Reilly house, Mary Ellen rocked the cradle, and she ruled the world.

Joseph was a simple, genial man, built like the side of a barn who, when upset, had a temperament like a runaway bull, unless he was in the company of his good wife, for Mary was the calming influence that kept him out of many a scrape.

The O'Reilly brood of Brendan, Mary, Patrick, Finbarr, Bridget, Maeve, Thomas, Margaret and Sean never once complained about it being a tough life, for they knew no other existence.

That they all would work hard for a living was a given. None of them expected to do anything less.

The children were brought up with good old-fashioned values, instilled with a solid work ethic, and eventually released, one by one into the world to be decent, respectful people.

All of the O'Reilly's were good Catholics or as good as they could be, in a poverty-stricken Ireland at the beginning of the twentieth century.

Joseph worked twelve hours a day or longer when the light allowed, six days a week.

On the Sabbath, he rested, if you could call it that, by doing odd jobs for his family or anyone else who needed his help.

"I have some overtime digging out a new trench," the clerk of works on a building site might say, and in a flash, Joseph would volunteer his services.

"I'm available boss," Joseph would shout, and he would work all night if it added just pennies to the family pot.

Occasionally, on a Saturday afternoon after work, Joseph would go to the pub for a couple of hours, with a tiny budget, if Mary Ellen thought the finances allowed.

Finnegan's Bar was a tired, unapologetic pub, on the corner of their sorry street. The furniture inside was sparse, to say the least, mostly rude unmatched chairs and tables made of salvaged wood.

"Good evening, sir, come into my lovely establishment, tarry a while and make new friends," the landlord would say to passing strangers to drum up business.

"The beers for drinking, but the furniture's only for decoration and bonfires!" he would continue as he let out a huge belly laugh.

Ma' O'Reilly, as the women of the street called her, knew Joseph had to have his time with the men, to talk about men's things, to let off steam after six savage days of labour.

In the more bountiful times, when discussing their husbands and children, she would often joke with her friends.

"A little drinking and gambling with your mates, as long as there's enough food for the kids never hurt anyone!"

All the women in that poor Irish catholic community would nod in agreement.

"As long as he is not chasing other women about like some of them other fellas; he's a good, kind man, and I don't want him here under me feet. I have got enough to do with nine kids, and I don't want him here making any more!"

Clodagh and Shannon, her closest neighbours, would then conduct pretend charades of a male Irishman grabbing female breasts or worse, and they would laugh an honest laugh until tears rolled down their faces.

Just like Joseph's man time at the pub, this was Ma O'Reilly's woman time with her friends. Husband and wife had an understanding, and they loved each other more for it.

Everyone knew the big-hearted O'Reilly's and they all respected them. Not for their chattels for they had none. They loved them because they were pillars of the community who helped those less fortunate than themselves, who might at any time seek their assistance.

* * *

"Give me the boy until he is seven and I will give you the man!"

The words rang out over the billiard table, as the fifth Lord Esher of Buckinghamshire responded to the news that he had been born a son.

"Congratulations old boy, the Prince of Esher has finally arrived, the contract is completed!"

The flamboyant Earl of Gloucester, together with the aristocratic Lord Wiltshire, reached for the brandy glasses to jointly celebrate this long-awaited result.

Unbeknown to Lord Esher they had been betting on it, and the Earl of Gloucester was five pounds richer for guessing the year, in a wager laid five years previously.

"I didn't think the old boy had it in him, eh what!"

"Well, apparently so, here's your five pounds, don't spend it all at once!"

Three months to the day, from the birth of his one and only son, the father presented a baby boy to a well-to-do county set at his christening in the family church.

This was a titled, immaculately dressed gathering of upper-class relations and friends. Later that afternoon the well-heeled guests were served champagne and oysters from the priceless family silverware, at the private estate which had been home for many hundreds of years.

"Give me the boy" was a phrase used by the men of this ancient family on the birth of a son and spouted at the christenings of the first male born.

The words were only spoken about the child that would secure the family heritage, to carry their hopes and dreams on lonely shoulders into the distant future.

Seven years was all they had available to educate, indoctrinate, and influence this golden child in the ways of the gentry.

Tradition had it that shortly after his seventh birthday, the child would be rudely plucked from his mother, unceremoniously packed, and delivered up to Eton School, where the ancestors had been sent before them, to ensure they remained a cut above all other classes of person.

When an Esher barked people listened. You would be a fool not to give them your ear, lest they take a lot more.

The House of Esher had power. These were distant relatives of Queen Victoria, who whilst not top of the titled tree in Buckinghamshire, certainly had a lofty view from their impressive stately home.

The difference between the two heirs born so many miles apart was simple.

In the House of Esher, the hand that rocked the cradle was his father.

* * *

The fifth Lord Esher was an arrogant, selfish man, who if not given his way, would resort to tantrums.

His wedding to Lady Isobel Cavendish was a marriage of convenience, in an age-old social equation designed to unite two noble families against the onslaught of the common man.

He had money and a disagreeable persona, but no suitors, while she had suitors, and was universally liked, but had no money.

Isobel was an only daughter, and her family's financial future could be guaranteed by marrying the caddish Lord Esher, who she did not respect and could never love.

The Cavendish line had been a handsome one over hundreds of years, Isobel proving testament to this with a soft, gentle complexion, beautiful long brown hair, and a winning smile.

Her parents were respectful people, but death duties and taxes, the lack of a male heir, and the march of time had made them vulnerable to the emancipation of the people.

Although she had many admirers, none of them had the financial resources that she needed to save the ancient, crumbling family home, and ensure her parents lived out their days in peace.

Isobel was made of resolute, determined, Cavendish stock, and despite months of self-doubt, she chose the most difficult path.

Being of noble blood, and therefore a suitable partner, she agreed to marry Lord Esher and give him a son. For his part, he would underwrite the finances to fulfil her family's wishes.

The wedding was attended by the full county set, but it was insincere and without love or respect.

Lord Esher did not get to the marital bed on the wedding night and preferred instead to drink port and play cards with his ex-army pals until well after midnight.

When one of them asked if he was going to consummate the marriage in the early hours after the wedding day, he answered in his grotesque, arrogant manner.

"I told her to keep it moist and warm, I'm paying for it, so I'll have it when I bloody well want it, deal the cards!"

Liaisons between the two parties were cold and brief. The firstborn child was a girl named Abigail, who was quickly forgotten, if ever really noticed by Lord Esher, for he took no interest in his daughter.

A baby girl was a real disappointment, and this despicable man did not mind publicly calling his wife a failure, as he bemoaned his lot.

It was a bigger upset for Isobel, for she knew she must share the marital bed with the loathsome Lord Esher until the contract was complete. Not only did this mean loveless, purposeful sex but it also meant she played high-stakes poker with the chances of catching the latest brothel-born disease.

It took almost six years of self-sacrifice for Isobel to render the account even. A baby son was thankfully delivered at the next birth and Lord Esher's breeding arrangement was done.

In those first seven years of the baby son's life, Isobel tried desperately to dilute the influence of his father, to rock the cradle herself, but her efforts were to no avail.

The increasingly insufferable, single-minded Lord Esher, having fathered an heir, no longer sought the necessity of Isobel's bed, and she was frozen out of the natural mother-son relationship.

With his life's duty now achieved, Lord Esher's arrogance seemingly knew no bounds.

He occupied his time with hunting, shooting, fishing, drinking, gambling, and whoring, having aligned himself to the birds of a feather that existed in his social class.

At his private club, Carmichael's on the London Strand, he believed everyone was entitled to his opinion.

"I shall bed every woman in the county between the age of consent and the age of collapse, except the ugly, fat ones," and he would guffaw loudly with his obnoxious counterparts.

Lord Esher, much to the chagrin of Lady Isobel, had one last task to complete before he fully retired to his dark, decadent social whirl. As far as he was concerned it was his responsibility, as it was his father's before him, to make a man of his baby boy before he was sent to Eton.

The boy was christened Crispin after his famous grandfather, Cornelius Crispin Esher, who had fought in the British army with great distinction.

There was a long-standing military tradition of the firstborn joining the Queen's Guards, the noblest of the English regiments.

Baby Crispin's father, the woefully inept current Lord Esher, was a retired colonel, a rank gifted by status and not by deeds.

It meant that every single day, discipline and punishment were a way of life for the young boy.

By the time he had reached the pageboy's age of seven, Crispin had been nurtured into an unlikeable child, with an unfortunate, arrogant manner, in a mirror image of his father.

His manufactured personality was a combination of selfishness, slyness, and sullenness, which all added up to a basketful of emptiness, for he had no friends.

This isolation made him a spiteful, vengeful, and dangerous character, and there was nothing Isobel or Eton could ever do to change it.

Lord Esher, "had been given the boy until he was seven," and the result was there for all to see.

* * *

The contrast between these two male heirs, born on the same day in two different countries could not be greater. The expectations of each man were far wider than the three hundred and thirty miles which separated their hopes and dreams.

Brendan, the first son and heir of the O'Reilly's had inherited the granite physique of a traditional Irish navvy from his father, and his mother's genteel, genial manner, which endeared him to everyone he met.

He was, however, no pushover, and many a man foolishly mistook his camaraderie and bonhomie for weakness.

Outwardly, Brendan O'Reilly was a good, honest, and likeable man but inwardly, just like his mother before him, as tough as they came.

Crispin, the future sixth Lord Esher, the heir apparent and lord in waiting, had sadly been sculpted into a replica of his father, with none of the endearing qualities of his mother, who had lacked any influence in his upbringing.

He had a constant need for immediate attention, with intolerance of any person lower down the food chain than he, for Lord Esher had been taught he was the most important man in the room. He was arrogance and birth right at its worst.

Their paths were set, and one day they would cross.

* * *

Brendan, as the oldest son of the O'Reilly family, had worked for as long as he could remember, helping his father, his mother, and later his siblings in any task that added family value, in any function that helped ease their plight of poverty, in a tough, unforgiving world.

At sixteen, after much discussion, it was decided that he should continue his education further afield and shake off the surly bonds of need.

It was time to open the "box."

One Sunday evening in late June 1916, after a dreadfully cold, unkind, and harsh Winter made worse by the Easter uprising of the people against British rule, Joseph O'Reilly with a great ceremony took down the family box, which sat on a rude dresser in the living room.

The wooden vessel contained all the O'Reilly fortune, both spiritually and physically.

Inside, lay the total sum of their life's hard labour.

Opening the old, neatly polished, handmade oak box, inset with a rusty lock that didn't work, Joseph proudly pulled out the entire contents and placed them on the rough-hewn wooden table in front of the family. This was a momentous event that would, in turn, be repeated many times over in years to come, as each sibling left the nest.

First, he laid out two old, faded photographs of Mary Ellen's parents, followed by a thread-worn bible, and then the locks of hair from their nine children. These had been kept so that the parents would remember them always.

Next, he took out some fabric from a distance relative's wedding dress, and a hand-carved wooden shamrock, whose skilful maker had long been forgotten. Finally, he laid out all the money they had saved over the years.

Seventy-two pounds, seven shillings and two pence now lay on the table and the younger children stood wide-eyed for they had never seen such a vast sum.

This was the family treasure, the total wealth fund. Not bad for a man whose basic wage in a city of too many labourers and not enough work, was just one pound per week, for sixty hours of back-breaking graft.

It had taken blood, sweat, love and tears to build up their children's inheritance, and this was the first time so much as a penny would be spent.

With the absence of words, he took out £5 in coins of various denominations and handed them to the wide-eyed boy.

His mother, the toughest of them all, subtly wiped away a tear, lest someone see her moment of weakness.

Joseph looked his son and heir firmly and squarely in the eye.

"It's time my boy!"

They had spoken of this moment on many occasions and now Brendan stood up proud and true for he had always known that this was his destiny.

"It is to England you must go to make your fortune, for these are tough times in Ireland, and there is not enough food for all of us. You must take your chances over the water."

Mary Ellen, having regained her composure, confirmed that the time had come.

"Father is right, your two uncles are in London, so you'll have a start."

"Yes, Mamo."

Brendan spoke the term of endearment that he had used since he was knee-high to the height of an Irishman's working boot.

His dad interjected and concluded the arrangement.

"Then it's done, there is no need for fine words, you sail tomorrow, and we all wish you the very best, good luck my son, and God bless."

Brendan was humbled, sad, and elated at the same time.

"I'll pay you back Da, and Ma I'll send money regularly to help with the kids like, you know I will."

His mother looked lovingly through tired, misty eyes, at the little boy who had grown up too soon.

"That would be lovely my son, your Da, me and the kids will look forward to it."

Joseph removed himself to his favourite chair, while Mary Ellen O'Reilly baked too many scones for the journey, as Brendan's siblings circled and fussed around him like there would be no tomorrow.

They were right. At 5 am the next morning, with the house at peace, Brendan O'Reilly set out on the next leg of his life's journey.

In London town, he would meet head-on whatever triumphs and tragedies it may hold.

* * *

As soon as he was out of the hands of his wet nurse Lord Esher began barking orders at the unfortunate child, scolding continually, criticising every effort to please his father in trying to do something right.

Lord Esher was doing what he had learned to do at Eton, and that which Crispin would learn all in good time.

This was a measured, mirrored behaviour, just like the ancient public schoolboy pastime of fagging, where the smaller, newer children were made to run errands and perform tasks for the older boys.

All the while they knew that if they made any mistake there would be a beating or some other drastic, savage punishment.

The only outlet for these young victims was to pass their personal grief down the line to boys lower down the food chain, and so it went on year after year.

Dishing out punishment cleansed the soul, gave one a sense of power, and made one feel better about oneself.

It was the public schoolboy way, but unfortunately, it often manifested itself in many an adult, who had previously served his time in that famous educational establishment.

The nervous infant, a product of his father's ruthless discipline, was sent up to Eton just after his seventh birthday. He would be known, as was the fashion for a son and heir, by one of his father's unused titles.

Crispin was introduced to all and sundry as Lord Cirencester, one of a cluster of titles the family had acquired over eight hundred years or so, by supporting the winning side in both politics and battle.

As he was led to the servant-attended carriage, silently waiting at the front of the splendid Esher House, young Cirencester, a weak and sickly child at best, began to cry, for he wanted nothing more than to retain the status quo, and remain with his mother for a good while longer.

Change meant fear, and he took after his father, a born coward, who for all his bluster, would rather command a battalion from the officers' mess than engage in hand-to-hand combat on a level battlefield.

In essence, he was one of life's milksops, who would forever hide behind privilege and title.

He looked wantonly at his mother for salvation, but she was helpless against the will of Lord Esher.

The words he heard were short, sharp, and savage.

"Stop crying boy and grow up!"

Crispin, who had a deep fear of his father's anger, whimpered.

"Listen, boy, do not disgrace the good name of this family with your girlish antics or they will eat you alive at Eton!"

The father was prophetically right, for the good Lord Cirencester would be a round peg in a square hole, just like his father before him.

It took him less than a month to find his position in the hierarchy of his school year.

He proved to be useless on the sports field, showing not a hint of any backbone when the going got tough.

One morning young Lord Marlborough returned from the tennis court to the changing rooms, distraught at losing in the first round of the tennis house matches, having been randomly paired with Lord Cirencester.

His classmate the Earl of Worcester was tying up his laces ready for the next match.

"How did you get on, Marlborough?"

"It was so embarrassing, they murdered us! He's useless at everything and I was handed the short straw in the pairs match. Why me?"

"He's a chicken at rugby too, that's why we lost our house match because he is afraid to tackle," added Worcester.

"We need to teach him a lesson and toughen him up!" offered Marlborough.

At that moment the unwitting Cirencester walked in from the tennis court and a war cry of "get him," ran out through the open windows across the main quadrant.

Cirencester was stripped to his underwear, and Marlborough pushed his head down the toilet while Worcester pulled the flush.

His peers ran off to the tennis courts laughing, whilst Cirencester cried. He was bottom of the class physically, socially, and academically, except for a flair for art, which he had been gifted from his mother, which was never developed.

Eton so it seemed, would not just be an education, but an open prison with spot punishments from staff and pupils alike for all perceived misdemeanours, be they real, imagined or invented.

Cirencester survived but hated every waking moment.

For the rest of his life, he used his title as a mask of power, to inflict punishment on anyone whom his arrogance would allow, often for no reason other than his pleasure or revenge on mankind.

His mother died young at the tender age of fifty-two, from some unknown virus the doctor had said, but the rumours of syphilis abounded in the kitchens and servants' quarters.

On the demise of the fifth Lord Esher just two years later, the staff judged themselves to be correct, the nastiest of brothel-borne diseases confirmed in a post-mortem.

Aged just thirty, Lord Cirencester, by natural selection, became the sixth Lord Esher in title, land, power, and wealth.

He smiled a rare smile to himself as he buried the loveless, emaciated bones of his father in the family plot at the village church, which the family had supported for hundreds of years.

***

Wealth and title are rays of sunshine to those who inhabit life's shadows.

Crispin now surrounded himself with the worst people of his set, who fawned over him at every opportunity to ingratiate themselves, for he was one of polite society's brightest jewels, basking in the trappings of inheritance. The sycophants enjoyed the reflected glory, but not one of them spent time with him because they liked him.

By the age of thirty-six, he had truly become his father's son, with the same selfish, sour personality, and prickly, mean-spirited temperament.

Life was one long party of drinking, whoring, and gambling.

A playboy's life was a delight, especially when you were a Lord of the land, and given to expect every possible favour and grace from classes of people lower than yourself.

When, like his father before him, he had gambled and drunk to his heart's content at Carmichael's of the Strand, he would make a show of calling his unworthy accomplices to action.

"Let's go and find some virgins!"

A loud cheer would go up from the over-privileged unruly mob.

"What else is a gentleman expected to do when in London?

They would all laugh in unison, and then follow him like penguins to a house of ill repute, where they would fornicate, play Russian roulette with syphilis, and argue about the price of bought pleasure.

The Summer was well and truly in the swing when one Saturday evening at the brothel Lord Esher turned his mind to new entertainment.

"Remember chaps, we are at Ascot on Thursday, bring your wallets, I've heard there will be some new two-legged fillies in town, after all, it's the debutante season you know!"

"Hear, hear," replied the entourage.

"I'll see you all there!" concluded Esher.

Then he swept out, ignoring the doorman who in fifteen years he had never called by name, and flounced into the back of a taxi which took him to his London apartments.

After a couple of calmer days of relatively quieter drinking and gambling, Lord Esher pulled into the private member's car park at Ascot in his chauffeur-driven Rolls Royce, quite alone.

Shaking off the cobwebs, adjusting his clothing, and practising a crocodile smile he barked.

"Wait here!"

The instruction could mean anything from ten minutes to fifteen hours, and without a single thought for another human being, he gravitated towards the noise, the colour, the gambling and the splendour that is Royal Ascot in June.

***

The early morning was wet, but the excitement engendered a warm exciting feeling that countered the damp, sullen air.

For Brendan, it wasn't just a new dawn, it was like being reborn. A new life was about to greet him across the English Channel.

He was used to hard work, and no stone would go unturned in his quest to make his family proud, by sending them the money he had promised.

Brendan was at the ferry port an hour early, amongst the first of the itinerant Irish labourers and navvies making their way to the promised land on the other side of the Irish Sea, where industrious days guaranteed a steady wage and food in your belly.

The fare cost three shillings and sixpence for a one-way ticket or six shillings open return. He bought the former. Brendan did not intend to come back this way.

As the ferry left the dock on time at 8.00 am sharp, Brendan said a silent goodbye to Dublin and locked the memories in his saddened heart, but he knew he must go forward with his life if he was to prosper and better himself.

It was a wild crossing on heavy seas, but the young traveller enjoyed every minute of this nautical experience, even though he was a bit green about the gills. This was the start of a brand-new adventure; the shackles were off, and it was thrilling.

Arriving at Holyhead in north-west Wales just before two in the afternoon, the long hike to London began. If he got a move on, he could get a good four hours and 16 miles in before dark, before setting up a rude, temporary camp in an unknown field.

"Which way is London?" he enquired of a security guard as he exited the ferry port. The guard had a stock answer which he had offered to many an Irish prospector over the years.

"Go east young man, go east to the rainbow's end and there after some three hundred miles you will find your pot of gold," and with that, the guard bowed low as if he had delivered his main lines in some imagined theatrical masterpiece.

"Thank you kindly, sir, thank you kindly," said Brendan, repeating the message in a friendly, humorous way, as only Irishmen can.

"Heh friend, did you say you were walking to London town?" asked a tall, red-haired young man, strolling past at just that moment.

"I did, and it's a good stretch of the legs this gentleman has told me."

"I'm Flynn," said the stranger, as he thrust out his hand to Brendan "I'll be going that way to look for work meself, two is better than one in a strange land methinks, shall we team up?"

Brendan shook the outstretched hand of Flynn and in that moment made a contract that would last a lifetime.

With one touch of his cap to acknowledge the thespian guidance from the security guard, and Brendan leading the way, they were out through the main gate and away up the hill. By the time they got to the top, they only had another two hundred and ninety-nine miles to go to London Town.

Flynn was about two inches taller than Brendan, with a shock of red hair and a thunderstorm of freckles about his face that meant he could never deny his heritage, however many elocution lessons he may take in the future.

They were an ideal match, both set on the same goal of making their fortune in London.

Brendan was strong, determined, and purposeful, with a wonderfully accommodating nature and friendliness born of his parents.

He was complemented by the energetic Flynn, who was a real character, also from a large family of twelve, and driven by them to improve his lot in a sorry world.

Flynn O'Hegarty to give him his full name was impish, funny, a teller of tall tales, a dreamer, a schemer, a grafter and born for this moment it seemed.

Together this new partnership would make their way to London and strive to earn some of its riches for themselves and their fine families back home.

Brendan was lucky with the weather for there was little rain, just the occasional shower. It was the windy days that made the walking harder.

If he followed the old map his father had given him, he estimated that without any real hills to climb, and walking forty-five miles a day, he would be at his uncle's lodging house in Whitechapel on Saturday morning, one week after leaving home.

It was a faded, creased, and well-used piece of paper with illegible notes written on it, the very map that Uncle Ted had posted back to Joseph from London some ten years before with this day in mind.

For two days the young men ploughed on and on, meeting their daily needs by drinking water from streams and feasting on an endless supply of now stale Irish scones, which Brendan readily shared with his increasingly impressive new partner.

After the scones had all been consumed Flynn for his part, "needs must" he said, contributed to the arrangement by knocking on the occasional front door of an inviting cottage.

Upon its opening and with a unique Gaelic charm, he would bow grandly, a huge irresistible smile shining from that leprechaun's face.

"Would you have a drop of water for two young Irishman travelling to London town to make their fortune please?"

Next, he continued fluidly with a well-practised "and if we can do any jobs for you to pay our way, we would be more than happy to oblige?"

It worked about one time in ten, but it depended on who answered the door.

"If you don't ask you don't get," said Flynn roguishly.

Young men were avoided as they would perceive the knock and request as some sort of threat or challenge.

By contrast, young women would seem very interested but quite nervous, and they quickly learned to avoid them if possible, or keep conversation to an absolute minimum. They certainly did not want any trouble coming their way because of people misinterpreting their actions and deeds.

The winning targets for Flynn seemed to be old men and middle-aged women, on whom his genial countenance worked like a dream for reasons he never knew. "Just call it charm!" he said to Brendan.

They received water, cake, apples, hearty meals, accommodation in outhouses and barns, and on one occasion even lemonade.

On finishing the unexpected treat Flynn bowed low.

"Thank you, Mrs Fine Lady of the House, that was truly the nectar of the gods!"

The phrase and big-hearted "thank you" saw him awarded with a second glass.

In return, they cut hedges, dug holes, put up fences, laboured, and carried all and sundry as requested, for as long as it took to complete the work awarded by their temporary employer.

The planned week's journey became twenty-one days, including a seven-night stopover on a farm in Staffordshire, where they ate pork sandwiches, and drank rough cider in return for fruit picking.

By the time O'Reilly and Flynn arrived together at the guesthouse home of uncles Kieron and Ted, the two boys were a well-honed team, destined to work together in partnership for the rest of their lives.

* * *

In the twenty years since his arrival on the dock at Holyhead, Brendan had worked hard to earn a good living.

His uncles, through their connections, had given Brendan and Flynn the start they needed, digging roads and ditches for the local corporation, and moonlighting for cash as builder's labourers where opportunity allowed.

By the time he was twenty-one, Brendan had started his own business, with Flynn as his foreman, and they worked from dawn to dusk, selling their labour wherever it was needed, on building sites, in railway yards and on the ever-increasing road network.

At thirty, they had a hundred men engaged in good honest work, including four of Flynn's brothers and three of Brendan's.

On the last day of every month, Brendan and Flynn would go to the bank at lunchtime and send money home to Dublin, to grateful families, fulfilling the promises they had made years earlier, as part of their exit strategy from their most humble beginnings.

Brendan O'Reilly and Flynn O'Hegarty were well on their way to being millionaires and known all over east London as two outstanding Irish characters, who would drink, sing, and gamble whenever they had a chance, but they never missed a day's work, regardless of how hard the partying had been the night before.

They lent money to new arrivals from Ireland "so they could get themselves sorted," thus creating a loyalty that intrinsically bound these new men to the company of Irishman that Brendan and Flynn had amassed.

The company paid wages when men were injured, or on very rare occasions, they were sick.

Employees of this grand Irish-owned company and their wives slept soundly and contently under the patriarchy of Brendan O'Reilly, the leader of the merry band.

One evening in early June 1936 at The White Hart in Whitechapel, the regular abode and spiritual home of the incoming Irish, they held a huge shindig for the fifteenth anniversary of Brendan and Flynn's company.

The two founders took their proud Irish wives, but their eight children were legally too young to attend, so the landlord pulled the curtains, and it became an Irish street party in a pub, where grateful men, women and small children all attended regardless of age, with a few local policemen included on the exclusive guest list.

At 9 pm before the beer got hold of him, Brendan stood up and gave a simple speech on behalf of his family to all in attendance.

He thanked everyone for coming, and his parents for teaching him manners and respect, and for once in the past giving him the grand sum of five pounds from the family box.

An emotional Brendan spoke highly of Flynn for his friendship and support, before giving a rousing rendition of "Molly Malone", accompanied by what seemed like the whole of Dublin on tour.

There were tears and handshakes all around, and Flynn stood up to respond.

To a man, woman, child, and policeman, the pub fell silent.

"Ladies and gentlemen, I have known this man, this good honest Irishman, since fate threw us together one Summer morning when we got off the ferry in East Ireland, a place the English call Wales."

A loud cheer and round of applause rang out for their Welsh Celtic soulmates.

"Hush now, hush now," said Flynn, his accent stronger among his kinsmen and women.

"I could say much about this man, but I do not like to dilute the quality of what I must say, so I'll just say this," he said wiping a tear from his eye.

"He is a true man, a good man, a fine Irishman, for it was a good day for all of us when we met him!" and another cheer rented the air.

"Today we must acknowledge him as "the King of all Ireland", and I pledge my loyalty to him!"

Then Flynn hugged the gentle giant he had just lauded, and there wasn't a dry eye in the house.

The name stuck, and henceforth Brendan would be known as the "King of all Ireland", and in the streets of east London, Flynn would be known as "the Prince of Dublin".

Even as rich Irishmen, they remained true to their origins, maintaining the dignity, self-respect and work ethic that always endeared them to their fellow man.

The celebration did not finish in the pub that night, because on the following Thursday a trip had been booked for twenty-four mad Irishmen and women to go to Royal Ascot.

The women planned to dress up and taste champagne for the first time, whilst the men couldn't wait to let their hair down with a little drinking and gambling.

Brendan and Flynn's company, "Dublin Construction Ltd.", had agreed to pay for everything. It was to be the celebration of a lifetime.

The men hired magnificent trendy Ascot regalia, set off with Irish-themed emerald-green cravats, each lapel sporting a shamrock for the sake of the old country, and the loved ones they had left behind.

The women bought expensive dresses and hats, all paid for by calloused Irish hands, and felt for once in their tough lives, just like royalty.

When they stood in the presence of the King of all Ireland, they almost believed it.

The bus picked them up outside The White Hart at 8 am on Gold Cup Day.

"This will be a Thursday to remember!" said Brendan as he got on the bus.

"As long as you don't drink too much!" replied Flynn.

The women had one ambition. They all hoped to see the King and Queen of England.

"Good luck with that," said Brendan prophetically, "none of the toffs will be looking out for us!"

* * *

In the homes of the gentry, they may still say "give me the boy until he is seven and I will give you the man" but the question they never ask is "will he be a good man?" It is simply assumed that he will be, but on this fine day, the Lord of the English would be measured against the King of the Irish.

Lord Esher, the privileged, uncaring, selfish playboy, would have his chance to assert his authority over the little man, the common man, and the peasant.

It was in the natural order of things, for he was born to title, and that lofty inherited position in society came with a great advantage, for it automatically suggested to everyone that he was a class above the rest, and that it must be recognised without question.

In contrast, despite the poverty, the trials, and the tribulations of an uncertain start in a Dublin slum, Brendan O'Reilly was a lover of life, and respectful of his fellow man.

However difficult and impossible things sometimes seemed, he was the eternal optimist. As far as he was concerned "every cloud had a silver lining", as his mother had ingrained into him so many years before.

On Thursday, June 18th, 1936, at Royal Ascot, the two unlikely combatants, with nothing in common, except a birthday, would meet for the first and only time, when two very different worlds would collide.

The two heirs would be pitted against each other for the entertainment of others, but only one would emerge as the better man.

* * *

The Irish party were having a fantastic time enjoying fancy clothes, gambling, and drinking to their heart's content, but bothering no-one.

Brendan decided he wanted a bet on the second race and went over to have a £1 each way wager on Dublin Adventure at twenty to one. It made no sense as the horse had run five times and only been placed third twice against lesser opposition, but that was what made it fun.

Meanwhile, Lord Esher was sat with his cronies on the balcony of the members' bar, drinking gin and tonic, whilst ogling the new crop of young women being eagerly paraded like lambs to the slaughter, by title-hunting mothers.

Bored with the charade, Lord Esher also decided on a whim to rush down and back a horse in that race.

Without warning, he leaned over and picked up his blazer from the back of the seat, and making no announcement, slyly slipped away.

The horse he had chosen was a two-year-old named Upper Class in a five-furlong sprint. This filly had been tipped by Snuffy Cartwright at the club last week.

Snuffy had a distant cousin, who knew a landlord of a pub near some racing stables in Newmarket, in which the stable lads of the horse regularly drank.

"Not quite from the horse's mouth but close enough," thought Lord Esher to himself.

With less than five minutes to the "orf", as the toffs referred to the start of a horse race, and not wishing to share his inside information with anyone else, he tripped quickly down the stairs, past security, and out into the bright sunlight, which blinded him for a second.

Using his gambling experience, he rushed off towards the Tattersalls area of the racecourse, where the betting odds on offer from the bookmakers were always better than the silver ring or member's enclosure.

He looked up at the boards with seconds to spare, and chastised himself for his tardiness, as he quickly realised that the odds of Upper Class had dropped to sixteen to one.

Glancing around, with the defeated look of a drowning man looking for a lifeboat that wasn't there, he saw odds of twenty to one were still being given by a bookmaker who was arguing with a punter over a losing bet. The dispute was just enough intervention to cause a delay in reaction, and the price stood.

He turned quickly and barged his way through the thronging masses, paying little heed to his manners or the movement of other people. He charged right into a bright green cravat that demarked the forty-six-inch barrel chest of Brendan O'Reilly.

The Lord Esher bounced off the stationary Irishman like the rain off a windowpane, landing unceremoniously on his seat, as the crowd split their reaction between good-hearted laughter and kind assistance.

"Sorry," said Brendan "are you ok sir?" he offered, realising the self-inflicting victim was a bit of a toff.

"I'm fine you idiot!" came the rude reply from the preoccupied Lord Esher.

In a flash, Lord Esher was back on his feet and made it to the targeted bookie with seconds to spare, without so much as a glance back at his new acquaintances.

The Irish contingent ignored him and moved away from the bookies to gain a better vantage point higher up in the stand, whilst Lord Esher told the bookmaker he wanted £20 on the nose on number twelve in this race.

"Which horse sir?"

"Upper Class you fool, number twelve, come on man!" barked Esher with that time-served arrogance and disrespect that was his trademark.

The bookies assistant wrote the slip which read in printed ink at the top "Martin George, bookmakers since 1902." Handwritten below was "Upper Class £20 at 20/1 to win".

Lord Esher relaxed and reached into his blazer for his wallet, allowing himself a little grin, knowing that he alone had beaten the marketplace.

He tried one inside pocket, then the next, and then put his hands in the side pockets. A look of horror came over his disgruntled face.

Next, he looked to the floor in the vain hope that he had dropped the wallet, but it was nowhere to be seen. The £300 he had brought with him, and the wallet was gone.

"£20 sir or no bet, they are about to go, thank you."

"Stupid man!" said Esher, expecting the bookie to be at his beck and call like his adoring entourage.

"Can't you see I've been robbed, call the police!"

"Book closed no bet," shouted the bookmaker, as he turned to review his board and speak with his assistant, so they could work out their potential liabilities and profits on the race.

"Call the police!" Lord Esher barked at the bookmaker while checking his empty pockets one more time.

"You call the police!" said the heavily built bookmaker.

"Sling your 'ook," he said sternly, "we don't need time-wasting types like you around 'ere, this is for honest people, so buzz off while you can still walk!" thus confirming that amongst the real people, the title meant nothing, but honesty was everything.

Lord Esher looked around and not for the first time in his life, he realised he had not a friend in the place. He slunk off through the crowd, relentlessly checking his pockets for the stolen wallet.

As he took flight back to his island of privilege, he was serenaded by the on-course commentary of the second race.

Five furlongs for the cream of this season's two-year-olds would be over in just under a minute at Royal Ascot, where the finest young sprinters staked their claim for the following year's classic events, such as the One and Two Thousand Guineas and the Epsom Derby.

Upper Class did not get a mention out of a field of ten until both Lord Esher and the horse approached their final few yards.

As he breezed past security into his private sanctuary, the commentator wildly and enthusiastically lauded the fast-finishing rank outsider, who passed everything in its sights to finish first as tipped.

Lord Esher had lost £400 in winnings because some thieving Irishman had stolen his wallet, and he was beside himself with anger.

As he entered the sanctuary of the member's enclosure, he saw a uniformed officer talking to a security guard and made a beeline for the pair of them.

"You there, I say, you there, I am Lord Esher! Fetch me your most senior officer, I've been robbed by a gang of Irish thieves!"

The young policeman was immediately intimidated, and the threat of a Lord of the realm being robbed on his watch could be career-defining. It was the type of response Lord Esher was more used to, and he suddenly felt back in control.

The nervous junior office asked Lord Esher to accompany him to the steward's office, where he knew the chief constable was personally conducting security matters, with a royal presence at the event.

On arrival at the door, Lord Esher simply barged in, much to the astonishment of the race stewards and officials in the room, followed apologetically by the young policeman to whom Lord Esher had reported the crime.

Looking for the senior uniform in the room, Lord Esher, with an air of authority befitting his station in life said, "I am Lord Esher and I have been robbed of three hundred pounds by a gang of itinerant Irishmen, and I need your help now!" raising his voice to accentuate the immediacy of his requirement.

The chief constable was a long-standing, time-served officer, who had seen it all before, at least twice.

"And where did this happen sir?" he said, paying just the right amount of deference to his lordship and no more.

"In the betting ring, Tattersalls, they are there now, you need to arrest them and get my money back, and put them all in jail, do you understand?", Lord Esher instructed thunderously.

The back of chief constable Robert Mulcahy had been well and truly rubbed up the wrong way.

"King, Wilson, please go with Lord Esher and investigate this matter, whilst we finalise details for the royal party," said Mulcahy thus cleverly trumping Lord Esher's demands with that of a higher authority that even he would not question.

Lord Esher, followed by the two officers, walked swiftly and purposefully to the Tattersalls area of the racecourse, where the next race was about ten minutes away from starting.

Scanning the bookmaker's temporary signs, Lord Esher locked on to a big-shouldered man in fine Ascot clothing, surrounded by an exuberant gang of friends in a sea of emerald-green. As the big man turned to address one of the bookmakers the Irish cravat was unmistakable. This was the thief.

"There he is, there's the ruffian who stole my wallet, and no doubt many others, arrest him at once!" ordered Lord Esher, much more confident in Tattersalls with the long arm of the law on his side.

Under huge protest, Brendan O'Reilly was branded a thief, grabbed by the arms, arrested, and shamefully taken away in full view of the watching crowd.

He was manhandled forcefully to the member's enclosure, at which point his supporters were headed off by the security team, leaving the bewildered Irish thief to face the music alone.

With royalty to protect, Robert Mulcahy was a busy man, and he was not in the mood to suffer fools gladly.

He glared at the Irishman.

"What's your name?"

"Brendan O'Reilly sir, of London and previously Dublin, Ireland," came the short, uncomplicated reply.

"And did you steal this man's wallet?"

"No sir, not me sir, I'm not a thief!"

"He should be shot, they should all be shot, all these Irish layabouts coming over here just to thieve and steal!" complained Lord Esher.

By now, word of Lord Esher's dilemma had reached his compatriots in the bar. The door opened behind him and in swanned eight of his finest acquaintances, led by the pompous, thoroughly dislikeable, Lord Tavistock.

"I say Esher old man, sorry to barge in and spoil the fun and all that, but I think you've got my blazer," he suggested, offering an identical blazer to Esher to the one that he had been wearing in the Tattersalls enclosure, before putting it on the table for the chief constable to examine.

"In your effort to bust the bookies, you've taken mine by mistake, you cad!" said Lord Tavistock, saying in jest that which everyone had believed for years.

"Is there a wallet with £300 in the inside pocket?" asked the bored chief constable.

"Yes, I believe there is!" laughed Tavistock, enjoying this schoolboy moment, as he plucked the missing article unceremoniously from the blazer in a drunken fashion.

Lord Esher was now full of self-anger for looking like such a complete fool in front of the lower classes. He hadn't been bested since he inherited his title and became a lord of the land.

He glowered at O'Reilly with that arrogance and swagger that endeared him to no one.

In his hallmark surly fashion, he took off Tavistock's blazer before throwing it to his playboy associate.

Next, he hurriedly put on his blazer, and then spun around and targeted the door for a swift exit, without so much as a word to those assembled in the chief steward's office.

Lord Esher's weak-kneed, sycophantic entourage paid homage to their compatriot by avoiding eye contact and stepping aside to let him take the lead as they fell in behind him.

The chief constable of Berkshire, a man who himself had risen from humble beginnings, stood in the noble Lord Esher's intended path. He moved not a muscle and not even Lord Esher would have the temerity to barge such a senior-ranking official out of the way.

Brendan O'Reilly stood at the table, an oasis of calm in a sea of fools.

Looking a picture in his hybrid Ascot and Irish finery, he maintained his dignity, suppressing his anger with great aplomb, whilst just wishing it would all be over soon, so he could go back to his friends and the racing.

As Lord Esher made to step around the chief constable it was the latter, immaculate in the uniform befitting such an esteemed office, that stepped in front of him, blocking the path of the retreating complainant and his band of merry socialites.

"Out of my way!" barked Lord Esher with not so much as a please or a thank you.

"I think you have forgotten something, don't you?" replied the chief constable holding his ground, thus preventing the easy escape of his quarry.

"Forgotten what?" snapped Lord Esher trying to intimidate the senior officer.

The chief constable glanced at Brendan O'Reilly who remained motionless at his station, expressing nothing but the politeness and respect his parents had taught him in old Ireland.

"I think you owe someone an apology."

For not the first time in his life, Lord Esher was not in control. His mind travelled back to that lonely and vulnerable place Eton, and the vicious memories it held. He was rattled, and his sullen manner gave away his anger.

Lord Esher knew exactly what the policeman wanted him to do, but he couldn't stomach the thought of it. To countenance apologising to an Irishman was unthinkable. As far as he was concerned, the Eshers were Lords of the land, the landed gentry, a class above the common and criminal classes, who had been put on this earth to serve them.

"Out of my way, I have nothing more to say, come on let's get out of here," he retorted, expecting his arrogance to win the day.

Adding nothing to the conversation he scowled back at Brendan O'Reilly, and with his head at boiling point, tried to squeeze past the chief constable one more time, but the policeman held firm, his bagman now adding himself to the blockage in front of the frustrated Lord.

"Lord Esher, I must tell you that if you have nothing to say to Mr O'Reilly then I'm afraid we may have to invite you down to the station and engage in a discussion about wasting police time," said a calm chief constable Mulcahy, for he had now assumed the upper hand.

It was a standoff, a siege, but it was a battle that Lord Esher could not win, as he made one more attempt to use his position to gain an advantage.

"Do you realise who I am Mr Policeman? I am Lord Esher; a cousin of Queen Victoria and I have friends in very high places!"

He emphasised the word high, to separate the distance in social standing between all assembled.

"That's very interesting Lord Esher, but unless you have something to say to Mr O'Reilly, and I'm sure you do, you will have to talk to your friends in high places after our little discussion at the station. Your choice, I won't ask again."

With that Mulcahy stared straight at Lord Esher who was beginning to melt under the pressure.

There was a cold, sullen, extended pause.

"Very well, but you shall hear more of this!"

In a closing scene to this unexpected equestrian pantomime, two impassive policemen watched Lord Esher turn to Brendan O'Reilly and address him directly.

"What's your name again?" he asked Brendan, truly expressing a lack of empathy for his fellow man. His followers sniggered, thus making matters seem just a little worse than they were before.

"O'Reilly sir," said Brendan touching his head respectfully in that wonderful Irish way, his cap removed as a mark of respect on entering the building minutes earlier.

"Well O'Reilly, I'm sorry if I've caused you any bother and here is £5 for your trouble," he said as he pulled a crisp, white, unused note from his wallet.

His friends billed and cooed and assumed freedom had been bought.

They looked at the two officers of the law to see their response, but none was forthcoming, and the door remained closed.

The accused thief looked Lord Esher straight in the eye, and there was a long pause whilst everyone in the room awaited his reaction, wondering what he was thinking, but they would never guess.

Brendan thought of his tough childhood in Dublin, his hard-working parents, his siblings, and his arrival in London town.

He remembered meeting Flynn and the hike to the capital city, finishing with an early morning thirty-mile walk into town to find his two uncles.

Most of all he remembered the signs they saw, as he and Flynn passed some of the guesthouses used by the working men who were building that great city.

Sign after sign simply said, "No blacks, no dogs, no Irish."

It had been the first time in his life he felt unworthy, and ever since then, even on a good day, he felt he was a second-class citizen at best, in a country whose social hierarchy he never quite understood.

The dawning of reality had left a mark on that early June morning as they strode towards London.

It had lingered all these years, despite his business successes and positive contribution to society.

"Was he as good as the next man?" he asked himself for the last time.

Brendan was a man of his word and respected by all. It was in his breeding, in his childhood education, and "in the manner of the doing" as they said in Dublin.

He stared at the sad, pathetic figure of Lord Esher, surrounded by his sycophants, but alone in this life, and at that moment, Brendan knew he was the better man.

"Thank you, sir, I accept your apology," said the gentle Dublin giant to Lord Esher, "but please I don't need any handouts, I've money of me own, money I've worked hard for, so thank you but no thank you!"

Lord Esher recoiled at this semi-scolding and could not wait to get away.

Before he had the chance to leave, Brendan, perceived by Lord Esher as a lowlife, uneducated, itinerant Irish thief, looked at the chief constable, then glanced at the assembled crowd, and said as his parting shot. "I need to apologise also."

Lord Esher spun around and took a step towards him, desperate for any crumb of solace, some justification for these onerous circumstances he found himself in.

"We both made a mistake sir, you thought I was a thief, and I thought you were a gentleman," said Brendan, leaving no chance of any possible comeback.

Lord Esher's blood ran cold, his face went white, and the chief constable and his bagman smirked, while the decent, fun-loving, intelligent Irishman said no more.

Witnessing the way Brendan conducted himself, you could easily imagine he was indeed the superior man, the King of all Ireland, for he had acted with the diplomacy, respect, and good manners his parents had always taught him.

To the uninitiated onlooker, the good Lord Esher appeared to be a peasant, in the company of a fine Irishman, with a touch of class.

The hand that rocks the cradle rules the world.

Chapter 3

NAKED AND AFRAID

I was as naked as the day I was born.

Beckoned by the bright, golden light of a clear Somerset morning, I reluctantly removed my unshaven, unsteady body, from the unbearably hot bed.

One half had not been slept in, whilst my side was strewn with cast-off, crumpled and creased bedsheets.

If my wife had seen the state that the bed and I were in, I had no doubt she would hit the roof. We were both a complete mess.

Next, I made my way barefoot across the carpet and stubbed my toe on a bedroom chair, cursed loudly, and then walked past the full-length mirror on the landing.

I stopped for a moment to regroup and could not help noticing that my birthday suit needed ironing, but it was a tiny distraction from my mother, father, and son of a hangover.

"I'm getting too old for this!"

I descended the stairs to the kitchen and salvation.

"Never again will I drink with the pub landlord, and I mean it this time; me and The Three Ferrets are finished!"

My head was pounding, beating brutally, like an oversized hammer on the side of an industrial waste bin, echoing with every accelerated heartbeat.

I was hot, sweaty, thirsty, and focused on just two things, water, and headache tablets.

As I hit the bottom stair of my new home, the telephone rang.

I unsteadily picked up the receiver, holding the bannister rail for balance.

After a short delay came a curt, unfriendly voice, that I did not recognise.

"I'm watching you!"

"And I'm watching you too!"

Flippantly I had replied, expecting my twisted friend to laugh and reveal his true identity, but not so.

The stakes were raised.

"I'm watching you right now!"

This was the voice of an angry, elderly man.

I was just about to put him straight when he shouted.

"The people who live in that house are on holiday!"

He was correct, I had bought the house three weeks previously and had been away for the last two of them, returning just last night.

"Well, I'm back!"

"No, you're not!"

"Yes, I am!"

"No, you're not!"

"Yes, I am!"

The pantomime continued, getting louder and louder, angrier, more stressed, with every contested exchange.

I decided enough was enough, and that I would impolitely invite him to leave the conversation when he screamed at me.

"Have you or have you not got a silver car parked on the drive outside that house, right now?"

It was so aggressive.

I froze, I was now as still as my stationary silver BMW on the driveway, the very car in which we had returned from our holiday last evening.

This was no friend and certainly no joke. Whoever it was, had the advantage.

I felt like a rabbit in the headlights of an oncoming vehicle, not knowing which way to turn for salvation.

My pulse began to race.

"Who was this menace?"

In my nakedness, I stole a glance through the blinds, looking studiously at the other houses from different angles, like a super sleuth seeking a clue that no one else could see.

My head was spinning.

I rushed upstairs to a better vantage point and carefully peeked through the curtains, but I could see no one.

The man at the other end was now raging at me.

"The people who live in that house are on holiday, have you or have you not got a silver car on their drive?"

"Am I still dreaming?" I asked myself.

Then the final killer blow.

"I have been filming your every move, and my camera is focused on you right now! There is no escape; I'm going to phone the police!"

I gagged.

I choked.

I could not take it all in.

I was speechless.

My hangover was at once suspended by the adrenalin surge.

Questions, questions, questions!

Do we own this house?

What has he been filming?

Am I being stalked?

I was naked and afraid.

* * *

Then I seemed to enter a state of suspended animation.

My thoughts were scrambled in a sort of dreamlike virtual reality.

Rapid ideas, bullet after bullet raged through my fragile head.

"It was the estate agent!
"No, it was the solicitor!
"No, they were in it together!
"We have been robbed, and we don't own the house!"

Having considered all the possibilities, I came to an unsavoury conclusion.

"No, it was my fault. I did not pay enough attention!"
"What will my wife say?"

I was terrified we had been conned.

* * *

My wife and I had bought this lovely new home just three weeks ago, before going away for a fortnight.

Until our return last evening, we had only spent seven nights in this new abode.

It was a small enclave of a dozen detached Georgian family homes, with strikingly neat front lawns, which announced to the world that the residents therein had too much time on their hands.

Retirees and pensioners, with wonderful interests such as wine tasting, rambling, and vegetable growing, were the denizens of this civilised Utopia.

Yesterday evening we had arrived back in Bristol from a fortnight skiing in France, to discover my wife's father had been taken ill and admitted into hospital in Romsey, just outside of Southampton, where he had lived his adult life.

Sally set out to visit him, whilst I stayed at the property to supervise the previously scheduled installation of a new kitchen the following morning.

She arrived at his bedside to find all was well with her father, and the panic subsided, but then decided to stay the night just in case of any turn for the worse.

It was Friday evening, so I arranged to go to the pub and share some bonhomie with the local landlord, a very good friend of mine.

One drink turned into far too many, finishing with, "one for the road," "one for luck," "one for Ron," and "one for later on".

My dreamlike state was broken by a hysterical voice coming through the telephone.

"Get out of that house right now, I know what you are doing, I'm going to call the police!"

On a sixpence, I bit, I snapped, my aggression surpassing his previous efforts, and my voice dropped three decibels.

I replied most firmly, expunging just enough aggression to make him consider his options.

"You CAN do what you like PAL!"

My stalker was good at dishing it out, but he didn't expect this reaction.

He was quickly on the back foot, less confident, diminished, and suddenly defensive.

The unknown, uninvited caller shouted back.

"Are you or are you not speaking to me on the telephone right now from 26 Wilson Road, Bristol?"

I gasped, I hesitated, I composed myself and forcefully said.

"NO, I am not!"

"Oh dear, I'm awfully sorry, I think I've got the wrong number!"

Chapter 4

FAINT HEART

THE beautiful teenage goddess smiled a perfect goodbye.

Now resigned to failure, they stared at each other through fixated teary eyes, and both lamented an opportunity missed.

In a gesture of surrender to the inevitability of fate, she leaned towards the window and waved goodbye to her unnamed, unknown suitor.

This vision of loveliness would affect him for the rest of his life, but now it vanished into a Mid-West sunset, like a beautiful princess disappearing into a children's fairy tale castle.

Standing alone, heartbroken because of his lack of confidence, all caused by a faint heart, he vowed that never again would he let shyness prevent him from taking a chance.

Chastising himself, he whispered out loud.

"The faint heart will win the fair maiden!"

Olivier Cartier, never saw Juliet again.

* * *

The previous evening at 10 pm his father had shouted to him in an overly theatrical French accent designed to hit the chosen target. His voice carried across the tired upstairs hallway of their small, comfortable, Chippewa Falls riverside home, penetrating the sweltering, early summer Wisconsin heat.

"Bon nuit my boy, don't be late for the bus in the morning! The windy city waits for no man. Not even the magnificent Olivier Cartier!"

"Hardly likely," Ollie thought, for as hard as he tried, it was proving impossible to do the teenager thing that year.

It was too hot for him to lie in bed till lunchtime, while away the day, and wait for the excitement of the night-time with his friends, and the unrelenting task of impressing the girls he dreamt of meeting along the way.

That Summer of 1978 was insanely warm throughout the Mid-West and staying in bed was proving too difficult. Tomorrow would be an important day, one that could change his life. There was no way he would be late in the morning.

This ninety-mile trip to the state capital and his interview at Capitol Oil Inc. might decide where he would be in ten years' time, what he would earn, and maybe who he would eventually marry.

"Best get to bed," he suggested to himself.

Come rain, come shine, come anything, Friday would come soon enough, and the young career seeker would be on time for the bus, the train and anything else the interviewer could throw at him.

His mother was already in bed, tired from long years of shift work washing dishes in local hotels, and more recently working as an assistant in a nearby mental hospital. They were both menial jobs, but the latter paid slightly more.

Cash was hard-earned and softly spent, for money was tight and times were always tough.

His parents had given everything they had, working all the hours God had sent, but they didn't have much to show for it, except a lack of credit cards which they had never applied for, a bank account that was never allowed to go into overdraft for fear of getting into debt, and their three children who they would love until the end of time.

Only through his efforts could he realise the ambitions they had set for him to better himself. Their greatest hope was to get Ollie away from the social handcuffs that were freely provided by blue-collar living.

"Education and drive are the keys," his mother would always say in their more philosophical moments together.

His father went to his bedroom, and he instinctively knew he had picked up his clock.

"Clocks wound tight, arms wound tight, dodgers tight," he said as Ollie heard him go through his pre-bed routine, ensuring the clock went off as planned at the pre-appointed time.

Where he had learned this eccentric behaviour, and what dodgers were, Ollie never knew, but it worked. His father was never late for work in forty-six years of employment, man, or boy.

Excitement gave way to fatigue, and he thought of what tomorrow may bring as random thoughts danced through his confused teenage head.

Ollie thought of the future, he thought of all the best-looking girls he knew in school, and as he drifted away to sleep, he focused on the prettiest girls in his class and singled out this month's favourite.

"What would our children look like?" he mused and drifted away.

The Tuesday dawn stole in bright and early amidst clear skies, but it gave no sleep concessions to tired old men. Military style, the old chap was up before the bell stopped ringing.

It was exactly 6.30 am. The sound of the dodgers springing into action had travelled seamlessly through the thin bedroom walls, easily conducted by the warm summer air.

Without exception and unsurprisingly, so did every other sound and movement travel equally well in that low-budget late fifties home. Bathroom noises, bedroom noises, sleeping and waking noises, all were regularly conveyed to his bedroom, as they had been forever.

The chance of sleeping after the dodgers automatically woke themselves and everybody else up was exactly zero.

His father was old-fashioned and single-minded. Everyone knew how it went.

"Dad's up, everybody's up."

That's how it was every day. No prisoners. No excuses. No apologies.

On this day the excitement Ollie felt meant that he was already awake when his father reached for the clock. Teenage nerves will do it every time. They are the most natural alarm clock ever.

"Good luck Ollie," said Dad as he went off to work in his pride and joy; a sporty, white six-year-old Chevvy with red leather seats and interior.

Sanctity quickly returned to the house, but Ollie was already washed and dressed by the time his father had turned the corner of the street.

* * *

If Ollie could pass this interview, he would be offered a sponsored place in university and a fast career path with one of the world's greatest companies. As the seventeen-year-old senior high school student mulled over the idea, he began to feel quite excited. This was a big day.

Unusually, he was at the Chippewa Falls bus depot ten minutes early. Normally, he could see the bus driving into the station from the front room of the house, even though it was four hundred yards away. A quick sprint would always get him to his required stop with about fifty yards to spare.

"No racing today!" thought Ollie, for he could not afford to miss it.

The Amtrak bus trip to Milwaukee Railway Station proved uneventful. Several inconsequential people got on and off and chatted about insignificant events and boring grown-up television programmes.

At the train station, Ollie bought his ticket to Union Station, Chicago, and showed it to the guard to gain access to the platform. He scowled at the ticket and grunted "platform two 7.45," whilst mentally slinking back into the scruffy outfit that passed for a uniform.

The train was packed but he had gained a seat by the window on the left-hand side.

Better still it was facing the way he was going.

Just where he would be going in the future was uncertain.

He had been to Chicago before, but only on one occasion with the school, safe in the security of an organised trip, and now at seventeen, he felt he knew it all, as all teenagers feeling their feet do, but nothing prepared him for his arrival at Union Station that morning.

What a zoo, what a carnival, such a circus, how fantastic!

Arriving at the taxi stand in a whirl of anticipation he jumped into the first one available.

"Where to boss?" asked the Asian taxi driver.

"Capitol House please sir," he replied confidently as he checked his arrival notes.

Looking at his watch it confirmed the time was 9.55 am, so Ollie was on target for his 11.00 am appointment, which he now nervously anticipated.

The job application process had begun nationwide in the previous September, with over three thousand applications for just eight sponsored places at the company.

Ollie alighted from the taxi at 10.15 am outside the magnificent modern office building that had been financed by the impressive revenues of the oil giant.

It stood like a comic book hero straddling the entrance to the Great Lakes, unwittingly guarding the wealth of Illinois.

Nerves rose unexpectedly in the pit of his adolescent stomach, the butterflies sending a signal that this was a grown-up's world. The opinions of all interviewee's parents would be futile here for each candidate was well and truly on their own.

Ollie strolled casually into a nearby coffee shop, ordered a straight black coffee and drank it inside, staring out of the window at the Chicago moving theatre of life, whilst simultaneously checking his watch to ensure he killed no more than twenty-five minutes.

The handsome, fifth-generation Frenchman had passed and survived a series of written tests and regional interviews and at 10.45 am, expecting a fight to the end, he entered the inner sanctum of the international oil giant.

After a warm greeting and introductions, the hopeful candidates were given tea, coffee and biscuits and allowed to mingle with each other and members of staff, whilst being watched all the while by the prospective employer. If lucky enough to be selected, the eight successful applicants would be on a dream ticket to success.

As the conversations settled into a kind of natural rhythm Ollie quickly realised that he was the only blue-collar boy in the room, and suddenly felt the pressure of jousting with the cream of the private American school education system.

The accents in the air came from the realms of New England, the deep south and the Texas oil fields, but these were not common American drawls, they were educated, intelligent, cut-glass infusions of assured confidence and birth right. They did not have any variation in their tones, they simply spoke classical American English of the variety heard in the old black-and-white films, each speaker oozing superiority.

These rival candidates surely belonged here, but now each time that Ollie spoke in his state school colloquial brogue, he felt as if he was an underachiever sent as cannon fodder to the lion's den.

Despite his appearance, his fortitude was now badly dented, and he feared for maybe the first time in his life that he may be out of his depth.

After lunch, all the candidates were sent for psychometric testing to a nearby cutting-edge human resources laboratory aptly named the Vocational Guidance Association.

This process involved interviewees completing a two-hour series of questions and answers about a vast array of random topics. The information gleaned from the completed papers allowed the laboratory to produce startling results.

The test confirmed Ollie was not cut out for art or religion, but strongly suggested he should be in business management or creative writing, the latter being shown as the role that would suit him best in later life.

Nothing of course was certain, and as the years rolled by only time would tell if there was any merit in the exercise.

In the short term, it gave the prospective employer a tiny ray of light to shine onto the guessing game of career employment.

The shortlisted troop of sixteen candidates returned to Capitol House in mid-afternoon and at 5 pm, after additional intense interviewing, the day was over, and all were sent on their merry way.

The interviewing panel informed the youngsters that job offers would be sent out within two weeks, and at the same time, apologetic rejections to the unsuccessful candidates.

Mentally, Ollie was exhausted, and he decided to travel back to Chippewa Falls as soon as possible.

"Two weeks could not be that long!" he thought to himself.

* * *

In a dreamlike state, Ollie climbed into a cab and twenty minutes later, having handed his friendly Puerto Rican driver a $1 tip he was back at the crossroads of the Great Lakes, the world-famous Chicago Union Train Station.

Walking through the great hall to his appointed place of departure he was careful not to engage in eye contact with any of the other travellers, for he had learned this new social skill that very morning on the early train.

Ollie bought a copy of the Chicago Times for company and walked onto the platform, where he stood looking at the large electronic timetable.

A Milwaukee train was due in ten minutes.

"Excellent news," he thought.

"The next train at platform seven will be the 6.15 pm to Glenview, Fox Lake, Sturtevant, Diamond Pass, Buffalo Hill, Plains City, Milwaukee Intermodal and Whitefish Bay."

That was confirmation indeed.

"Milwaukee here I come, I'll soon be on my way home," his exhausted brain said to his tired body.

As the train arrived at the platform, three coins fell onto the concrete in front of him.

The tired young man sprang into action and instinctively bent down to pick them up and return them to their rightful owner.

As Ollie turned around, he looked up into the eyes of the girl he wanted to marry.

***

The unanticipated vision of loveliness was incredible. Her smile would light up the darkest night. There was just something about her. She was undoubtedly the personification of teenage beauty. All at once, he was smitten, and he had this overwhelming feeling that they were meant to be together.

Somewhere, sometime long ago, someone had written a script.

This was the beginning of their book, the very first chapter.

As Ollie handed her the coins she smiled again, appreciatively, almost willing him to speak.

He could not speak, his confidence had been sapped by the ragged interview process, so they simply looked at each other for a split second too long. Ollie just knew it was a thunderbolt moment. She was the only one for him, and he was sure he would be the only one for her.

At that moment the iron horse slowly screeched to a halt, the herding began, and the crowd started competing for a good seat on the train.

The lovestruck youngsters were pulled apart and towards different doors. Ollie glimpsed her climbing into the other end of the carriage, as he was roughly moved in the opposite direction. She looked back at him as she entered the train and once again smiled with her beautiful, blue eyes.

In the melee, he grabbed an inside seat about halfway up the carriage, but this time facing back to Chicago. There was already someone opposite and quickly the seat next to him was taken.

A man was causing mayhem with an oversized bag in the opposite doorway, and as he eventually sat down, she appeared in the aisle.

His newfound Aphrodite saw him as he glanced up, fixated on her flowing skirt and beautiful athletic shape. There were two seats left in the carriage, but she walked casually past the first one and intimidated by her beauty, Ollie looked away as she sat in his section.

The last remaining seat in those four was now taken.

She was so close he could almost touch her.

Ollie's heart rate increased uncontrollably as he resisted the temptation to stare. He averted his longing gaze to the window as a form of self-protection, so that he did not give away his shyness or his incompetence.

This was easy, because after all, as a teenager he was assured, cool, and used to giving the impression he knew it all.

All at once, in the safety of her reflection in the window, he focused on the girl of his dreams; this young lady he had never met.

There and then, Ollie decided that he was going to marry her.

She was hypnotic, magnetic, and all-consuming.

"I wonder what her name is. Well, if I am to play Romeo, she shall be my Juliet. Why not?"

Ollie couldn't stop sneaking peeks at Juliet and then it happened, she tilted her head sideways, her shiny auburn hair and perfect complexion looking straight at his mirror image in the carriage window.

Panic overtook him, and he pretended to look past her into the distance as the train began to pull out of the station.

"Damn fool," he said to himself as his courage left him wanting.

This failure brought a never known burst of emotion that reached every part of his physical and mental being.

His fear of embarrassment prevented him from looking her in the eye and so he gave himself a stern telling off.

"How pathetic, this beautiful girl would never marry a man who could not even introduce himself!"

It was time to regroup. The train ploughed on towards Glenview, accompanied by the sounds of weary commuters vying for the best standing positions in the oversubscribed carriages, shuffling newspapers, or simply making small talk with strangers.

"If my fellow passengers can talk to each other then why can't I?" was the question repeating itself in his less-than-confident head.

The answer was simple, they were older than him, more experienced, and more self-assured, but more importantly, they had nothing to lose, so they didn't have to pretend.

If Ollie spoke to this girl in front of all these other people, it could go horribly wrong.

Perhaps he had read it incorrectly, and he suggested to himself that maybe she was just a friendly person, a nice girl.

"Stop making excuses!

"If you are ever going to see this girl again you need to break the ice. Smile, wink, just say or do something!"

For twenty minutes he stared resolutely ahead, wrestling with his conscience, trying to portray confidence, but he was not sure if he fooled anybody, let alone himself.

Occasionally he pretended to look at something of interest out of the window, but he didn't think he was very convincing at that either.

Every single minute he could feel her glancing at him, almost willing him to turn and look at her.

"She must be feeling the same way as me. This is not a teenage imagination. It's real. It's love at first sight. Surely, there could be no greater magic than this!"

Ollie continued to give himself a mental thrashing, while out of the corner of his eye he sensed her looking straight at him, measuring, imagining, longing.

The emotional pressure of unfettered desire, combined with the fear of failure, became overwhelming, as he looked away through the window once more.

* * *

The man sitting on her left appeared to be a veteran commuter.

Ollie loved people-watching and he named him "Gingerbread Man" or "Ginge" for short, as he was the image of his school headmaster, who according to himself was Wisconsin's gift to education.

The ginger passenger was about fifty years old and looked to all intents and purposes as if he was born that age.

Pomposity, pretence, and purely fabricated importance oozed from every pore of his being. The receding hair that remained on a raised forehead, had been tinted a ginger brown to give the appearance of youth.

His three-piece suit included a rather natty paisley waistcoat which made him look like a fugitive from the 1960s. Just like him, his silk pocket-handkerchief listed to port, and it had lost the vibrancy it may once have had.

As his long commuting day came to an end, Ollie imagined him going back to his two bedroomed apartment and his pussycat in Glenview, or maybe Fox Lake, where he lived alone eating TV dinners, living his life through his favourite soap operas.

There was a distinct absence of any friends in his life, so he told his neighbours that in Chicago he was a hotshot and that next year after a big promotion he would be moving away.

He concluded that "Ginge" was a lonely fifty-year-old gingerbread man, who would always be old before his time, who would never be important to anybody, and whose promotion would never come.

"Ginge" began to fall asleep and was most definitely listing towards the window. His arm rested on the hard plastic sill, but the combination of its smoothness and rounded shape meant that each time he began to nod off, his elbow slid slowly and surely off the edge.

Every few minutes he awoke with a start, but his fatigue made him oblivious to Ollie and his fellow passengers, all of whom outwardly chuckled without looking each other in the eye.

Juliet almost laughed out loud as she glanced sideways at this hilarious behaviour and began openly smiling at his tired antics.

Once again, Ollie's attention was caught by "Ginge," as his arm slid spectacularly off the window, causing him to wake up sharply and sit bolt upright.

Ollie glanced away to the window and for the second time, he looked straight into the eyes of that Venus-like reflection that travelled with him. He was transfixed, but joy of joys so was she.

Her eyes did not just smile, they lit up as they both realised, they had made contact.

Over the next fifteen minutes, their virtual relationship went from strength to strength, as they exchanged glances and little smiles in the safety of the reflected glass.

He wondered if she thought he was a bit odd, just looking at her in the window reflection, but her body language told him she was as besotted with him, as he was with her.

As the train trundled relentlessly onwards towards Milwaukee, it seemed impossible for them not to glance at each other at every opportunity.

His cloud nine experience was soon shattered as the train slowed gently, accompanied by a squeaking of metal and a smell of friction when the braking mechanism did its job.

"The train now arriving at Glenview is the 6.15 pm from Chicago. This train will call at Fox Lake, Sturtevant, Diamond Pass, Buffalo Hill, Plains City, Milwaukee Intermodal and Whitefish Bay."

"Oh no, what if she is getting off here? Disaster, I don't even know her real name, never mind her phone number or address. What can I do?"

Ollie squirmed in his seat as he set the fear of losing her against the nervousness of his teenaged embarrassment.

"Make a decision, be positive!" he silently shouted at himself, but words often speak louder than actions and he did nothing.

In his hesitation, his fears went unfounded, and she remained on the train.

"I bet she was thinking the same as me.

"Where is she going? Where does she live? I hope it's Milwaukee and maybe Chippewa Falls!

"All roads lead to Chippewa Falls, don't they?"

Quizzing himself, he wondered how this relationship was going to work if her destination was not his hometown.

Ollie quickly decided that he was putting the cart before the horse.

"Man up, you have to talk to this girl!"

The train snaked onwards to Fox Lake, and after ten minutes of jockeying for positions, the new passengers settled down.

A kind of serene fatigue enveloped the coach as passengers began to fall asleep or just doze.

This calmness was broken when a guard arrived in their compartment and began to randomly check and validate tickets. He held brief conversations with passengers as he did his job and remarkably seemed to know some of them.

The lovesick interviewee concluded that they must be regulars, if indeed there could be such a thing on a Milwaukee train.

"What do I know about train travel, never mind the girl I'm going to marry? Ah yes, Olivier and Juliet Cartier, my blushing bride, it's got a nice ring to it!"

As he daydreamed the guard asked for his ticket.

"Milwaukee?"

"Yes," he said quietly, completely lacking any confidence because of his emotional ordeal.

"Thank you," the guard said, clipped the ticket and handed it back to him.

Inadvertently, as he was now facing away from the window to the walkway, he looked straight up at Juliet. She smiled nervously and Ollie could not help but smile back.

Progress, real physical contact had been made. Well almost.

He was so wrapped up in this minor development that he completely missed his chance to start a conversation with his bride-to-be.

Ollie chastised himself.

"All I had to ask was, "Are you going to Milwaukee?", and we would have been star-crossed lovers in no time.

"The shyness is killing me, as well as our children before they are even born.

"Get a grip, time is running out!"

As the guard small-talked his way into the next carriage they arrived at Sturtevant. Many travellers alighted there, but all seats were taken as the new arrivals boarded. Not one of the four passengers in Ollie's section moved a muscle and so the journey resumed.

Surveying the scene, he felt sure that "Ginge", now wide awake, and the passenger to his left, the one sitting opposite Juliet, had realised there was tension in the air.

Next to Ollie on the walkway side was the fourth passenger in their group.

She was a well-groomed lady of about forty years of age; very smartly dressed and clean-looking in an understated sort of way.

This lady seemed accomplished, purposeful, and yet kind and understanding at the same time.

Ollie was sure she knew what was going on.

As he took a sideways glance, he realised she looked a little bit like his Aunty Joan.

He found this a little disconcerting and certainly did not need a family member with him when he was trying to organise both a hot date and a wedding proposal. Her perfume was the same as the one his mother used, but he had no idea what it was called. It was spooky.

The proximity of this lady was comforting and off-putting at the same time.

"You wouldn't want your mother with you at your first kiss, and certainly not when on bended knee to the girl you love!"

The four travellers sped on across the sunlit, windswept prairie lands to Diamond Pass and Ollie realised the significance of the station name.

"Maybe I could get an engagement ring there?"

His nerves were frayed as he realised that he had his aunty, his mother and his headmaster all assisting in his failed courtship of Juliet.

"Talk about pressure, am I making this too complicated, am I overthinking this? Juliet is just a girl who wants me to talk to her, at least I think so anyway," he said silently with a total lack of belief.

"Chuff, chuff, chuff" went the sound, as the love machine trundled on, and the prospective young lovers went from strength to strength.

With contact made, they kept looking directly at each other, catching each other's eye, smiling together, and raising their eyebrows at the exaggerated behaviour of some of their fellow passengers.

Even though they did not speak a word, their subtle little exchanges were a form of bonding, which sealed their embryonic relationship as the metallic odyssey continued westward into the evening sunset.

"Ginge," and the lady who looked like Ollie's aunty, both departed at Diamond Pass and disappeared into the warm sultry air.

They went their separate ways up the exit ramp to very different existences.

In the early evening moonlight, "Aunty Joan" disappeared towards a sea of tranquillity and a neat future, whilst Ginge shuffled in crablike fashion to his universe of imperfection, to be forever trapped in loneliness.

Ollie vowed it would not happen to him because he had Juliet, and who could need more than that?

As he watched them disappear, Ollie began to pluck up the courage to make his long-overdue introduction.

They both seemed much more relaxed with their two oldest friends departed, but right at that moment, a large, fat, obnoxious salesman in a crumpled, worn-out pinstripe suit sat down next to Ollie and opposite Juliet.

Disaster had struck.

"I'm too slow to catch a cold!" he complained to himself.

This new addition to the company wore a loud shirt with a very wide, old-fashioned, kipper tie that matched his personality. Ollie could not help wondering if he had wax in his ears.

It was obvious that he did not consider that Ollie and Juliet should be classified as adults, and so he talked loudly and constantly across the aisle to anyone who would listen, about nothing of any specific interest, but even more annoying was that he talked at people and never actually with them.

In his world, everyone was entitled to his opinion, whether they wanted it or not, unless they were kids like Ollie and Juliet and then of course, they luckily didn't qualify for his free expertise.

It was impossible to open a conversation with Juliet as this buffoon rode side-saddle right next to him. The upside was that the knowing glances and exchanges between Ollie and Juliet became more blatant, and in a strange kind of way, even deeper in meaning.

It sounds ridiculous but they had a full-blown conversation without saying a word.

"Is this what married life could be like?" Ollie mused.

Buffalo Hill came and went with the status quo remaining in place, but then Ollie became more nervous as they arrived and departed Plains City.

Juliet, Ollie, and the sales buffoon continued to ride the lowlands towards Milwaukee Intermodal.

"She must be alighting at Milwaukee, as it's the main station on this route."

Exactly on time and to everyone's surprise, the train pulled slowly into Milwaukee Intermodal.

Those passengers Ollie had perceived as regulars commented humorously about this momentous event, which deflected his sense of purpose.

The buffoon stood up to leave, and Ollie nodded to Juliet with a smile of anticipation as he followed the larger-than-life character into the aisle.

She smiled back with a face that was full of love, kindness, beauty, and expectation.

"Success, Juliet's getting off here, so we can finally make our introductions!"

He walked about twenty feet along the train carriage and out of the exit doors on the left.

As Ollie stepped onto the concrete platform, he was joined by many of the other passengers, who began rushing off to meet loved ones, and to connect with taxis and buses for onward journeys.

Anticipating finally being able to speak to his dream girl he turned and waited, but Juliet was nowhere to be seen.

Quickly Ollie looked along the windows of the compartment in which they had travelled.

Halfway along he saw his empty seat and then realised the love of his life was still sitting on the train and panic immediately set in.

"It's now or never. What to do, what to do, what to do?"

A loud piercing whistle beckoned everyone's attention and signalled the train doors were about to close. The lovestruck teenager urged himself to get back onboard but once again he hesitated as his courage failed him.

Ollie's brain was in a fog as the announcer told all and sundry, young lovers included that "this train is now on its way to tonight's final destination at Whitefish Bay."

The doors closed; he was too late.

The inappropriate words of his mother ran through Ollie's brain.

"If stands stiff in a poor man's pocket!"

The moment was gone.

* * *

Forty years had passed after that fateful day on the train and much had happened in Ollie's lifetime. No doubt much had also happened in Juliet's world, but it could have been so different for them both. If only he had found the courage to simply say "hello".

There was rarely an occasion where on seeing a pretty girl in a restaurant, at the mall, or just walking in the park, Ollie didn't reminisce about that extraordinary train journey of self-discovery and love lost.

He was not offered the career-defining opportunity at Capitol Oil Inc., but it was one of the most memorable days of his life.

Ollie often thought about it and wondered what may have been with both the oil giant and of course the love of his life that never was, the vision of loveliness that was Juliet.

Three thousand four hundred American senior school students, the cream of 1978, applied for those eight places with Capitol Oil Inc, and he reached the shortlist of sixteen. Not bad for a blue-collar boy from a small, backward town like Chippewa Falls, but far from good enough.

In the fall of that year, Ollie went to Milwaukee University and ironically, years later, one of his old student friends became a Vice President at Capitol Oil Inc., but life's paths are well-trodden, and oftentimes take the strangest turns.

It's funny how things work out. Nothing in life is ever quite what it seems.

Eventually, after university, Ollie came back to Chippewa Falls and melted into the social background as an average Joe, playing sports and chasing girls, as is the way of most young men everywhere.

Each day he would look in the mirror in the morning and make a promise to himself.

"Never again will I let a lack of confidence deny me an opportunity. The faint heart will win the fair maiden!"

It became his modus operandi and the newfound confidence worked well. In the Summer of 1986 at the age of just twenty-five, he married Amber, the best-looking and most sought-after cheerleader of his school year.

His new wife immediately sweet-talked him into quitting Chippewa Falls, selling his bachelor pad and jettisoning his extremely promising career as a career accountant with a state-wide public utility company. They moved to Chicago, bought an overly expensive two-bedroom apartment on the waterfront and Ollie started his own business as a private accountant in his own right.

His trophy wife wanted nothing more than for Ollie to work long hours, earn vast amounts of money and at every available opportunity to parade her at the country club in expensive clothes and make up.

Alas, in life it takes two to tango and one not to.

Ollie quickly found he was dancing through life alone, whilst funding the increasingly expensive playgirl lifestyle of a stay-at-home wife who he was growing less fond of year after year.

The learning curve of a public accountant to a private accountant was a steep one with many pitfalls and problems along the way, but bit by bit and yard by yard he became established, even if he did feel worn out before the age of thirty.

Economic recession came to the USA in 1990 and it had a severe effect on the businesses of Milwaukee over the next few years. Farming, transport, defence, and especially small businesses in the supply chain were hammered in the short term. Interest rates went north of what was considered reasonable with clients pulling their horns in on their spending, whilst Amber continued to haemorrhage cash like tomorrow would never come.

Despite burning the candle at both ends in work and play, Ollie's heart was no longer in business or in love.

Having struggled on in an over-committed, self-destructive spiral for two years with no support from his wife, it all came to a head in July 1992 when he discovered she was having an affair with "Flash" Fred Zimmerman, the news anchor of a high-profile Milwaukee TV News Station.

His well-practised parting words to Amber were the stuff of theatrical dreams, that many an actor would wait a lifetime just hoping to be given, but for Ollie, it was an honest, truthful, and no-way-back exit speech.

"Well Amber, you've done it this time, so let me tell you how it is for a change. Here's a news bulletin just for you.

"First the weather, thunder clouds are gathering, it's going to get rough out there.

"Now the local news. The rabbit is out of the hat, and everyone knows the cheerleader is in the sack with the news guy and it seems I was the last to know.

"Here are the headlines. Our apartment goes on the market tomorrow. I've closed the business today and cancelled our joint bank accounts and credit cards.

"Finally, we are now equal on a level playing field. We both have nothing. That's not quite true, I have my dignity back, you might get bed sores if you're lucky.

"One last thing, please thank "Flash" Fred for me; that guy has saved my life.

"Never contact me directly again. My lawyer will be in touch. Goodbye!"

Ollie picked up his case and left Amber in the middle of the lounge weeping crocodile tears to an empty audience. The marriage was over.

The last bus to Chippewa Falls carried a happy, penniless accountant back to his parent's house where at just thirty-one years of age he vowed to rebuild his life. It wasn't long before the utility company came knocking and welcomed him back with open arms.

He was now a man full grown with emotional scars and life's bitemarks slowly moulding him into the "catch" he would eventually become.

The second time around is tough, and Ollie worked hard to kickstart his life, but after ten years of playing the game and nearing his fortieth birthday he resigned himself to the fact that he was "on the shelf". This was despite having plenty of girlfriends both before and after being married. None of them it seemed were the right one for him. He was never going to make the same mistake twice.

"There must be something wrong with me," he regularly said to himself or "am I trying too hard?"

For some men, no woman could ever live up to that consciousness of perfection that is their mother. Perhaps for Ollie, no woman could ever live up to the stunning beauty and teenage glory that was Juliet.

On some days he wondered if meeting Juliet on that train was the worst thing that had ever happened to him.

"Does it mean that every other woman can only come second to the beauty that got away?"

Ollie couldn't put his finger on how it happened but one day he decided to stop searching for love.

"Just live," he decided.

At that moment Ollie's fate was sealed, and his destiny was fulfilled when he decided to buy a new beachfront house in the much sought-after paradise that was Whitefish Bay.

In April 2001, for three months, he had been living back home with his parents, as he had recently sold his own house and was actively looking to purchase something new.

This was going to be a special purchase for he had acquired a budget that afforded him to look at some very expensive neighbourhoods. In his mind this would be the last house he would buy, for he wanted to settle down and just live out the second half of his life in peace, taking every day as it came.

As soon as the latest home particulars from the realtor landed on his mother's doormat, he knew it was for him.

On arriving for a first viewing of his prospective new abode the door was opened by the delightful Natalie and her two small boys.

It was apparent that she had her work cut out with those two boisterous little chaps, and a house viewing with a stranger at the same time, but it all went like clockwork.

She had a lovely smile, a hint of a distant French accent and a great sense of humour.

Natalie was a brilliant organiser. Her packing in the lounge was a testament to this, with everything neatly stacked and ready to move out at the drop of a hat.

Her marriage separation from her lawyer husband meant the property had to be sold.

Ollie and Natalie chatted for ages, and both got on like a house on fire, quite forgetting the purpose of their meeting.

This coming together of two strangers was so natural, so perfect. It was like they had known each other forever.

Natalie turned out to be third-generation French.

"Ah well, you cannot have everything," Ollie remarked when she told him, and they both giggled like schoolchildren at the innocent jovial comment.

"What do you do for a living?" Natalie casually enquired.

"Well, by training I'm an accountant but not anymore. Twelve years ago, I got divorced, came back to Chippewa Falls and had a lot of spare time on my hands. I started writing books part-time and it just took off!"

"You're a writer?"

"I am now. I slowly realised in my thirties it was all I ever wanted to do. Years before it had been suggested that I take up writing, but I was too busy getting on with life to try it. Working full-time never gave me the opportunity. At least I can thank my ex-wife for empowering me to do something about it. Divorce was the best thing that ever happened to me! It gave me more spare time than I knew what to do with!"

"What type of books do you write?"

"Business thrillers about corporate shenanigans and murders. Intellectual property theft, international fraud, adultery, alimony, love, good luck, bad luck, success, and failure. Oh, and I have a detective who solves it all. A bit like Agatha Christie, except my guy is a gal and she's second-generation French living in the USA!"

"And your name is Olivier Cartier?"

"Yes, fifth-generation French, the real deal!" and he winked at Natalie to let her know he was the genuine article.

Tongue in cheek she retorted, "Well, I've never heard of you but good luck. I'll look out for your next book!"

"I'll have to try harder!"

Ollie did not let the cat out of the bag for he did not write under his name, and not even under his sex. In local society he was anonymous.

His pen name was a pseudonym. Natalie would certainly have heard of an author named Marie Louise, even if she had never read one of her books.

Marie Louise was published by one of the USA's largest publishers, Falcon West Publications Inc., out of Los Angeles. The author had sold over five million books to date and the star performer in the series was the French detective, Adrienne Dubois.

This character was written as a serious, no-nonsense, red wine-loving, mousy-looking woman with a penchant for red lipstick, black stockings, and garter belts, which created a contrasting sexiness and simmering ancillary plot that bubbled under the dialogue of every chapter.

Hollywood was knocking on Falcon West's door to buy the film rights and unbeknown to Natalie, the successful author Marie Louise and the prospective home buyer Olivier Cartier were one and the same.

In 1978 the Vocational Guidance Association in Chicago, Illinois had either been extremely lucky or entirely correct when forecasting that Olivier Cartier was well suited to book writing, for he was now a comfortable millionaire, and his star was still in the ascendancy.

Whether Ollie would buy the house was never in doubt. What he did not expect was a readymade family to come with it, but he never regretted it for one moment.

Two weeks after moving into his new beachfront home and quite by chance, he bumped into Natalie at Easter in the local pub restaurant. They were reintroduced by mutual friends and the future was written then and there.

After a couple of years of easy courtship, she moved back in with Ollie to the home she had sold to him a couple of years before. It was the best thing that had ever happened to him, and he loved it. Three years later they were the happiest married couple in town.

The kids grew and flew the nest, but over the years they all travelled, partied, skied, cycled, played soccer, football and laughed loads in everything that they did. Memories were truly made of times like those.

As his life moved on, Ollie rarely thought of Juliet and that day long ago on the Milwaukee train, except for when he lamented the fact that he had never pursued his life's ambition to write a book of short stories because that teenaged train journey was a gift of a story to tell. He had even worked out the title.

Ollie would call it "Faint Heart."

Several times he almost began the short story project and constantly squirrelled ideas and story titles away on bits of paper whenever he felt inspired, but it was so much easier said than done to get started whilst he was still committed to the international publisher.

In January 2016 Olivier delivered his final full-length novel to Falcon West, for he had decided that the series had run its course. Adrienne Dubois was killed off by her jealous husband after discovering her long-standing affair with a news anchor for a well-known Mid-West TV channel. Sometimes fiction is more intertwined with fact than we realise.

Ollie was now free to write one final book for himself.

"Short Stories for Book Lovers" would be his holy grail, the pinnacle of his life's work. He already had plenty of ideas for various chapters from the copious notes he had made over the years.

There was one story that still touched his soul after all this time, and he just had to tell it.

It was a tale of paradise found, paradise lost, and paradise never regained. This was his teenage love story of a young man meeting a girl called Juliet on a train bound for Milwaukee. It was nearly forty years ago, and he had to get it out of his system once and for all.

Ollie was a born writer, a teller of tales and he wanted to tell the world about Juliet, the girl he left behind, all because of a faint heart. Only then would she finally be gone from his life, and he could say, "goodbye my love goodbye," and it would be done.

He didn't need the money from this final writing effort. Ollie decided he might even break the mould and use a new publisher but more likely he would publish it himself, as the book industry had changed dramatically in recent years.

Instead of beavering away day after day on his keyboard, this project would be different. He would ease himself into retirement by slowing down and writing when he felt like it.

Once the final book was completed life would be about Natalie, the boys, daughters-in-law, grandchildren, golf, and anything else the world threw at them, and he was determined to enjoy every minute.

The new tome started well enough, and nine chapters were completed by Christmas 2016 but there the impetus stopped. He typed into the computer "Chapter Ten" but over the next three years, he found every excuse under the sun not to write it. The page remained blank.

He blamed lots of things. He was too busy. It was writer's block. He even questioned whether it was fear of Natalie knowing how he had truly felt about another woman so long ago.

Whatever it was, the laptop was fired up every day on the table in the lounge, but not one word was added to the book. It became a standing joke between Natalie and Ollie. She called it "the book that never was!"

Ollie would stand in a bookshop somewhere, wondering when he would write the final chapter in his book of short stories and inevitably memories of the Vocational Guidance Association in Chicago would come flooding back. They had been right about almost everything.

Firstly, his vocational leaning towards business management. He was good at business, and he had learned much from his accountancy experience in Chicago. The utility company had certainly paid him handsomely enough for his efforts.

Secondly, they had singled out above all things Ollie's natural ability at creative writing. Time had proved the forecast to be spectacularly correct. Marie Louise and Adrienne Dubois were translated into more than twenty languages and published in over sixty countries worldwide. The television series and the Hollywood film and sequel were the icing on the cake.

The only thing they had failed to forecast was Ollie finding and losing Juliet on the train that day, but no one is perfect.

* * *

During their fifteen years together, Ollie had often spoken with Natalie about his dream of writing a book of short stories under his own name, free from the exacting demands of a hungry publisher. They jokingly referred to it as his "bestseller," and both knew it would be a milestone in their relationship.

On rare occasions, when they would bicker or argue, Natalie might throw into a heated conversation, "why don't you give us all a rest and go and write your book?"

Usually, they would laugh at this and then regroup, to go on the same as before, that is until March 1st, 2019.

Ollie blamed the butcher as much as anybody for what happened, but it is to him that he owed possibly the greatest debt of his life.

Every weekend Elijah Horvath the local butcher, known as "Sausage Fingers," to his friends, owing to their huge size, delivered a selection of meats to their house.

Before the children flew the nest this always consisted of copious amounts of steak, beef, and bacon. All of it would be consumed by the two growing sporting enthusiasts and swallowed without touching the sides.

"I don't know how you can afford it!" Elijah used to say as Ollie paid his weekly invoice.

"I'd rather keep a horse than keep those two!"

Whenever Ollie asked the boys if they wanted more meat, the word "no" never crossed their minds, as is the way with ever hungry teenaged boys.

The children were long gone, so the weekend order now amounted to a small joint of sirloin beef, sometimes a chicken, or occasionally a leg of pork. On this occasion, Natalie had requested that Ollie order a joint of beef for two.

She had gone out shopping earlier in the week and bought the vegetables to accompany this feast. Broccoli, her favourite green beans, and fresh carrots were awaiting Ollie's amateur chef routine in the kitchen.

As they were having beef, she had also bought some frozen Yorkshire puddings. This much-loved English delicacy is a great accompaniment to beef, especially when your mouth is watering at the thought of a classic Sunday roast, even if you have cheated a bit. Add in the Idaho roast potatoes and a nice bottle of French red wine and who could ask for more?

The Sunday routine was that Ollie played golf in the morning while Natalie cleaned the house, and Ollie cooked dinner later when Natalie went out with her friends to her dance class, which, with coffee and biscuits, and then catching up on the news and gossip, usually lasted about three hours.

It worked well, but unfortunately, it was not to be on this occasion.

Having won a small competition, Ollie arrived home from golf in good spirits just before noon. The word "bandit" still echoed in his ears. You can win as many golf trophies as you like, but they mean nothing. You know you have arrived when your friends call you a "bandit," thus suggesting you are a lot better than your allotted golf-playing handicap.

Just before 1 pm, Natalie went off to do her thing at the dance school, and that's when he discovered the butcher's mistake.

Ollie went into the fridge and opened the package Elijah had delivered the morning before, to discover a chicken looking back at him. Chicken and Yorkshire pudding is not and would never be an option in the Cartier house. It just wouldn't work. "Yorkshires" went with beef.

"No problem," he thought quite calmly as he put the chicken back in the fridge, before hopping off to the local supermarket to buy a replacement piece of meat. It was a roasting joint of some description, but on Sunday afternoon just before closing, it was the only roasting joint.

Ollie quickly gathered up this "last supper" before anyone else had the opportunity.

It was now just past 2 pm and the supermarket, to the relief of the staff, closed as he exited the shop, so that everyone else could start their Sunday too.

He had already prepared the vegetables, so next Ollie preheated the oven and opened the beef.

It was rancid, and the grotesque smell permeated the house, forcing him to open all the doors and windows.

Inspecting the source of the awful odour, Ollie noticed that the vacuum-packed wrapping was punctured underneath. This joint of meat had been festering for days and all the smart shoppers had left it behind.

He wondered how to solve this problem, and then Ollie began watching television, putting on the golf channel to inspire his thought process.

"We'll just have to have pizza."

Naturally, with golfed out, tired old limbs, and fresh air wafting into the house through all the opened orifices, Ollie fell into a deep sleep where he won the US Masters and British Open golf titles in less than an hour.

* * *

The planned dance session was a disaster.

Natalie happened to get stuck in a lift for an hour and missed the session.

Fuming, she later returned to the car park to find that her pride and joy silver-open-top Porsche Carrera had been bumped by another vehicle, causing thousands of dollars' worth of damage.

To make matters worse the culprit had fled the scene, without leaving any contact information.

A distraught Natalie came home much earlier than expected. She was tired, frustrated and naturally very upset.

Walking into the house she discovered the stinking scarlet beef on display in the kitchen and saw red herself when she found that Ollie was missing in action.

"What else can possibly go wrong?"

Out of nowhere, they had a huge argument about what Ollie had ordered from Elijah the butcher.

"You just don't listen, I said sirloin of beef, and what is that rotting carcass you bought at the supermarket? They must have seen you coming!"

Woken rudely from his golf championship dreams he bit back.

"I did order beef, and the rotting carcass is all they had left. I went and bought it as a substitute while you were out enjoying yourself!"

Whoops.

"Too late," he thought. The words just slipped out, but as they left his lips, he already regretted it.

Ollie knew nothing of Natalie being stuck in a lift, or of the car being damaged. He should have realised she was in a high state of anxiety, but he was just a man, not a mind reader.

In response, Natalie's eyes flashed not only red but fire and thunder in the same stare.

Her body was animated yet rigid.

"Another job you never finished, just like your book!"

"Serves you right, you deserved that," Ollie thought, yet he could not see the logic between Yorkshire pudding, rancid beef, dancing, golf and writing a book but she clearly could.

"I'm having pasta, you can have what you like!"

The truth sometimes hurts and glancing at his laptop on the table he knew that her description of his failed book was entirely accurate.

He had written nine chapters of his ten-chapter masterpiece and was procrastinating for all he was worth.

The book of short stories was almost complete but for over three years he had been unable to finish it. Something was missing but he didn't know what.

It was a search for the impossible dream, the perfect story to end his career, but whatever Ollie considered, nothing was ever good enough.

This final story had to be special. It had to be something significant to complete this career pinnacle, this labour of love, and in setting the bar so high his search for the Utopian dream had drifted on and on.

Two years ago, instead of using a traditional publisher he had decided to self-publish and retire in a blaze of glory.

Ollie had designed the cover himself, costed the project, and obtained the ISBN number and barcode to make his publication legitimate, but he had not completed the task.

Natalie was correct.

Then against his better judgement, he bit back again.

"You've solved the Sunday dinner issue. If you are so clever why not finish the book yourself?" Ollie said sarcastically.

He was on a roll and his dander was up.

"You enjoy your pasta, I'm off to the golf club," was Ollie's flippant comment, as he exited stage right and out through the door for a Sunday afternoon lunch of beer, pretzels, and salted peanuts.

* * *

Making his way on-foot to the golf club bar a half mile away, Ollie realised how stupid his reaction had been, but foolish pride meant he would have to stick this out. It was a man thing.

"How could I suggest Natalie finished my book?"

That was taboo.

Ollie only began writing it on one condition, and that was secrecy. He made her promise him that she would not read any of the stories until the book was published. That was the deal before he put pen to paper.

He entered the private members club which Natalie often referred to as his "second home" and in no time he was sitting drinking with his golf friends as he guzzled cold beer and talked with them about golf matches played in days gone by. Every time he tried to leave the club someone else came in from the golf course and inevitably, Ollie stayed there for about five hours.

He was seriously drunk, for peanuts and pretzels are not a great Sunday lunch, especially if washed down with six pints of imported Mexican lager and a Scotch Whiskey for luck.

It was already dark as Ollie approached the house at 8.30 pm, and he mentally prepared himself for an extended chastisement.

"What's done cannot be undone but I'm sure we'll work it out!"

He thought back to when they got married and the vicar's advice freely given on that occasion.

"Never go to bed on a row, stay up and fight all night!"

Ollie giggled to himself, "this could be an all-nighter!"

Quietly, he opened the front door and there she stood staring at him through weepy, red eyes.

"What's wrong?"

"Nothing," she said and burst into uncontrollable tears.

Ollie strode forward and hugged her.

"What on earth is wrong?" he repeated, but Ollie was now as sober as he could be.

Sense and fear had kicked in. He had never seen her like this before. She blurted out through more tears.

"I got stuck in a lift and someone bumped the car, and the Yorkshire puddings are wasted."

Ollie tried to process the unexpected message.

"This makes little sense, and it certainly does not explain her erratic behaviour."

Stepping back, he looked at her quizzically.

"Maybe she has been drinking?"

Her behaviour was totally out of character. She was irrational, like a teenage girl out of synchronisation with her emotions. There was no logic he could follow. It didn't add up. Natalie did not normally behave like this.

Then it escalated to a whole new level of drama.

"You don't understand Ollie, I love you, I love you, I love you!" she exclaimed and started kissing him like it was the first time they had met.

Ollie's mind was swamped by crazy emotions, but it was better than any additional arguing, so he decided not to try too hard to work out what was happening.

Then she moved away and grabbed him by the hand, leading him forcefully into the lounge and over to the table, giving him the most wonderful smile and bellowed.

"I love you and I've finished your book!" and more tears streamed down her face.

Ollie's emotional being was immediately kicked into gear.

Surprise at not having another argument was mixed with anger that she would even dare to look at the book, let alone write a chapter.

She had broken the code, broken a promise, broken his heart.

"No, no, no, no!" he protested in self-anger.

Natalie felt Ollie's disappointment and his instant negative reaction, and it cut her to the quick.

"Please don't say anything, just read it," she begged.

Ollie looked at the contents page and saw the chapter titles of his nine completed stories, beginning with chapter one, "Faint Heart".

"Ouch, now she knows how I felt about Juliet all those years ago."

He had wanted to let her down gently with that one, but she seemed unaffected except for the bizarre emotional antics.

Ollie's eyes scrolled down to chapter ten where the title space had previously been blank.

This gap was now filled with the title of the final story as written by Natalie.

It simply said, "Fair Maiden".

Quickly, Ollie tried to work out the logic of this title.

Chapter one was his very own story of unfulfilled love at first sight, "Faint Heart".

This was followed by eight chapters of other experiences and events, some real and some imagined.

Now, this last chapter was to be called "Fair Maiden".

"How could that possibly fit in?" he wondered.

Natalie's excitement prevented Ollie from getting angrier and exploding.

He was hooked but the failed chef could not work out why Natalie thought that she could finish his book and get away with it. He whispered inside his head.

"One chicken that should have been sirloin beef, combined with a forgetful butcher does not a novel make!"

Ollie scrolled down to look at chapter ten and there was the story just as she had typed it.

The heading "Fair Maiden" stared back at Ollie as if it was set in stone.

Slowly, he began to read the newly added words and for the first time in his adult life, he began to cry and then to weep inconsolably, until he vibrated with pleasure, security, and sheer joy.

Turning sideways, and looking away from the computer for a moment, he hugged Natalie and they said everything and nothing at the same time.

Their happiness was immeasurable, personal, complete, and it would be forever.

Ollie looked into Natalie's beautiful blue eyes, wiped away her tears, and saw her smile that smile.

The smile that meant you are "mine" and I am "yours".

"Our book," Ollie said authoritatively, is complete.

"I should say so, I can't wait for us to write life's sequel together."

With huge pride, Ollie looked down at the opening words of chapter ten, "Fair Maiden", that his wife had written whilst he told shaggy dog stories at the golf club.

Natalie realised what Ollie was doing and took him gently by the hand.

Then with smiling eyes, they looked at that first sentence, and together they read aloud in perfect harmony.

"I was a teenage girl stood on a train platform at Union Station, Chicago.

When the train arrived, I accidentally dropped three coins onto the floor in front of me, and a stranger rushed to my assistance and picked them up.

As he turned around to hand them to me, I looked down into the eyes of the boy I wanted to marry."

Trembling with overwhelming joy and emotion they both turned away from the screen and stood just inches apart, gazing longingly into each other's eyes.

"Je t'aime Romeo".

"Je t'aime Juliet".

Chapter 5

THE MIGHTY CARIBOU

RECOGNITION was instant.
They stared at each other, but neither flinched, as bygone memories of romance stirred.

Two squirming seconds of uninvited, unexpected, emotional trauma elapsed. Both were fascinated by the vision that greeted them, and so they held their gaze.

Thirty-three years had passed since the age of puppy love, when their desperate, love-starved, teenaged lips, had entwined for the first time.

Rachel's husband and her two grown-up children walked by her side, oblivious to the dramatic love scene being played out in front of them.

Secretly, she asked herself that burning, unanswered question, which eats at the soul, and had haunted her for a lifetime.

"Does first love ever die?"

* * *

Rachel Williams was seventeen years old and looked great in a netball skirt, but she had never kissed a boy.

Some people just develop later than others.

It's often down to the pressures added by parents, who because of their own worries, fears, and experiences, either unwittingly or occasionally deliberately, aid in helping their offspring suppress very natural tendencies.

Rachel was a good girl, and you would be forgiven for thinking that butter would not melt in her mouth. She was from what the teachers described in the staff room as "a good family", and an easier pupil to teach was hard to find.

It was late November 1977, and her head was more focused on the mighty caribou than it was on boys, but only just, and the balance was rapidly changing.

She never missed school, she didn't answer back, she represented her high school in hockey and netball, and excelled at her three chosen senior school subjects of geography, history, and English.

The model schoolgirl was tipped to have a great career, whatever she should ultimately choose to do in the future.

When Rachel announced to her parents that she was staying on in school for higher education and that she wanted to go on to the well-respected Oxford University to study modern history, they were delighted.

She later added that her ultimate desire was to become a teacher, just like her mother.

At that moment they were the proudest parents in Swansea, that dramatic Welsh seaport town, second only in importance to the capital city of Cardiff, further to the east along the edge of the Bristol channel.

Rachel took the first year in lower sixth in her stride, and whilst not coming top in class, easily achieved the academic standard required to fulfil her future dreams.

* * *

Rachel Williams and Gareth Evans were in love with each other. They had been since that first day in Glyn Mawr primary school aged five, but neither of them quite understood their invisible bond in their formative years.

Once it dawned on them, they were certainly not brave enough to mention it to the other, for fear of rejection.

Rachel laughed at all of Gareth's jokes, and when she played hockey on the girl's pitch, she couldn't help but watch him out of the corner of her eye, as he strutted his alpha male routine on the adjoining rugby field.

She found him to be magnetic, mesmeric, magnificent, and she was getting more excited all the time, as hormones began rushing through her runaway teenage body.

Gareth, for his part, was the pick of the boys for manners, looks and humour. He was besotted with Rachel, and he could barely keep his eyes off her in class.

He longed to hold her, to kiss her, to stroke her, to look after and protect her. The machismo, rugby-playing star, would eat her if he could, but despite all his boyish bravado, he just couldn't ask her to go out with him.

What if she said no?

* * *

Excitedly, Rachel climbed out of bed, throwing to one side the Minnie Mouse duvet that she had long since outgrown.

"Tuesday, 27th November, just one more mock exam and Christmas here I come!"

History and English exams had fared well, as had the first geography paper, and her teachers expected that the final test would be much the same.

Rachel would be quietly confident in this second geography exam, for she had an ace up her sleeve, courtesy of Bronwyn Davies, her wonderfully supportive, enthusiastic geography teacher, who had instilled in her a love of that subject.

Mrs Davies was a likeable, long-serving, popular teacher, who had fostered in her pupils an above-average interest in the annual migration of the mighty caribou, in the great northern plains of Canada.

Rachel had always liked animals and her laid-back Siamese cat, hilarious cocker spaniel dog, and impassive goldfish were testaments to this.

In the first week of the lower sixth form when geography lessons began, Mrs Davies had shown the class a thought-provoking documentary film about one of nature's great annual events, the migration of the mighty caribou.

This had struck a chord with Rachel. It was from that moment onwards, that she wanted another extremely large mammal to add to her private menagerie at home.

"Aren't they magnificent Mrs Davies?"

"I think so Rachel, I've been teaching classes about the mighty caribou for twenty years and I never grow tired of watching them!"

"They are so big and strong Miss, and they just take everything in their stride, and the countryside is incredible, and they are so tough, oh and their baby caribou…… I want one!"

Cleverly, the seasoned teacher brought the conversation back to earth, and to education.

"I'm glad you all liked it, because these mighty caribou may give you an advantage in your final exams!"

The class looked mystified, and Rachel put her hand up and asked the obvious question.

"What advantage Miss?"

"Every year for the last eight or nine, the migration of the caribou of the great north has featured on the geography paper. It is a sort of banker question and if you enjoyed the video, it's one of the easier topics to learn, so I suggest you do.

"It could mean the difference between being selected for the university of your choice or having to take something you are offered as a consolation prize."

On returning home that evening, whilst having supper with her parents and her fifteen-year-old younger brother Jack, she enthused them all about the magnificent caribou.

"Mrs Davies says it is a, now let me get this right, "a cast-iron, nailed on, sure-fire certainty of a question" for the geography exam, and those extra marks could get me into Oxford University!"

Mrs Williams, an English teacher herself, and well-versed in examination technique, silently applauded Mrs Davies.

"Well, you know what you have to do then darling, study those caribou until there is nothing else to know about them!"

The following Saturday morning Rachel's parents went shopping in Swansea city centre, with their daughter's education and future career in mind. They were in search of the mighty caribou, which they found in the entertainment section of Virgin Records and Black's bookstore.

A VHS video of migrating caribou, and a beautifully illustrated coffee table book on their daughter's chosen specialist subject, were bought without hesitation.

Returning home, her parents casually left both gifts on Rachel's bed as a surprise for their outstanding little girl, who they loved unconditionally.

* * *

Each subject in Wales was made up of two papers, each one being three hours in duration. Rachel had to answer four out of twelve questions in each paper, so in reality, each one of the eight questions attempted was worth twelve and a half per cent of the total subject marks to each pupil.

The first five exams had come and gone in the blink of an eye and only the second geography paper stood between Rachel and Christmas.

All the children in the class realised that the caribou were heaven-sent and could indeed make a substantial difference to their futures, but none more so than Rachel, who couldn't wait for the final exam, and what questions she might receive about her friends in the north.

Rachel was streets ahead because she loved the subject of geography, worshipped the caribou, and was constantly reading about them in the library, or watching wildlife programmes on television with the hope of seeing one.

There was no time for boys when you had a herd of beautiful caribou to look after, endangered by the heartless, uncaring march of mankind.

Nervously, she sat at her desk in the examination hall with her fellow pupils, as the invigilator handed out the mock papers.

The second-hand on the clock at the front of the hall raced towards the tipping point until it reached the appointed time.

"Ok, turn over your papers."

The hunt was on.

She carefully opened the exam paper, and in a mirror image of her co-examinees, quickly scanned the page for what she had described to her friends as, "our free go".

No one had to look far, for Mrs Davies was correct, one question stood out like a caribou on heat in a windswept, tundra-infested arctic desert. This was question five.

"Compare and contrast the benefits and challenges of the caribou migration to the indigenous peoples of the Canadian North." It was a cinch.

Her eyes lit up as she grabbed her pen. She could not wait to get started.

Rachel's intense focus meant she missed noticing how every other person taking the exam that morning did the same.

"I love geography and the caribou are ok too!"

She wrote of decreasing habitat, variety of diet, local tribes being pushed north, illegal hunting, the fur trade, predators, the other four migrating animals of the world, disease, lack of education of local peoples, mating habits, and other facts and figures that no one else in the room could even guess at, including Mrs Davies, for Rachel Williams was a caribou expert.

The exam was over before she knew it. Rachel had completed all four questions and wrote and wrote until she could write no more.

* * *

"Time please, put down your pens." It was over.

Her mother came rushing through the door from work, eager to know all about the exam.

"How did it go?"

"Aw mam, it was brilliant, the caribou turned up just as expected, and I nailed it!"

"Fabulous, that's my girl, Oxford here you come!"

They took a moment for a mother-daughter hug.

Rachel's life then restarted with a jolt, for once a teacher always a teacher.

"Right miss, I know Christmas is just around the corner, but you make sure you keep studying, because the real exams in June will be a lot harder, and now is not the time to take your foot off the pedal."

"Yes mam, I'm going to Oxford University, and that's the end of it!"

The steely look in her eye suggested that here was a girl who had more to offer than most.

* * *

Gareth Evans knew what Rachel had to offer, he could not keep his eyes or thoughts off her.

The opportunity to finally do something about it could be coming his way, with eighteenth birthday parties and Christmas celebrations coming up thick and fast. This Saturday would be an ideal opportunity.

Rachel's best friend Sandra Morris was having her eighteenth birthday in the local Craddock rugby club, one of Swansea's finest, and all the class A-listers had been invited.

The exams were forgotten by lunchtime the following day, and Sandra spoke of nothing else other than her party which was now just days away.

"All the boys are coming!"

"Which ones?"

"Don't pretend, you know exactly who's coming Miss "Goody Two Shoes", Gareth Evans of course, and the rest of the rugby team."

Rachel's face went cherry red.

"I was only asking!"

"We all know you fancy him, and he fancies you, so it's no secret is it, you two have been an item like forever!"

Inner heat increased the scarlet colour of Rachel's cheeks, as she felt that her biggest secret had been exposed to the world.

"Do you think he will finally ask you out, or do you think he is too shy?"

"There will be lots of girls there for him to choose from. What are you going to wear?"

Rachel changed the subject and with that, the inquisition was over, and a scarlet complexion slowly returned to flesh tones.

The rugby club had been booked months before by Sandra's well-organised parents. With a squeeze, you could fit just over one hundred people into the room if you kept the obligatory buffet in the back office until the parents served it as standard at approximately 9 pm.

All the girls looked lovely and had spent the week comparing notes about dresses, music, and boys. Everything was quite normal, but it would never quite be normal again for seventeen-year-old Rachel Williams.

Up until 9.00 pm, Sandra's and Rachel's parents and their adult friends mingled with the excited teenagers.

Some of the children's fathers, courage infused with cheap rugby club booze, put on peacock-like displays of dad dancing, which impressed no one except themselves, and least of all their embarrassed wives and children.

Preceding the opening of the buffet at 9 pm prompt, John Morris, the father of the strikingly pretty, blonde schoolgirl Sandra, addressed the crowd with well-chosen emotional words, wiping tears from his eyes, as he recognised her journey from infants' school to womanhood, wishing her a wonderful future.

He was hugely emotional about her striving to achieve her university grades so that she could read medicine at Bristol University and become the first doctor in the family.

Mr Morris finished by inviting everyone in the room to sing "Happy Birthday" to his daughter, and an impromptu Welsh choir did her proud.

Following the speech, Sandra gave a nervous, hurried, thirty-second response, which culminated in her cutting the cake with her mother.

All the girls cried while the boys acted like love-starved cockerels, displaying their muscles and lack of emotion in the false belief it made them more attractive in the game of love.

They were too young and immature to realise that humility, understanding, compassion and vulnerability, were the most powerful hidden ingredients of attracting the opposite sex.

Sandra's mother took the cellophane off the sandwiches. "The buffet is open!"

The starving teenagers almost swallowed her whole in trying to get at the sausage rolls, pasties, ham sandwiches, and cheese and pineapple sticks.

Gareth Evans stood next to Rachel in the buffet line, in an impromptu appointment expertly fixed by Sandra, who shoved them together at the right moment.

"Wow, you look amazing, so grown up!"

Rachel's face lit up with this attention, but her courage failed her, and she blushed, looking at the floor to avoid eye contact.

"Thank you, I didn't know you cared!"

She regretted it immediately; in case a negative reply was forthcoming.

Surfing the buffet together, the verbal game of snakes and ladders continued between them, but the teenage curses of lack of confidence and indecision saw them go separate ways as they passed the serviettes and cutlery at the end of the line.

"He said I looked grown-up!" Rachel said to Sandra, stamping her feet with excitement.

"Gareth said I looked amazing!" she quietly whispered to the birthday girl, not wanting to attract anyone else's attention, lest her cheeks give away her secret love.

"He's desperate for you! he's been watching you all night."

Rachel, despite her self-control, went bright crimson anyway, and recognising this involuntary beacon of love interest and discomfort, moved to a darker corner of the room, where her flushed face would not be noticed, such were the trials of teenage love and discovery.

As the older women distributed the cake, the DJ began to play his musical set, starting with the huge disco hit Staying Alive by the Bee Gees.

The girls responded as if they had been called to arms by an overwhelmed soldier general, and formed circles, where they danced around handbags, in a kind of tribal bonding ceremony.

The boys did nothing, except avoid the dance floor at all costs.

As it was the rugby club, they ordered alcoholic drinks from their older teammates, who were putting in a shift on the other side of the bar, whilst ogling the new crop of young ladies, many of whom had never graced that place before.

A pint of lager with a dash of lime was the fashion of the day.

Now the male teenage contest of proving who were the big dogs and who were the lightweights in the "downing pints" competition began in earnest. It would last a few years yet until maturity entered the fold, and at that time the ritual would be passed to a younger, dafter generation.

At 10.00 pm in a silent prearranged tryst, the parents began to drift away, thus confirming that it was no longer their time.

This night was about Sandra with her friends.

It was their rite of passage to the beauty, and sometimes the despair of adulthood, depending on which choices they made, what effort they put into life, and fate's fickle hand.

"We're off now," Sandra's and Rachel's parents said in unison, hugging and kissing the girls before they disappeared into the night as the words, "have a good time and behave yourself!" and "don't do anything stupid!" rang in their ears.

With the buffet removed and the parents gone, it was not long before the party got going.

As unaccustomed swigs of alcohol hit their emotional button the girls danced, showed off, laughed, sometimes cried, and occasionally screamed, as is a teenage girl's way to attract the attention of the boys they pretend not to be interested in.

Gareth Evans was the pride of the pack, strikingly handsome in tight-fitting cream, khaki drill trousers, with a dark blue, open-neck, short-sleeved shirt pinned onto a bronzed Adonis-like chest.

It was neatly set off by a navy, double-breasted blazer, which he threw off as soon as the older generation exited stage left so that he could be more informal and relaxed.

Gareth was used to a couple of pints of alcohol in the rugby club, having played there since being a junior player aged seven, and at sixteen, on joining the ranks of the youth team, soft drinks just seemed to evolve into lager and beer. That is how it was in Craddock and every rugby club throughout the land of Wales.

On this night he had consumed three pints by 9.00 pm, already one more than his customary two, which as a big, strapping, fit youth, he could handle with ease, but he wasn't counting, for he was on a mission.

Gareth had one goal in mind, and it was not dancing the conga.

He only had eyes for Rachel Williams, the love of his life, and he dared himself to do something about it.

As the evening wore on and the alcohol hit the spot, some of the other boys began to tap the girls on their shoulders and ask them to dance in a performance that subsequently witnessed many of them pair up for final school-year courtships.

From a distance, Rachel watched a confident Rhiannon Jones approach Gareth at the edge of the bar, where he had been rooted for an hour.

Until then, he had been happily exchanging knowing glances that lasted a millisecond too long, before finishing with them both looking quickly away as if it had never happened.

Rhiannon was a slim, pretty girl with a vivacious smile, who with makeup ably applied by her mother's fair hand, looked a million dollars on this special evening.

Any boy in the room would jump at a chance to have Rhiannon, and she and all the other girls knew it.

She was a real stunner, with a great personality that made her popular with both sexes, who everyone thought could be Miss Wales if she entered the annual beauty competition.

Rachel stared and went weak in the knees as it was obvious that Gareth was being asked to dance by Rhiannon.

"Horror of horrors, I will lose my love before he even knows I love him!"

There was no need to worry, Gareth seemed to point to his knee making excuses about an old rugby injury and rejecting a beauty that no man in the whole of Wales would ever refuse.

"You like Rachel, don't you?" Rhiannon whispered, "don't worry I won't tell anyone, if the rest of the school doesn't spill Swansea's best-known secret first," and smiled knowingly as she said, "go on Gareth, ask her to dance, you are made for each other!"

Rhiannon tipsily and maturely accepted the refusal and walked away.

Rachel breathed again, as life came back to her body, signalled by sweaty palms and palpitations.

She knew her heart was ticking because she could hear it beating in her ears.

"Is this what love is meant to be like?"

Gethin Thomas, who played scrum half to Gareth's outside half in the school rugby team leaned over.

"You must be mad; how could you turn that down?"

"There's plenty of fish in the sea, Thommo!"

Gareth sipped his pint and ignored the increasingly effervescent and drunken Gethin.

He quickly returned to the night's chosen sport of Rachel watching, when she wasn't looking at him, of course.

The lively and fast music had been playing for two hours non-stop, and it began to slow down as the end of the evening approached.

Sandra and Rachel had danced themselves silly, the former now hand in hand with Tom Jenkins, who she would snog at every drunken opportunity.

Unbeknown to them, this liaison would lead to marriage eight years later, three children and six grandchildren, in the way that these unscripted pairings just happen.

Some of the girls now sat openly with boys that they had hunted this year, this term, this night, while boys sat with girls, they thought they had hunted, where nothing could be farther from the truth, the boys being just too immature to realise that they were, in fact, nature's prey.

Over the speakers, the DJ announced that the evening was concluding, and put on Evergreen by Barbra Streisand, the theme song from the smash hit film A Star is Born.

The remaining single girls and boys earnestly looked around, to see what remained on offer at this unofficial cattle market.

Andrew Willmott, a large prop forward made a beeline for Rachel, but Gareth having bolted down the remains of his fifth lager and lime in an instant, proved why outside halves played where they did, and slow lumbering giants gasped for air in the pack.

Gareth passed Andrew on the inside and was in front of him before he knew it, having unwittingly found the courage he lacked by increasing his alcohol intake, which had aided nature's urge.

As Andrew stopped in his tracks, beaten by the better, quicker man, Gareth reached out to the delighted, nervous Rachel, and smiled through glazed eyes, looking like a puppy dog awaiting his next treat.

"Will you dance with me?"

Rachel went weak at the knees, her heart beating like a trip hammer.

All at once she felt like she wanted to cry, cheer, and smile at the same time. A nervous feeling in the pit of her stomach metamorphosed into one of complete safety, security, warmth, and love as he embraced her for the first time.

Gareth felt nothing but the gentle response of the girl he had always loved, and a warm feeling oozed over his body.

Somewhere in the darkness, Rhiannon found another rugby player, and Sandra wiped tears from her eyes.

"At last, I've been waiting over ten years for this!"

The music played gently in their ears, as they felt each other's passion, and tried to interpret the song in this most special of moments,

The lyrics rang true to the embryonic young couple.

"One love that is shared by two, I have found with you, like a rose under the April snow, I was certain love would grow."

They mimicked the words to each other through watery eyes, and it just happened, Gareth leaned forward, and his lips were met by those of Rachel, who had felt the same urge at that very second, and they kissed their first kiss.

As the music ended, they both giggled, and Gareth took Rachel's hand, giving the impression that he would never let it go.

Rachel held on tight, hoping he never would.

Over the next few days, Gareth was introduced to the family as Rachel's boyfriend, and everyone at school, including the self-sacrificing beauty Rhiannon, believed that the strength of this perfect bond would not be broken in a hurry.

* * *

In early January Rachel announced, "it's been the best Christmas ever," before her mother redirected her daughter's thoughts, as only mothers can, to the topic of school, the caribou of the north, examinations, university, and her future chosen career as a teacher.

On Monday 5th January 1978, Rachel walked joyously and eagerly to school, anticipating a brilliant new year, and just dying to see her boyfriend Gareth Evans.

Gareth had decided he would not go on to university after the sixth form, for he would be joining a kitchen installation company as an administrator.

The decision was made because he wanted to concentrate on his budding rugby career with Swansea RFC. He had moved from his local club

Craddock to the Swansea youth set up at Christmas. They had unofficially told him he would be signed on professional terms for the following 1978/79 season.

The job had been arranged, as was traditionally the case, by one of the club's sponsors. It was a coveted role only given to the most talented prospects, of which Gareth was heralded as the most outstanding.

Gareth was receiving rave reviews in the local press, attracting much attention from the rugby fraternity, and from the young female camp followers who sought a rugby-playing bovine mate.

True love repels all interlopers, and all efforts to win Gareth's attention by the pack of celebrity-hungry good-time girls were refuted out of hand.

He was a one-girl guy, but alcohol changes personalities, and oftentimes creates unwanted opportunities.

Gareth managed to get himself seriously drunk after winning the Welsh Youth Cup in March, at the national stadium in Cardiff in front of fifteen thousand adoring fans.

Rachel, her family, and their friends had all been there and watched their hero have the game of his life, for he was an international player in the making. It was only a matter of time before he pulled on the famed red jersey of his home country.

After everyone offered their congratulations, Rachel left Gareth to celebrate with the boys and gave a promise of seeing him on the morrow.

Staying close to his side would have been a far wiser decision.

The joy, adrenalin, adoration, alcohol, and the opportunity, turned out to be too much for a young man to resist.

Euphoria, immaturity, and too much to drink are potent mixes that can change personalities and dilute responsibility.

By 11 pm the new Swansea rugby starlet was drunk out of his mind, and devoid of any logic.

The writing was on the wall as his teammates egged him on and on, down a dark path to a lifetime of regret.

The resulting meaningless, sexual transgression in a scruffy bedsit with a popular pub barmaid, destroyed the teenage dreams of a wonderfully innocent, naive, trusting girl.

* * *

Word travels fast in a small city and by Monday morning the genie was out of the bottle, the Chinese whispers inexorably making their way closer to the school playground.

Rhiannon was well connected, and she heard it first, and then passed the bad news on to Rachel's best friend, Sandra.

They talked all morning between classes about what they should do and finally Sandra suggested.

"Shall we tell Rachel?"

"Sandra, you are her best friend, maybe it's better coming from you?"

"It's not my story to tell is it?"

"The rumours are spreading fast and everyone in school will know by this afternoon. We can't have them laughing at Rachel behind her back!"

"Then we must tell her. What a nightmare!"

"We?"

"Yes Rhiannon, we! I cannot do it on my own, it's not fair."

"Oh Sandra, we are damned if we do and damned if we don't!"

The two young ladies, thrust into the woes of adult romance, agreed to break the news to Rachel during lunchtime before she heard it elsewhere.

When school ended, a distraught, inconsolable Rachel, left class in floods of tears, never to speak with or see Gareth again.

As far as Rachel was concerned her life was ruined, and her future marriage to Gareth was over before he had ever proposed.

Gareth's remorse mattered little, for the trust was broken, and as Sandra said, "the magic is gone, it can never be the same again!"

The rest of March and April witnessed an uncharacteristic parent-child dogfight, with Rachel's broken heart, broken relationship, and broken trust, plunging the teenage romantic into a dark and dangerous place.

Her schoolwork suffered terribly, especially as she refused to attend lessons, in case she bumped into her lost love.

Parents visited the school, teachers visited the house, and as the exams started, although woefully behind in her subjects, the general belief was that she might still be good enough to achieve the grades to get into Oxford University, where a new life and bright opportunities would unfold.

A chink of light appeared on the horizon when least expected for Gareth left school in the middle of April and did not return, having taken the weight of his misdeed heavily on his shoulders.

It availed Rachel the opportunity to go to school, and have three extra-curriculum lessons with Mrs Davies, who was painfully aware that her most outstanding pupil had not completed enough of the geography syllabus to cover all bases, and that getting high marks was in the balance.

Time waits for no man or woman and just like the migrating caribou the school examinations arrived right on cue.

Rachel wasn't confident the first two history exams had gone well.

"I think I did ok!"

Her mother was delighted, for she knew that her daughter was her own worst critic.

"If she said "ok" it means she has done "ok" if not better," she told her husband that evening.

English was next, and with additional coaching from her mother, she was better prepared than for the other subjects.

Once again, having sat both papers, she thought she had done ok and as her father said, "two "ok's" should make two good grades, but let's hope it's enough for Oxford!"

Rachel sat the first geography paper and reported to both her parents and Mrs Davies that she thought it was her best so far, which considering the time she had missed at school, was an unexpected reaction.

Now Rachel's future all hinged on that last paper.

"Can lightning strike twice? Will she do well again, this is the paper that always has the caribou question, it might be just enough to save the day!" said Mrs Davies to her colleagues.

After one more final lesson, the time had come for the showdown, the last throw of the dice, before young futures across the land would be decided on a set of not-so-random geography questions, which might or might not involve the mighty caribou.

In a private moment, Rachel and Mrs Davies stood in front of the blackboard as pupil and teacher for the last time.

"Let's hope your banker question comes up, for you are truly the world's foremost expert on that subject!"

For the first time in months, Rachel managed a smile, followed by a flood of tears at lessons learnt, and things lost.

"I hope so Miss, I hope so!"

The older woman comforted the younger woman until the pain and tears on both sides subsided.

"Good luck, you will be fine and say hello to the mighty caribou for me. See you tomorrow."

They hugged each other tightly, ending a seven-year relationship built on enthusiasm and respect and then gently parted and waved their sad goodbyes. The stage was set for the second and final geography exam, which would decide a bright, sparkling girl's future.

It was a fifty-fifty evening for Rachel, as she split her thoughts between her lost love and geography revision.

Rachel cursed the first day that she ever saw Gareth, and she scolded herself for falling victim to love's illusions rather than remaining firmly in the pragmatic world she had always known, and in between thoughts, she read about the reliable caribou, her best friends in the whole world.

The clock went off at 6.30 am in her parent's bedroom next door and functioned as a call to arms for every member of the household, and with passing conversations and good wishes for the day ahead, the family would soon be whisked off to the four winds.

Mum would go to a comprehensive school on the far side of the city, whilst dad would go to work as a chartered surveyor. Her younger brother Jack would go off to school as normal with his friends, to study for his big exams the following year.

Rachel would walk in through the main entrance of her school for the last time, directly into the examination room to meet and wrestle with her fate, a future that she alone could influence.

As the clock approached everyone's predetermined departure time, a knock on the door summoned her younger brother Jack to arms, and he was immediately up and away with his mates, without so much as a second thought for his emotionally traumatised sister, kicking a soccer ball as they went.

Next to leave was her mother, who understood the game of love, and was wise to every secret her daughter held, in the way that mothers just know things.

"Forget mean old boys today and do your best. Knock them dead and make sure the caribou have a good run out!"

Mrs Williams hugged her daughter, and then shouted goodbye to her husband, before driving off to work.

Now only two remained in the house of doom.

Dad had deliberately played about with his tie, repeatedly doing, and undoing the knot, until he was finally left alone with his daughter.

"Come here, darling!"

The only man in the world she felt she could ever trust, gave her a fatherly hug and kiss, which reaffirmed her faith in herself and human nature.

"Boys will be boys, and I know you can't imagine it, but I was a boy myself once you know!"

Rachel wiped away her free-flowing tears and blurted out.

"But I loved him, dad!"

"I know darling, it's all part of growing up and I understand."

It was an obvious clichéd response, offered by her father whilst knowing that not in a million years would he ever understand a woman's mind, let alone the extraordinary impulses of the female teenage daughter.

Cometh the hour, cometh the man. He recomposed himself, before saying what he had planned to say.

"Rachel there are three things in this world which are important."

"Which are?"

"Yesterday, today and tomorrow."

"And how does that work dad?"

"There is yesterday which we can learn from, there is today, which we must make the most of, and there is tomorrow, which, if we take the positive from the other two, we can influence for the better.

The words struck a real chord with Rachel, and she vowed to remember them always.

It was a father-daughter moment that no one else could ever invade or understand.

"Now go into that exam room, show them the real Rachel Williams, and give it your best shot. You know we will always be here to support you in everything you do."

Rachel cried, dad cried, while the Siamese cat, and naturally the goldfish were uninterested, but the cocker spaniel whimpered, suggesting he was rooting for the cause.

His parting shot offered further clarity and inspiration.

"Remember the mighty caribou of the great Canadian north, they could make all the difference, and look out Oxford University because here you come!"

Dad had worked his fatherly magic, and they hugged again.

As her father drove away to work, Rachel was now upbeat, his precious daughter waving him a loving, grateful, confident, goodbye.

Rachel's head was spinning, yet she still wisely took the time to do ten more minutes of revision, before checking she had everything for the exam.

Taking one last look in the mirror she suddenly saw her.

The young foolish girl who had fallen in love, who knew that no matter what happened in the future her parents would love, cherish, and support her.

Rachel gazed at her reflection for a moment and challenged herself, and then the steely determination of an excellent athlete came to the fore, as Gareth Evans's spell of magic crumbled to dust.

"I might have given you my heart, my trust, my love, but I still have my soul, and I will be needing that today. Look out school and look out Oxford University because here I come!"

The emancipated schoolgirl, a woman full-grown, walked down the passage from the kitchen to the front door, exited calmly, and closed it gently behind her, as she went in search of the mighty caribou.

* * *

Rachel strolled into the exam room with a new air of self-belief and greeted all she met with an assured, winning smile.

"She's like the old Rachel," said Sandra to Rhiannon, as they welcomed Rachel back from life's shadows.

It was almost 9.00 am.

This was it; the future lay between her and the exam board. The journey from this room would determine not only her education, lifelong friends, and connections, but also her career path and she wondered, "maybe also a husband who I could truly trust, who doesn't play rugby and let girls down!"

Rachel regrouped and reigned in her overspilled emotion.

"Cheap shot! Gareth is so yesterday, and from hereon in, the old Rachel is back in town. I have learnt from yesterday, I'm going to give it my best shot today, and in the future, I'll make the best of the results I get!"

With that, the invigilator announced the exam had begun.

"Look out caribou!" she thought, and quickly scanned the paper for the head start she needed.

She read the twelve questions twice, lest she had missed something, but there was not a migrating caribou in sight.

Those mighty animals, her best friends, had abandoned her in this hour of need, for this paper was caribou free, and the timing could not have been worse.

One more time she read it again, taking solace in the fact that despite her limited attendance and lack of knowledge of the full syllabus, there were three questions which she could answer well, thus giving good marks, but she was still a question short.

Rachel hesitated, then bit the bullet and started to write the answer to a well-rehearsed climatology question on the South American rainforests and Amazon delta, making sure she only spent forty-five minutes doing so, as Mrs Davies had previously taught the class the exam technique of using their time budget wisely, and not panicking.

Her geography teacher's exam mantra ran through her head.

"If you can only answer three of the four questions you are supposed to answer, DO NOT spend an hour on each!"

Rhiannon had asked. "What must we do then?"

"Spend three sets of forty-five minutes on each answer, which will leave you forty-five minutes at the end.

"You will not get any more marks for spending an hour on a question instead of forty-five minutes!

"The last forty-five minutes should be used to use your mental prowess to eke out some marks by attempting another question.

"It could be the difference between a pass or a fail."

Rachel, before her love affair and very public break up with Gareth, had been a good pupil and a great listener, and she remembered these words verbatim.

Her second question fared even better and allowed her to expound on the theory of coastal erosion, with a particular emphasis on longshore drift.

It was the halfway point, and her tail and confidence were up, despite lacking the gift question about her long-standing missing friends, the caribou.

The third question she answered was another gem, for it was all about the weathering of mountains over time.

She wrote of corries, cwms and tarns, extreme hot and cold temperatures, glaciers, and wind erosion. It was the mirror of a similar question she had answered in the mock exam the previous November, in which she gained full marks.

Extra marks, no matter how few, would be critical in deciding her future. There were exactly forty-five minutes left, and with three great answers completed, Rachel scoured the paper to find one last question she could attempt.

Her eyes kept coming back to question seven about New York.

It read.

"Write about the northern hemisphere city of New York, USA, explaining in geographical terms why it is such an attractive place for people to migrate thousands of miles to live in, considering it's given to extremely hot Summers and harsh Winters."

She studied it and a plan began to form.

"Remember what Mrs Davies said, I've answered three great questions, I've got plenty of time, maybe there are one or two more marks left on the paper if I can just write something about New York City!"

Then it dawned on her. "I'm going to make Mam, Dad and Mrs Davies proud because I'm going to Oxford University!"

She stared at the New York question.

"Could this be a gift from the examiner Gods, put there just for me?" The words jumped off the page, "northern, migrate, thousands of miles."

It was a sign. This was the question that she must answer, for she could not even try the other eight.

Rachel had seen New York many, many times on television and in the movies.

King Kong, Cary Grant, and Deborah Kerr all spent time at the Empire state building. The New York Yankees played baseball, and there was boxing too at Madison Square Garden because Gareth had made her watch Muhammad Ali one night, even though she loathed the whole experience.

Her mind raced onwards, "Saturday Night Fever was shot there, and the theme music was Staying Alive" she thought, and then her mind wandered off course for a moment, as she thought of that fateful night at Sandra's party.

Rachel sat up straight as her pretty disposition turned to a steadfast determination.

"I'll answer the New York question, I'll add some marks, and I'm going to Oxford so look out, here I come!"

Picking up her pen for the last time as a school pupil, the liberated young woman and daughter, of whom all mothers and fathers would be proud, began to write.

"There are no caribou on the great streets of New York City, but if there were............"

* * *

Epilogue

By the age of just twenty-one Gareth's dream of success was cruelly cut short by a serious knee injury, as is often the case in professional sport, and with only basic qualifications, his fading star was at the mercy of life's behest.

He rapidly fell from the dizzy heights of fame to a career of menial administrative and clerical jobs, supplemented by bar work at the rugby club, and part-time coaching, where he tried to relive the glory days from week to week.

Rachel would never know what marks she received for the answer to her final geography question, but academically and career wise she achieved everything she had strived for and deserved.

Following a successful spell at Oxford University, she entered the teaching profession, later rising to be the headmistress of a well-renowned private girls' school just outside of London.

On her dad's 80th birthday in 2010, not long after her 50th celebration, Rachel was returning to Swansea for the weekend with Charles, her barrister husband, and their two children.

Charlotte and William were now aged 23 and 25 respectively, and the tight knit family had all travelled together in one car, just as they did when the children were young.

The Mighty Caribou

Rachel decided to go via Marks and Spencer at Cross Valley Roundabout, just off the M4 motorway on the outskirts of Swansea, to collect the gorgeous birthday cake from that fine shop, which stood like a Welsh castle opposite the superstore Tesco, clearly pointing out the pecking order and shopping authority in those parts.

They parked their comfortable, new Mercedes CLS class saloon on the Tesco side of the facility, as all the spaces on the Marks and Spencer side were full, because of a snap, half-price sale.

All four family members exited the car like synchronised swimmers, stretching after a long five-hour journey from St Albans, their expensive hometown near London.

In the fading light, Rachel had a flashback, as she half recognised a shadowy figure entering Tesco. It was too dark to tell, so she just continued walking with her brood in close attendance.

Despite the huge numbers of bargain hunters in Marks and Spencer, they stuck boldly to their task, and within thirty minutes they were through the tills, with cake and party food in tow, on the return journey to their shiny, metallic, silver chariot.

Perchance by fate, as the neat family group walked once more past the front of Tesco, Rachel looked up, and the misty figure she thought she had recognised earlier was not twenty feet from her, carrying a heavy box of cheap cider, man and cans lit up like a beacon by the lights of that discount shopping emporium.

She looked at him; he looked at her. No words passed their lips.

Rachel stared at the barely recognisable, balding, pot-bellied man with his T-shirt hanging over his scruffy jeans, who was accompanied by an equally poorly presented female, clearly past her sell-by date, with a larger stomach than him.

This scene was offset by the ugliest conglomeration of tattoos on a man that the headmistress had ever seen.

Gareth Evans had left the building, and it seemed an old tramp was using his body.

He stared at Rachel, who he had not seen since the day he had transgressed all those years ago, for once the spell of love had been broken, she had dismissed him out of hand.

For a moment, her heart skipped a beat. She cursed her lifelong best friend, Sandra, as a flashing vision of an 18th birthday party long ago, appeared and disappeared.

She averted her gaze from her ex-teenage lover and compared the twilight vision she had just seen with that of her handsome, trusty, caring and loving husband, who she had met at Oxford University some thirty years before.

Next, she proudly looked at her children, a teacher and biochemist, both with great prospects, and she silently praised the Lord.

Her eyes turned one more time to Gareth Evans, the dishevelled fallen star, and she took one final mental picture, that she would privately keep forever, in the way that females do, of love found, love lost, and a life saved.

Regrouping, she thought about her wonderful parents and how she had come to Swansea that weekend, to celebrate the birthday of her loving father.

Fondly, she remembered the support they had given her in the age of puppy love, and she felt warm all over like her naked body had been kissed by the gods themselves.

On a whim, she turned to her husband and children.

"Do you know?.............. I've got the best parents, husband and kids in the whole wide world!"

They all looked at each other for answers, whilst trying to work out where this curveball had come from.

Gareth's brain clicked slowly into action at the distinctive sound of Rachel's voice, vaguely hearing her parting shot, as the blurry vision of his one true love's persona, spirited itself away, into the darkness.

Memories of better, youthful times, stirred his brain to action, creating a wave of happiness that he had not felt in years, but that fleeting dopamine moment disappeared as he thought of his two money-grabbing ex-wives and his three estranged children. Then he glanced at his current concubine and concluded, "not much better, I'm definitely on a downward spiral!"

He thought of primary school, eighteenth birthday parties, rugby tours, casual love affairs, drinking games and excesses, a host of thankless jobs and a lost future.

One more time he looked at the athletic, successful, happy figure of Rachel, as she stood by the car with her family, and from just over thirty years and fifty feet away they stared at each other for the last time.

At that moment Gareth Evans finally came face to face with what he had always known.

He had won and lost the most beautiful, kind-hearted girl in the world, the love of his life, and it had taken him a drunken, remorseful, immature lifetime to realise it.

As Rachel drove away, the greying figure of the once dishy, handsome Gareth Evans faded into oblivion, her devil finally exorcised by the unwitting comfort of her family.

Her mind drifted to her father's eightieth birthday party, and then to the words that he once said to her, before she went on a fruitless caribou hunt one early June morning, which had, with a little ingenuity and presence of mind, turned up trumps in the end.

"Dad was right, life does happen in three stages.

"I have learned so much from yesterday.

"I am loving today; can it ever get better than this?

"As for tomorrow, I can still influence it and I cannot wait for all the good things yet to happen!"

She looked over her shoulder to the back seat and impishly said to the kids.

"When are we going to have some grandchildren?"

Chapter 6

KING OF NEW YORK

"THE King is dead, long live the King!"
Quentin Prendergast spoke the words out loud and clear to his reflection in the mirror.

His death was imminent, and if he was lucky, his end on this earth could be counted in months.

Death and taxes were the two certainties. He had paid his taxes up to date, but soon he must complete the contract.

"To be or not to be?" was not the question. His impending demise had taken that phrase out of his hands.

"To act or not to act? that was the question!"

The physically fading Broadway and Hollywood star, slowly and carefully stretched himself up to his commanding height of six feet tall, before gazing at the heavily rouged reflection in the mirror.

He stared boldly ahead, drawing on all his thespian experience, and then addressed the haunted image that stared back at him with perfect elocution, timing, and emotion.

"Should I play the part the crowd expect, portraying the image they crave, or do I announce to them the uncomfortable, uncompromising, unbending truth!"

* * *

Walter Wyatt Palmer was a weak, sallow, sickly infant, bereft of love, warmth and affection, from the day he was born under the sign of Taurus on 28th May 1957.

His birth and life were simply an interference to the liquor fuelled world of his haphazard, unmarried parents, and that was the highest rating they ever gave him.

He remembered his first day at school vividly, making his solitary, lonely way behind the other kids, as if to the beat of a drum.

It began, when at five years old and with his father at work, his mother Maria, devoid of any maternal responsibility, pushed him casually through the front door, whilst nursing yet another hangover.

Despite his undernourished appearance and absence of social structure, Walter was a naturally good and kind child.

His blue eyes, hopeful, innocent smile, and open countenance suggested something almost angelic about him, that in some way he might be special, and a little bit different to his counterparts.

"He must get it from his grandparents, whoever they are!" said Missy Clarke, the secretary to the school principal Mrs Osborn, at the end of the first semester.

"Yes, we'll have to keep an eye on young Walter if he is to become anything in this life, because, with parents like he's got, he has no chance!"

Growing up in the small cowboy town of Great Falls, Montana was purgatory for Walter.

No matter how much he tried, he never fitted in. His few friends were all girls, who mothered, pitied, and protected him from the aggression of his masculine male counterparts.

He told the girls how lovely they all were, remarked on how kind to him they always seemed to be, and it served to encourage them even more to love and defend him.

Walter had quickly realised that being soft, gentle, polite, and non-threatening, with a little bit of vulnerability, would endear him to most people. It became his modus operandi. His biology teacher once remarked in senior school, "you can catch more flies with sugar than you can with salt!"

Unwittingly, she had defined the mantra by which he would live the rest of his life.

To the teenage schoolgirl at William Rodgers High School in Great Falls, Montana, the young man known as Walter Wyatt Palmer was a safe pair of non-predatory hands. They could practice "talking to boys" with Walter because he seemed to understand girlie things like makeup, fashion, irrational emotions, and walking arm in arm without being embarrassed.

No one spoke about the unspeakable subject of being gay. It was taboo. All the girls knew he was gay, and all the boys too; his parents and teachers knew also, but no one ever voiced it in public.

The last guy in town to believe it was Walter because he was the only one fighting it.

It was the first of only three fights he would ever have.

***

He was a born pacifist and would avoid confrontation at every opportunity.

Many years later if you bumped into him in a bar and spilt his drink, he would apologise to you and offer to buy you one back for "his mistake".

When Walter drove his car as an adult, he would invite pedestrians and other drivers to go first at traffic lights, crossings, and interchanges, much to the frustration of his fellow drivers.

He had never argued in his life, let alone been involved in an altercation that he had started. Walter would always concede the point and hope to remain friends. It was his way.

His father Joe was not a big man, but he was a strong-minded, stern individual, an ex-marine with little sense of humour, who was a loner until the drink hit his good time button.

Joe had met Walter's mother Maria when they were both out surfing the local bars in years gone by, opportunistically looking for casual lovers. It seemed they never wanted the party to end.

Walter was more the product of Jack Daniels and Stella Artois than he ever was of the mean-spirited, serial alcoholics, Joseph Palmer, and Maria Wyatt. The new-born baby was anything but the fruit of love.

When Joe was on a high in a local dive, his favourite toast was "beer, helping ugly people have sex since 1800," but here was a man who despite his happy-go-lucky drunken outward appearance, was a two-sided coin.

Walter's father could change his personality on a dime. In the house, he was a completely different personality to the "great guy" who people experienced in the drinking dens of Great Falls.

On one hand, it seemed you had a clear, shiny, happy face, but on the other hand, was an unpredictable countenance hidden from the sun. It was more of a silhouette than a painting, and it haunted the boy throughout most of his childhood.

Walter never knew which face would greet him on any given day. Every waking hour in the house was a walk on eggshells. The more he failed to be "like the other boys," the more he was punished. There were chores, slaps, punches, and threats.

Without fail every single day, and worse on weekends, the small boy suffered both physical and mental torture. Drip, drip, drip, it was agony.

Joe would get out of his mind on cheap booze, lose his money chasing slow racehorses and fast women, and then take it out on Maria and Walter. Violence and disorder were a way of life.

Fear contributed to Walter wetting the bed until he was twelve.

"You wet the bed again boy!" followed by thump, thump, thump, but Joe was too clever to ever mark Maria or Walter where anyone would see any damage. Hits were restricted to clothed areas. Joe's "treatment" could hardly be construed as a solution to Walter's nervous disposition.

The phrase "man up," still echoed in Walter's brain years later. There wasn't a day in his adult life when he didn't hear it somewhere at the back of his mind.

The school was a saviour for Walter, for it brought a sense of belonging and a feeling of warmth and security. It was his first-ever family.

Walter was average at most subjects but bottom of the class in sports and physical activities.

However, when it came to drama his teacher noticed a spark in Walter that he nurtured for all it was worth, for it was obvious that there was something special about this boy.

In music he was a late starter in forging ahead of the other kids but once his voice broke the school music-master realised that this boy could sing like a bird. Walter easily performed any musical genre from easy listening to rock anthems and could effortlessly sing any male solo from the leading musicals.

He spent most of his time with the girls, in the way that birds of a feather flock together.

His favourite was Emma Wilson, the daughter of big Mickey Wilson, a no-nonsense second-generation Irish traffic cop. From the moment Walter met her on that first day at school they were inseparable.

The strong-minded little girl was Walter's saviour. She was beautiful, kind, and thoughtful, but beneath the pleasant exterior, she had her father's iron will. It would be unwise to try and bully Emma or any of her friends, for she feared no-one.

At the end of the first week, Mick witnessed Walter walk Emma safely to their porch. They were just five years old, and he had watched them hold hands from the school gates less than half a mile away.

"I'm Walter, I've brought Emma home for you, Mr Wilson," he beamed through misty blue eyes, and then delivered the hallmark smile that would later in life be a passport to his world of hopes and dreams.

Mrs Wilson looked out of the kitchen window and shouted.

"Would you and your friend like to come in with Emma for some cake Walter?"

"Friend?" said Emma as she looked back some twenty-five yards behind them.

Another classmate with a sullen disposition stood there, who unnoticed by them, had followed the two youngsters home. He was big for his age and had a noticeable turn in his left eye; the imperfection being immediately noticeable to adults and children alike.

"That's Dexter, he's not with us mom, he's weird!" said Emma.

Dexter heard every word, and in a tantrum threw down onto the pavement a half-eaten apple he had been carrying, thus expressing his frustration at not being included. He stared at the Wilson home for an uncomfortable two or three seconds in some sort of silent, belligerent challenge, and then turned around and without saying a word walked back towards the school, using his good eye as his navigational tool.

"Oh, wow! I wasn't expecting that. Right, anyone for cake kids?"

"No thank you, Mrs Wilson, I have to get home, my father said I have to do chores."

With that Walter was gone, despite the fact he was hungry and longing for the perceived sanctuary and security of the Wilson household.

Whilst Emma ate cake, Walter ate humble pie, and suffered death by a thousand insults, at the hands of Daddy Joe.

"You know what Mick; I think Emma has met her husband-to-be!"

"I agree he's a nice kid, but don't get carried away, there's something there that's not quite right."

"What do you mean?" said Mrs Wilson who was slightly taken aback.

"I don't know, something's not quite right, no other boys are lining up on our front path, that's all. Anyway, they are only five years old."

***

Maybe she got it from her dad, but Emma oozed confidence, and Walter, a nervous infant, was happy in her shadow.

One day when Mick turned up in his shiny patrol car, wearing his trademark Aviator sunglasses, and gave them both a lift home, Walter somehow felt protected and safe for the first time in his life, at least until Joe's next erratic outburst.

Everyone knew about Walter's poor domestic situation, including Mick. The police department were regular attendees at "Joe's Bar" as they called it, as Maria often called the sheriff's office to say she had been punched or threatened by her raging husband.

When the police attended Maria would never press charges. The officers would go through the motions, with Walter as scarce as possible, in case he said something he shouldn't, for fear of later incurring the wrath of his father.

His terrified mother would either change her story, or just clam up and break down, while Joe denied everything, and just brooded in his special dark way.

Eventually, the police would leave, and the circus would begin again, with Walter nervously awaiting the next intervention for an imagined minor misdemeanour.

Not all policemen worked by the book, especially in a small old-fashioned town like Great Falls.

Some of Mick's colleagues would occasionally "rough up" Joe a little, with a backhand across the cheek, a punch in the solar plexus, or a crack with a nightstick behind the thigh.

"Is that how you hit your old lady Joe?"

The threat of increased violence on a return visit from the local police force would create enough of a mental note in Joe's pickled brain for him to see reason. He would behave himself for a while, or at least a few months anyway, and then once again he would see the differences in Walter to the other boys, target him as the focus of some deep inner anger, and it would all reignite.

Joe, alcohol, and gambling were incompatible bedfellows. This was a dangerous combination for someone with a bad temper. Sooner or later, they would conspire against each other, and the violence would begin again. He was an obsessive, compulsive character long before the term OCD was invented.

In the canning factory where he worked in the finishing section, he was legendary for the way he lined up "his ducks". His co-workers marvelled at the way he set out the cans for labelling like rows of soldiers awaiting inspection from a higher authority. All ducks inline, all uniform, all the same, every time. He couldn't do it any other way.

Everything had to be just so and in its place. Six o'clock meant six o'clock and now meant now. Any deviation at home brought punishment, in a swift, uncompromising military style. If Walter or Maria were late for anything, if something was where it shouldn't be, Joe would snap.

***

Just after Walter's fourteenth birthday, the problem solved itself.

Rumour had it that some money lenders caught up with Joe in a bar where he was "on one".

The truth was far simpler and, in many ways, inevitable.

"You can only play with fire for so long without getting burned," said Mick to the boys at the station.

Joe had been losing heavily at cards for weeks on end.

He borrowed two thousand dollars at a ridiculously high rate of interest from an Italian loan shark named Carmella and stupidly chased his bets with it.

When it was time to pay, he hardly had a dime to his name. The only money he possessed were the coins of shrapnel from a borrowed $20 bill. His smooth talk had won a short-term loan from the new barman at his favourite haunt The Copper Mug Bar & Grill on 2nd and 5th.

In fairness to Chuck the barman, he had only given it to Joe because he was an ex-marine. He felt obliged to tide over a down-on-his-luck army veteran.

Joe was just so plausible and entertaining at the bar, telling exaggerated soldier stories of days gone by, of battles fought, women bedded, and lessons learned.

It was the last Chuck would see of his night's wages.

Carmella's men arrived at seven o'clock in the evening and Joe gave them a weak smile. He offered them a seat and suggested they talk.

"Let's go sit in the corner boys, we can discuss our business there, what would you like to drink?"

The Luigi twins were identical, which made their presence even more frightening when set against the serenity of the downtown bar.

These tough Italians were not only professional collection agents, but they were also two granite, no-nonsense, man mountains, with square jaws, and absolutely no sense of humour.

No answer was the stern reply. They never moved a muscle.

The twin on the left had a vertical scar down one side of his face, obviously won in battle, distinguishing him from his brother, which underlined his unmade claim to be a member of an unmentioned, underworld organisation.

He discretely and professionally whispered in Joe's ear.

"Mr Carmella would like the money you owe him, plus the interest you agreed to pay, and he's asked us to collect it now. You are already two days late."

Joe sobered in an instant, turning from a drunken Joe Palmer to sober Jack Rabbit in the blink of an eye.

"They might be big and strong, but they will have to catch me before they can hand out any punishment!"

Out of his seat in a jiffy, Joe pulled it across in front of the two swarthy Mediterranean giants, obstructing their plodding way for a couple of seconds.

The ex-soldier made his bid for freedom, as if on manoeuvres in some foreign theatre of conflict.

In a flash, he was out through the side door, up the alleyway, and across the main street to make his getaway.

He got away all right, but further than he planned.

A vegetable delivery truck on Main Street, delivering to the Great Falls Wholesale Market, hit Joe up in the air as he ran through the traffic in his futile bid to escape. The ex-marine landed in the local cemetery ten days later.

There were seven people at the funeral. Walter, because his mother made him go, Maria, the local priest, two gravediggers at a respectful distance, and way over in the car park two policemen.

One of the officers was wearing what appeared to be a pair of Aviator sunglasses. He simply stood by his vehicle throughout the grim ceremony, as if to witness the occasion and make sure it was true.

Once heartless Joe had died, Walter could breathe a little and tried to "man up" by taking several part-time jobs, to assist with the now non-existent family finances.

Selfishness and ignorance cast long shadows. The demise of Joe cut away the weeds smothering a beautiful rose; those weeds that had been preventing it from realizing its full potential.

* * *

Two years later, by the time he was sixteen the young man had put on twenty-eight pounds in weight and grown four inches taller.

Walter, free of emotional bondage to his father, now worked two-weekend shifts at the soda shop. The girls were delighted because he was funny and did wonderful impersonations of all the pop stars and TV personalities. It seemed he was a born actor, but nothing could be further from the truth.

It was a charade, an escape, a diversion from the pain of reality, a social mechanism to get people to like him, for with that attention, he felt loved, wanted and temporarily secure.

Unbeknown to Walter, it was a scenario being played out by gay schoolboys and girls across the nation, but he was too young and innocent to understand his plight.

Years later, as he looked back on his life he would say, "as a misfit in life you often become an actor, and pretend to be someone who fits, especially in an environment where not being "normal" could bring rejection or violence at any time!"

The more he was encouraged with smiles and applause, the better actor Walter became, spending many lonely hours in front of the mirror, perfecting his characters, and secretly applying makeup to make the illusion complete. It made him feel good, but no one else needed to know. It was his secret.

On Friday and Saturday evenings, Walter worked his soda shift.

Returning home at 11 pm on Fridays, he would arrive to the dishevelled silence of an empty house and go to bed exhausted.

Somewhere in the sanctity, serenity, and salvation of the darkness, he was sometimes dragged back from his midnight island of calm, by the sound of his mother talking to one or more strangers in the living room below.

At 6 am he would promptly get up and do the Saturday paper round for old Mr Johnson at the newsagents.

Walter would arrive back from delivering newspapers at 9 am, and his mother would still be sprawled out in the lounge, surrounded by empty wine and beer bottles.

Occasionally she would bring home a chancer from a local bar, just to prove to herself that she was still worthy and loved.

Oftentimes, Walter would walk in and see two half-naked bodies just lying there amongst the party debris, comatose, and oblivious to the schoolboy's needs and wants.

Only state welfare and the goodwill of the town prevented Walter from falling through the cracks. Everyone loved him because he was a trier, and against all the odds, he turned out to be a model citizen.

Walter would freely offer help to anyone, whether it was an old lady crossing the road, a teacher whose car needed a push start, or an elderly neighbour who was grateful to have their lawn cut.

He just wanted the company, the gratitude, and the adoration.

Above all things he just wanted to be accepted.

Friends and neighbours would invent small paid jobs and tasks for the unwitting Walter, just to help him out.

He washed cars, mended fences, ran errands, and if he washed Mick's patrol car, not only did he get $5, but he got to spend time in the place he called "Normalville", with cream cakes and sober, sensible conversation.

Normalville was the clean, tidy, well-ordered, safe, and secure place that Emma called home.

"One day I'll have somewhere just like this if I work hard enough!" Walter thought to himself.

About a year after his father's untimely death, Walter spent one Sunday afternoon with Emma's family at Normalville, which he often did if he had valeted Mick's car before lunch.

It was a favoured appointment because the afternoon that followed would bring the delightful company of that wholesome family, and a proper square meal.

This was a day he would never forget.

"So, Walter, fifteen years old now, what are you going to do when you graduate school in a couple of years?" asked Mick, still licking his lips after consuming one of Mrs Wilson's jam doughnuts in two bites.

Mick was a force to be reckoned with, a man who knew right from wrong, and practised it professionally every day for a living, however tough the circumstances. He was a plain-speaking individual, and not someone to mess with in that town.

Walter warmed to this doctrine, for it let him know exactly where he stood, what he could do, and what he could not do. Life had rules, and if you all stuck to them there would be no violence, no anger, and no distress.

A teenage boy's mind can sometimes be a wonderfully simple universe, especially under the paternal wing of a guardian angel. It was no surprise that Walter had adopted big Mick as the father he never had but always wanted.

"I'm not sure sir, I'm thinking of either going to the University of Montana to read business, or becoming a policeman just like you," Walter replied, saying what he thought Mick wanted to hear.

Mick was flattered, but he was very long in the tooth. He couldn't help wondering if Walter was giving him an answer that fitted the scene.

"Once a policeman always a policeman," he cajoled himself.

At that point, Emma and her mother went out to wash the dishes and uncharacteristically left Walter and Mick together.

Next came a spark that lighted a flame, which in turn lit the way to Walter's future.

"Walter, can I talk to you man to man?"

"Yes sir, Sheriff Wilson," said Walter delighted to be called "a man," by someone he respected.

"As you know, I deal with some rough types in this town, a lot of young punks and suchlike. I've managed to get some of them into the sport of boxing through friends I have.

"These guys, not all of them you know; the discipline of boxing has changed their lives. They have a new sense of pride, a sense of belonging, and a sense of worth.

"They have in a way, taken a different path to the one they were on, I suppose they have found themselves."

"I don't think boxing is for me!"

Mick did a great job of not laughing.

"I know that Walter, we are all different and that's my point. I knew you weren't a boxer the first day you walked Emma home from school!"

The subliminal message hit Walter between the eyes, unsettling him, and making him hot and nervous.

Walter knew that Mick had long since realised he was not like the other boys, and that he might be gay. What would the policeman say next?

"I know you have had some tough times Walter, and I admire and respect you for the way you have handled it all. You never fail to impress me.

"There is room in this world, especially in Great Falls, for people of every race, every creed, every denomination, and every sexual orientation under God's heaven.

"God made the world, not us. We are only the gatekeepers."

Walter could feel his face reddening at Mick's use of the word "sexual".

The Irishman never reacted, never faltered in his good-hearted monologue.

"I have watched you grow up and fight your way through all manner of problems. Life has put many obstacles in your way, but you are a hard case, even if you are not a boxer.

"Between you and me, don't let the girls know, I told everyone at the station, that pound for pound, you are the toughest guy in Great Falls!"

Tears came to Walter's eyes. The daddy he never knew was talking.

The release of stress that someone finally understood and acknowledged his plight, the things he had put up with all his life, his misery, his dilemma, and the frustration at not being "normal," were too much to bear, and Walter burst into uncontrollable tears.

Big Mick never flinched, and then in his deep western drawl, added a comment that would forever live in Walter's heart and mind.

"It's not about the size of the dog in the fight, it's about the size of the fight in the dog!"

Good-hearted Mick was on a roll.

"Walter, I am going to give you some free advice, that I want you to think about.

"For ten years the Wilson family have watched you develop, we have seen you entertain people, get them on your side, make them happy, and very often make them feel better about themselves, just by you being in their presence.

"The thing is Walter, you are truly gifted, a born actor and showman, even if you are the only guy in town who doesn't know it.

"In the end, Great Falls may turn out to be too small for a personality like you, who is certainly a little bit different from his fellow students.

"My advice is this, let the real Walter stand up and be recognised. Leave the past behind. Do not set your horizon at the Great Falls city limits but set it at the bright lights of Hollywood Boulevard or Broadway.

"Don't you ever be restricted by the fear of failure, go where your heart takes you and be true to yourself!"

Big Mick welled up a little himself, but his experience allowed him to keep his composure.

"You are a man now, so be a "man's man" for the rest of your life, because going forward you are going to have to make some very tough decisions."

Mick continued as Walter listened, not taking his eyes off the Irish giant for a moment.

"Don't let the good people of Great Falls down. The people who have supported you forever and ever, even if you have never realized it.

"You are truly something special, because you add value to people's lives and that is a rare and enviable gift that you have.

"Walter Wyatt Palmer was put on this earth to do something great.

"Grab the opportunity with both hands, take your talent, work hard and soar with the eagles!"

In the absence of the women who could return unannounced at any moment, Mick drove his point home.

"Go where you are celebrated, not where you are tolerated!"

Walter consumed the prophetic words for all they were worth.

"Only then will you be free. Only then can the real Walter Wyatt Palmer stand up and be counted."

In such lightbulb moments, destinies are decided.

Big Mick looked Walter in the eye, as he concluded his advice.

"Somewhere at the rainbow's end you will find your dream, your pot of gold, and I wish you every success, whatever path you may choose."

Walter was breathing hard, silently hysterical with the release of emotion, but the tears were gone.

The man he respected above all others had accepted him.

"One more thing, we will never speak of this again. Understood?"

"Yes, sir," Sheriff Wilson.

"I won't let you down."

They watched the ball game for the next fifteen minutes when suddenly Mrs Wilson and Emma reappeared with more coffee and cookies.

Their female intuition told them that something was different, but it was imperceptible to the human eye.

"What have you two been talking about?" they asked together, as their curiosity got the better of them.

"Men's talk!" they said in unison.

All four laughed a knowing laugh.

* * *

Having now received Mick's seal of approval and encouragement, Walter felt emancipated, freed from the shackles of doubt, and released from the yoke of uncertainty.

Buoyed by the pep talk, he began to believe in himself.

He could be someone.

Walter had never felt quite comfortable in school despite everyone's best efforts. His early years were torture because he knew deep inside that he didn't fit in, that he was different from the other boys, although he tried to reject reality in his mind.

Whilst the boys had enjoyed playing sport and chasing girls, Walter would rather flick through fashion catalogues, looking longingly at the new look that would be this year's vogue, but hesitating to turn the page, as his fingers ran over the bodies of the male models.

He was different all right, he was gay. Why couldn't he just be himself? Mick had released him from his self-imposed bondage to an imposter's dream, and now he finally had the confidence to face everyday life as the real Walter Wyatt Palmer.

The pernicious, all-enveloping, smothering and evil shadow cast by his father Joe, had evaporated in one sunny Sunday afternoon, punctuated by cream cakes, coffee and cookies with the people and the family he would always love.

Time moved on and with the vacuum that Joe had left, his mother's attention continued to be focused even more on wine and sexual gratification. It did not matter anymore to Walter, because he now had a new vision and a real sense of purpose.

The increasingly confident, outgoing, and handsome young man thrived over the next three years and as school graduation approached, he flourished both physically and socially.

He was six feet with a tape measure but now ten feet tall with happiness.

Freed of the social handcuffs of the parents he would not have chosen Walter rapidly developed his personality.

He entertained everyone he met with funny stories, jokes, even funnier walks, and a wonderful singing voice which his music teacher had said "was truly outstanding", so much so, that he was chosen to sing the male solo at the school prom.

The budding entertainer had only ever seen the ocean on television, so singing Rod Stewart's "Sailing" as the goodbye tune at that year's school crescendo event felt a little weird, but there wasn't a dry eye in the house.

Walter's magnificent performance struck a chord in the heart of every pupil and parent alike, as they realized that the flowers of Great Falls's youth would all be sailing on to a new world in the coming weeks.

In the end, that song was the catalyst that changed his life.

Despite his domestic difficulties, Walter had turned from an ugly duckling into a beautiful swan. One day he would fly, and it would be sooner than he thought.

Only one person in the audience did not clap. In the dark where he belonged, Walter's nemesis and lifetime bully just glared through the cheap sunglasses that hid his lifelong squint, as he sat alone at the back of the prom night congregation.

Dexter Munro was a sly child who had become a sullen and sulky adolescent. He was now on the brink of adulthood, and the chips on both shoulders occasionally made him seem level-headed.

His attitude meant that socially his peers avoided him. The girls couldn't stand him or the cannabis he smoked. He was the most unpopular pupil at William Rodgers High, and he was a thug and a bully, but only if he could get away with it, so he chose his victims well, as bullies always do.

Dexter couldn't try it on with the jocks, the sporty guys who could hold their own against such an apology for a man. Furthermore, he would not dare to try and take on the girls because they would gang up, and the things that came out of their mouths when addressing him would be fit for many a sailor's haunt. They all despised him, and it was mostly because he had been bullying Walter for over ten years.

On this night, Dexter skulked alone in a corner, whiffing of weed, until he disappeared into the night at around 10 pm as the evening concluded, alone as usual.

Walter had sung his heart out, and now on a natural dopamine high, he danced with all the girls and was truly the queen bee, his newly acquired confident, ostentatious flamboyance, making him the obvious centre of attention.

"What a transformation in just a few years, what a triumph!" thought Walter, as he left the prom that evening and wondered where, after reaching this dizzy height of popularity, life's path would take him next.

He walked the prom queen to her home. Emma had begged him to be her partner on this landmark evening, and big Mick thanked him for the courtesy he had shown to his daughter in escorting her on such a momentous occasion.

Mick invited him into the Wilson family enclave, and Walter spoke of times gone by and days yet to come, as they drank coffee and ate scones.

Walter left Emma's house before midnight, buzzing with adrenalin and the excitement bestowed upon him by the best night of his life, but he couldn't switch off from the emotion of it all and sleep would therefore be impossible.

As it was such a lovely summer evening, he decided to take a casual walk a mile down to town, where maybe he would call into Gino's Soda Bar and tell them all about his fabulous night.

Walter thought he might recreate characters and events from that evening of celebration, impersonating some of his fellow pupils and teachers, and maybe finishing one more time with his new signature tune "Sailing," using the excuse of assisting them to lock up at the customary closing time of 1.00 am.

**

The prom night superstar did not arrive at Gino's as planned.

An ambulance driver called Chico Nelson was returning to the hospital from an earlier call and said he was lucky he did not hit Walter with his vehicle, when by chance he found him at midnight lying bloodied, battered and confused on the side of the road.

The graduating student was badly beaten up and had lost consciousness. Walter had several contusions to his face that were the result of heavy fists and probably pointed cowboy boots, as the black marks on his head were stained with polish. The heavy bruising and swollen face were testaments to the good work of his invisible assailant.

At first, the ambulance man who had found him thought he had been drinking, possibly wandering into the road in a drunken stupor and then being hit by a vehicle, such was the damage done.

Immediately going to his aid, cleaning him up and checking him out, Chico Nelson identified the boot polish shining on the facial swelling and realised Walter had been assaulted.

He called the police to attend to what he described as an attack on a "white male, Caucasian".

There was no threat to Walter's life, but he was given tranquilisers and the police could not interview him until the following day.

The William Rodgers High School rumour mill began in earnest, and it was suggested that Walter had made a gay pass at some guy leaving The Dark Horse Saloon Bar, and his "beating up" was therefore the result of his stupidity.

More fuel was added to the fire as Walter, a lifelong pacifist, would not speak of the incident and did not wish to bring charges against anyone, no matter how much the police tried to coax the information from him.

The girls refuted the rumours out of hand, and the mistruths died a natural death as common sense made it obvious that Walter would never have done what had been suggested. Over the next few days, things began to calm down.

* * *

The truth about the mysterious assault took almost a week to rear its head and only came to light when big Mick went to speak personally with Walter at his home, showing great diplomacy lest he tread on a fellow investigating officer's toe.

After some initial conversation and having won Walter's trust with some well-planted questions concerning his future, the young man began to weaken in the company of his mentor.

The victim felt that it was impossible to refuse the man to whom he owed so much, telling Mick within thirty minutes of his arrival, that the culprit was the repulsive Dexter Munro.

This was just what the Irishman had believed from day one. The school outcast with the wall eye was the menace who had broken Walter's nose and blacked both eyes, damaged his ribcage and left him looking like a mess on that midnight tarmac.

Dexter was a cocksure, boastful loser, who, when things were not going his way, would pick on anyone lower down the food chain than himself. The girls in school all loved Walter and hated the lifelong school bully with a similar passion. They had wished "that loser" as they all called him, would move to a new school or better still to a new town.

Walter's story made perfect sense to the big brooding traffic cop when the gentle victim recounted the events of the prom night.

"Well Sheriff Wilson, Dexter had tried his luck with all the girls, and they blanked him as usual. He just sat in the corner with a face like thunder staring at us all. I thought that he was angry at me, possibly for the applause I received for singing that final song.

"Later I wondered if it was because the girls were dancing with me and ignoring him.

"Dexter approached Emma and asked her to dance but she flatly refused.

"Then he tried his luck with Nancy and Beth who also said no, and you could feel him getting angrier and angrier.

"Suddenly he started making obscene gestures to Emma, who he called "Irish trailer trash".

Big Mick ground his teeth, his temper rising at the thought of his precious daughter being verbally abused.

"What happened next?"

"It was quite scary, and the more he smoked the weed the more focused he seemed to become. Emma was upset, so then I decided to be a "man's man" like you said to me before, and I asked him to stop, but he just glared at me, grinned, and said nothing.

"Without warning, he simply disappeared, and we never saw him again, at least till I did shortly after midnight.

"I was walking down into town after leaving your house and I heard voices on the other side of the road.

"As I strolled past the Dark Horse Saloon Bar there was a big commotion out front, where they were throwing Dexter out, and I heard one of the doormen say, "come back when you are a real man!" and then I realised it was Dexter they ejected.

"I'm ashamed to say I carried on walking on the other side of the road, as I knew he was bad news.

"I didn't want to get involved. I guessed he probably deserved it!"

"Did he see you?"

"Oh yes definitely, we had eye contact and just stared at each other, full recognition, kept our thoughts to ourselves and then we went our separate ways or so I thought, but I was wrong, and Dexter's self-anger and venom turned to what he considered to be easy prey as per usual."

"Do you want to press charges, Walter? I know from experience that your friend Dexter is trouble, and he's going to cause a lot more trouble around here before he's done. I don't want him messing with my daughter or you, or anyone else for that matter!"

The steely look in Mick's eyes left no doubt that he meant every single word.

"No sheriff, I don't want to draw any more attention to myself, I don't like violence and I just want it to go away, I won't be filing charges if that's ok with you?"

"It's your choice Walter and I respect your decision, and I thank you for being a knight in shining armour to my daughter. You have my respect; I owe you one!"

* * *

Time is a great healer and the swollen eyes and contused face slowly returned to a kind of normality.

Within two weeks the bruising was gone, but Walter had something to thank Dexter for, something quite unexpected.

The second fight of Walter's life provided a surprise bonus to the victim.

The aggressor had been wearing a ring, and one of the right-hand punches had cut his victim's cheek. When Walter's image stared back at him in the mirror, he had a small scar below his right eye that looked like a cute sort of dimple.

Unwittingly, Dexter had made Walter look more handsome, more vulnerable, and even more boyish in a delightful sort of way.

While he sported his injuries Walter would not leave the house for the next two weeks, and despite the encouragement of his girlfriends, he would not press charges.

He didn't need to, as justice in a small cowboy town has a way of working itself out.

After Dexter's violent attack on Walter, things did not sit easily with Mick, and it was now getting too close to home for his liking.

It rankled with him that a drug-pushing thug like Dexter Munro could get away with hurting such a gentle, honest soul as Walter, the boy who had tried to protect his daughter.

It incensed him that Dexter would bully, beat, and threaten one of Emma's best friends, but it terrified him that a cannabis-smoking loose cannon would even have the temerity to ask his daughter to dance, never mind being disrespectful.

"What could happen next time?" he kept asking himself, and day by day during the next week he brooded, and the voice in his head got louder until he decided on a little bully-boy tactic of his own.

Early one Saturday morning in the following week, Mick and a colleague were working the graveyard shift, finishing up with a final sweep along Main Street at 5 am.

Driving along to the station Mick instantly recognised Walter's nemesis in the shape of Dexter Munro.

Mick looked all about and checked the car mirrors to be sure, but there was not another soul in sight. In that moment he decided to let his brooding thoughts of the last week become a reality.

The patrol car stopped and Mick stepped out and assisted an unwilling Dexter into the back seat of the car on the suggestion he was drunk and disorderly.

Dexter protested his innocence.

"I ain't drunk Sheriff, you can't arrest me, I ain't done nothin, I ain't!"

"Shut it" said Mick, "you're coming with us!"

They drove casually out of town so as not to attract attention and up a lonely mountain road to a remote location known locally as Blanco Canyon.

Town rumour had it that they threatened him with violence if he stepped out of line again. The reality was much worse.

Dexter sat in the back of the car smirking and laughing in that sullen edgy way that endeared him to no one.

"You can't touch me, I ain't done nothing!"

Then he made the mistake of making a disparaging remark about Mick's daughter Emma, suggesting she was easy meat for the boys and went on to be equally offensive about Walter and gays.

"Park the car on the left!" Mick demanded.

"You can't touch me Sheriff, you'll be in trouble!"

The patrol car halted abruptly between two trees on a patch of barren ground, in a dark, foreboding, and isolated spot in the woods, as Mick's temper began to get the better of him.

Mick aggressively opened his car door and got out and moved to the rear of the vehicle.

"OK big boy, let's see how tough you are!"

Using one hand Mick dragged the tough-talking loser from the back seat and threw him heavily to the floor. His colleague pinned Dexter down on the muddy embankment as Mick loomed ominously over him.

"Dexter, all of your life you've been a bully and a coward.
"That's a great way to be until you meet a bigger bully!"
"You can't touch me Sheriff, you can't!" screamed Dexter as fear overtook his cannabis addled brain.

Next, with steam coming out of his ears, a racing pulse, and the strength of two men Mick took out his regulation police pistol.

Dexter visibly shook as Mick suggested to his quarry the weapon that he was now pointing at him was a gay man's appendage.

"Is this what you mean? he said as he thrust the loaded weapon into Dexter's mouth.

He forced it deep into the back of his throat until Dexter's eyes almost popped out of his head.

"If you ever threaten or touch my daughter or one of her friends again I will put a bullet in your brain!

"Do you understand me boy?"

A terrified Dexter could only nod his agreement, for his voice was muted by a mouthful of gun metal, precariously attached to a mad Irishman.

The night air was rancid with the smell of urine and faeces as the paper tiger lost control of his bodily functions.

Dexter was released without further harm to find his way home and told that if he ever touched any of his classmates, Emma, Walter, or anyone else again, they would come back up the mountain and complete their unfinished business.

"Gays might be gays, but they are our gays," said Mick to his colleague as they returned down the lonely track to the main road.

"I'd rather a respectful, law-abiding, decent, and honest "straight" gay than a waster like Dexter," replied his colleague with a smirk.

That was the end of the subject, for big Mick was confident he had squared his account with Walter.

With that, there was a call over the radio with an all-points bulletin to every patrol vehicle concerning an armed robbery at a local drug store.

Normality, it seemed, had returned to Great Falls, and the waste product-contaminated night air tasted a little sweeter.

* * *

Dexter did not have a physical mark on his body, the policemen were far too clever to leave any evidence of that, but their victim's mind was scarred forever.

The next day, without sleep, Dexter made his way to the Greyhound bus station and bought a one-way ticket to California. As far as anyone knew he never returned to Montana again, and everyone in Great Falls agreed it was a better place without him.

No one in town openly mentioned Dexter or the mountain incident again.

Whispered rumours persisted which served as a road sign to lowlifes and ne'er do wells everywhere, that justice had many forms in a small country town.

Walter was not himself after the attack by Dexter, and despite his improved looks was a troubled soul. He knew his attacker had "left town" because he received calls from his friends telling him so, but he never knew the details of how and why, and no one ever mentioned any of the rumours to him, so he was none the wiser.

Although he felt safer and more comfortable with Dexter gone, it brought him face-to face-with the reality of fear and violence. These were the two things he hated most in life. It was why he was a pacifist.

Walter could not stop thinking of his parents. Substitute the words fear and violence for Joe and Maria and the connection was complete.

After almost two weeks of not receiving visitors, his "cheerleaders" as he usually called them in jest, arrived uninvited and in no mood to take no for an answer.

A dozen beautiful eighteen-year-old teenage girls, tanned, lovely, hormonally charged, and ready to wallow in the drama of it all, stood at Walter's front door and begged him to come out with them.

It was every boy's dream and nightmare all in one go.

These A and B sides of emotion were matched by the present they brought for him.

They thought that their gift would cheer him up and send an invisible message that all his friends knew he was gay, and that they had always known, couldn't care less, and would support him evermore.

The present was a song recorded over two sides of a vinyl record. It was called The Killing of Georgie (parts one and two) by Rod Stewart, Walter's new favourite pop star.

They coaxed Walter out of his refuge to listen to it at Nancy Kovac's house while her parents were out shopping. Emma had suggested to the others that "it will cheer him up and focus his mind elsewhere!"

She was certainly right about the latter.

The music played over and over, and all the girls fussed over Walter like he was a film star. He was not very responsive, not because he didn't like the adulation, but because he had mentally left the house, the town, and the State of Montana.

His mind had been stolen away to a more vibrant, intriguing world. Once he had tuned into the track, "The Killing of Georgie" the seeds of change had been irrevocably sown.

It was a mesmeric song about a gay man, who had left home to go to a new city to find his real self. This gentle, innocent soul was later stabbed to death for no reason on the streets of New York City and then lamented by a friend who sang the song.

Walter memorized the lyrics and the melody almost at once, singing it repeatedly in his mind for the rest of the following week.

"Leaving home on a greyhound bus, cast out by the ones he loved, a victim of these gay days it seems!"

Powerful stuff thought Walter.

The song had romance and intrigue, a gay hero, an incredible backdrop, and a city with a culture that seemed to embrace people like himself.

* * *

The locals all knew about the assault, and they all knew Dexter had left town under a dark cloud. They also believed, that as Walter returned to his chores, day-to-day life would return to normal.

Alas, it could never be the same again. Living a lie was not an option anymore, because for Walter the assault marked a line in the sand, a time to grow up, a wind of change.

Throughout July and much of early August, the girls were talking as usual about boys, and now with a new maturity about which colleges and universities they would attend.

Beth was always a bright one, and she was off to MIT to read mathematics. Nancy and her twin sister Madison would leave for Harvard to read medicine, but mere mortals would stay closer to the nest.

Emma Wilson was going with most of her friends to Missoula, to the University of Montana. She would later graduate and excel at law in private practice.

Walter decided that he must also seek higher education, but just like himself, his university would be very different. The decision was gifted to him through that "get well soon" present the girls had brought him several weeks earlier.

The Killing of Georgie theoretically meant that there was at least one space in New York City for someone like Walter. It meant he could go there and join the University of Life.

On August 16th after a huge leaving party and endless good wishes and tears, it was time for the class of '75 to finally separate and move on to higher things.

That Friday Emma's parents took her to Missoula and on their return to Great Falls they confirmed to Walter that she had settled in and "was thinking of him".

At 6.30 am the next morning Walter rose from his bed, and as he washed and dressed, he took a last look around his childhood prison.

He skipped breakfast, for he did not wish to wake his mother, who was once more comatose in the lounge next to three empty wine bottles.

Opening the door for the last time at 7.00 am, he was surprised to see a large Irish policeman, wearing Aviator sunglasses, who stood uninvited, unexpected, and unannounced, next to a shiny Montana State Trooper patrol vehicle.

"Taxi for Mr Palmer?"

Walter smiled from ear to ear, as he acknowledged the kindness of his one and only mentor.

Big Mick silently drove Walter the fifteen minutes across town to the Greyhound bus station, from where Dexter had fled less than two months before.

Mutual respect is an unspoken book of memories, captured privately in the minds of all participants, with no need to discuss its details.

Not a sound passed their lips, for when you both know the story, clarity or back-slapping is not required.

Exiting the police vehicle, Walter turned to thank Mick.

"Thank you, Sheriff Wilson, I appreciate it.

"You once said to me "go where you are celebrated, not where you are tolerated!" so here goes, I'll let you know how I get on!"

"I salute you, Walter, I was right, pound for pound you were the toughest guy in Great Falls. We're going to miss you.

Don't be a stranger!"

There was a millisecond of awkwardness, for the moment had come to say goodbye.

Big Mick diffused the situation by offering Walter the open palm of a huge Irish hand.

Walter accepted the invitation and shook it, and then Mick gave him an unexpected fatherly hug.

As the young man withdrew his hand, he stared at the envelope which Big Mick then gave him from his jacket pocket.

"What's this? he asked in a surprised tone.

"Oh, it's just another one of those "Good Luck" cards from me and the wife, just like those you got from Emma and the rest of your cheerleaders, but please make me a promise Walter, won't you?"

"Sure thing, Sheriff Wilson!"

"Please don't open it until you get to your destination.

"You wouldn't want to see a policeman cry would you!"

"Fat chance of that Sheriff, I promise I won't open it until I get there."

"Oh, and Walter, one more thing.

I almost forgot!"

He stepped backwards and reached into the back of the patrol car. Next, he pulled out a huge plastic lunchbox and handed it to Walter.

"Here you go Walter, it's from Mrs Wilson."

They looked at each other and both laughed as they uttered the words together.

"Scones and doughnuts!"

"Exactly" said Sheriff Wilson.

"There are also a couple of soda pops in there and some other stuff she put together for you. We are sure gonna miss you Walter! Good luck, keep in touch."

"Thank Mrs Wilson for me sir, I appreciate it. I'll write you when I can."

With those final words it was done, and as Mick climbed into his patrol car, he reached for a handkerchief and wiped an unaccustomed tear from his eye.

"Damn conjunctivitis!"

Entering the bus Walter chose a seat facing forwards, but shaded from the sun, and put his rucksack holding all his worldly goods on the storage shelf above.

Walter now looked forward to a clean slate, a new beginning, and a place where he could breathe freely, unencumbered by the prejudice of the uneducated, unwise and unsympathetic.

He closed his eyes and spent the next hour working on a little conundrum that had to be solved by the time he reached New York City.

* * *

After her son's departure, the widow Maria, the serial alcoholic who had spent more time seeking love than loving her boy Walter, would soon find a path to an early grave. Guilt oiled the tracks somehow.

Following Joe's death, Maria's drinking got worse, her time for Walter even less, as she set out on a seven-year, one-way road to oblivion.

By the time Walter was twenty-one, she was a resident at the poor end of the West Great Falls Cemetery, mourned by no one, not even her only son who was no longer in touch.

Big Mick completed his career as a police officer, and after thirty years of exceptional service to the local police force, he went into youth counselling, a career for which he had unwittingly trained all his adult life. He loved every minute of it.

Emma Wilson graduated top of her law class at Missoula and went on to have a successful legal career in Helena, the State capital, eventually returning to Great Falls to set herself up in business under the title "Wilson Law".

She named her first son Walter, after a friend she had once known, who she had loved and admired.

* * *

One Saturday Summer afternoon in 1975, the new boy in town stepped out into a sunny Central Park, New York City.

He had $250 worth of blood, sweat and tears in his wallet, and he was hell-bent on succeeding in this brave new world. The money had to go a long way. It had to last him the rest of his life.

Buying a coffee from one of the local vendors, he sat on a park bench to enjoy the wonder of it all, and to tune in his thought process to the pulsating rhythm of this vibrant city.

He was handsome, chiselled, fit and very much available, and without realising it, he had already begun to attract attention.

As he sipped his drink, he remembered his promise to Big Mick not to open the envelope he had handed him as he left the bus station in Montana. Now was as good a time as any he thought.

Walter pulled the "Good Luck" card from his rucksack and as he studied the beautiful handwriting on the envelope it was obvious that this was the work of his favourite "aunty", the one and only Mrs Wilson.

The envelope was the only friend he had in New York, so he opened it without hesitation. As he unfolded the card $500 dollars in $50 bills stared back at him and tears filled his eyes.

He quickly squirrelled the money away into his inside pocket for safety and began to read the sentiment.

"Dear Walter,

Please do not be embarrassed by this gift we have given you. Ever since that first day you came home with Emma, we knew you were special, and special people deserve special help, support and treatment from their special friends.

It has been a joy to watch you grow up and we thank you for the friendship you have given to both of us and Emma over the years.

When you get to your destination take a good look around and realise that this is your time, your place and the first day of the rest of your life.

We wish you nothing less than the success you deserve.

Work hard, play hard and every night we will search the big Montana skies and look for your shining star which is surely in the ascendancy.

In life some things are written, they are meant to be, and all we have to do is make them happen.

If anyone can make it happen, it's you, the boy with a heart of gold, the dog with the biggest fight in him.

Look out New York, New York, a star was born today.

Good luck

Irene and Mick Wilson

Walter wiped tears from his eyes as he realised how much he had been loved by the Wilson family.

He slowly regrouped over the next fifteen minutes and felt in positive spirits, for Walter now knew he had a buffer of $750 to kickstart his new life.

* * *

A blonde, attractive young lady, wearing a tight blouse and hip-hugging jeans, chose to take a break from her lunchtime stroll and sat down next to him.

Excitement, born of his inspirational surroundings, spurred him on to make conversation with the vivacious new arrival.

"Wow, New York City is really something!"

"Are you a tourist?"

"Oh no, I've just moved here; this is my first day, my first hour to be truthful!"

"Well congratulations, I'm Shelley, welcome to New York!"

"Why thank you, Shelley!"

He knew that he must now introduce himself, and this proved to be more difficult than he had expected.

"I'm err, I'm Quentin, err Quentin Prendergast."

He had buried the ghost of Walter Wyatt Palmer on the long trip east, and in his place, Quentin Prendergast had been invented to take on this exciting new universe.

This had been his conundrum on the bus trip from Montana. Walter felt a new start demanded a new name and so it was he chose his forename out of respect for Quentin Arkwright, his drama teacher and then took his surname Prendergast from the legendary musical schoolmaster Paddy Prendergast.

Both of these men had taken him under their wing and helped to develop the talent that Walter hoped would one day lead to great things in his quest for success in New York.

"I'm an entertainer, I've got a lot to learn, but I'm going to make it big here!"

"Aren't we all Quentin, it's nice to meet you, let me know if you ever get famous, and I can tell people I met you on the way up!

"Are you a New Yorker?"

"No. I'm just another moth to the gypsy flame!"

"Have you been here long?"

"Six months, I came from Nebraska, there's no music scene there, so good old New York, New York was the obvious choice to kickstart my career.

"I'm a singer, a rock singer, but I've been working full-time in a restaurant to help make ends meet. It's so expensive here!"

"Any luck?"

"If you asked me last month, I'd have said it's been a disaster!

"I was singing in local bars; not much happening you know, but a guy came in a couple of weeks ago and we got talking.

"Turns out I had been spotted by a friend of his who knew he was looking for a singer. I've got myself a job as lead singer in an up-and-coming country rock band called Rockaria!

"We start making an album next week and go on tour in three months. I'm so excited!

"I've pinched myself every morning for the last week, to make sure it's really happening!

"I handed in my notice to the restaurant this morning. Today is my last shift!"

"How fabulous, "Shelley Superstar", it's got a ring to it, make sure you leave a little room at the top for me!

"Well, I guess I can tell people I knew Shelley on the way up, give or take the first few feet!"

On a sun-kissed Central Park stage, the two performers laughed out loud.

Quentin had made his first friend.

They continued to talk about personal hopes and dreams for a few minutes more, like old acquaintances comfortable in the knowledge that they shared a common goal.

Shelley finished her lunch, handed Quentin her visiting card in the mistaken belief he might ask her for a date, and headed back towards Broadway from whence she had come.

* * *

Freed of the shackles that the cowboy state had freely given, Quentin now looked every piece the quintessential American footballer who you would expect to see on the front of Time magazine, after leading his team to victory in the Superbowl, but the reality was far from it.

Quentin was an exceptionally good-looking, tanned young man, who had been attracted by the bright lights and glitter of that sleepless city with an urge to finally belong.

Like most newcomers uprooting themselves to New York City, he figured out early that the longer he stayed, the more difficult it would be to go back to the big skies of Montana.

It would be impossible to crawl back under the rock, to flee back to the darkness of a small town, whose inhabitants would never fully understand the social pressures of being gay in a man's world.

He was one of the thousands who had to tread that same weary road in the 1970s, but for Quentin failure was not an option.

The new boy in town needed three things: accommodation, work, and love. The latter could wait, but the first two were a high priority in a city full of strangers.

He finished his coffee and left Central Park and then booked himself into the Vanderbilt YMCA off Broadway but remained in his room for less than five minutes. He was a man in a hurry, and in double time he had walked to Times Square, the centre of his new universe.

On the way, he picked up a tourist map from a street vendor to help him find his way around.

Within three hours of leaving the YMCA and making polite enquiries in all the shops bordering the tourist areas, Quentin was offered a job delivering leaflets for Jimmy's Delicatessen on 42nd and 5th.

The money was paid cash in hand and the hourly rate was nothing to boast about. It was exploitation, but it was a start, and delivery work, however unsavoury, would teach him his bearings, help make acquaintances and give him the platform he needed to go forward.

He eagerly consumed all around him, quickly figuring out how it all fitted together.

The Empire State Building, Central Park, Broadway, The Rockefeller Centre, The World Trade Towers and The Statue of Liberty were emblazoned on his mind in the same way a taxi driver would look at signposts.

He knew them all from television, and within a week he knew them all personally, for he had visited every location including Grand Central Station, the majesty of which made him weak at the knees.

Next, he found Greenwich Village, where his eyes were like organ stops staring at the glamour, the fashion, and the exaggerated behaviour of the denizens of that fantasy island.

This city had a buzz, a beating heart, and he was dying to be a part of it. There was no going back.

In the second month, he moved up the working ladder and won a job as a singing waiter in the evenings at Monte's Bar & Grill. He stuck with it for six months, making new friends along the way. Mostly they were out-of-work actors "between jobs", who were only doing it for experience and practice they suggested. "More like for bread and butter," thought Quentin.

With tips, he was now making more than he was spending, and moved into an apartment share in Queens, with five other young men whose sole ambition was to make it in New York City.

It turned out to be the making of Quentin and with his arrival, there were now three gays and three straight men laughing, joking, and tolerating each other through the boiling hot Autumn, and the incomer was overjoyed at his acceptance.

He found New York City to be a very frank and direct place, where people called a spade a spade. His good looks meant many girls would often openly approach him and ask for a date. It was flattering, but he always said no. He wasn't interested in girls, but men were a different thing.

Love is a strange beast, for the harder you try the less successful you are. It bites you when you are not concentrating and when you least expect it.

Shelley's loss would be another suitor's gain, for it was a slim, handsome young man with a dashing smile who would eventually provide the attention that Quentin desperately needed.

Within the month he was in a fully-fledged adult relationship with Calvin, who had also moved to the city in January of that year from some small intolerant town in Pennsylvania. The apartment share had paid off in more ways than one, and with Calvin living in the room opposite, neither had far to travel for a night of love and romance.

Calvin was in theatre and encouraged Quentin to audition for small parts, either singing, acting, or dancing, so he could earn more money and develop his obvious talents.

Quentin, with Calvin's steadfast support, quickly gained huge experience and an extensive network of theatrical friends, by singing in bars and appearing in adverts for soap, flea powder, headache tablets and suchlike. He had been in this new city for less than a year and he was already attracting quite a following.

As the early years rolled by, he met up with Shelley from time to time, for they both had something to offer each other. He was a safe pair of hands for her, and she had enough limelight to shed some on him.

When she wasn't touring or making platinum albums, Quentin was the perfect partner for casual evenings out, away from the increasing public attention that fame had brought her.

"Quentin, you and I are the same!"

"How do you work that out, darling?"

"We both knew each other before we were famous!"

"But I'm not famous yet?"

"You will be darling, you will be, there's no doubt about it!"

She introduced him to her showbiz friends and the infamous Greenwich Village "inner circle".

In the classical late-1970s Greenwich Village gay scene, Quentin was hardly noticeable in the first couple of years as he slipped seamlessly and invisibly into any social background, but with personal introductions from a famous rock star, his new-born confidence created a greater presence.

This new aura must have pervaded Quentin's work because he was "spotted" by a rather famous gay director called Valentino Romano, who chose him to play a supporting role in a new comedy film. This low-budget role brought rave reviews, making him an overnight success from which he never looked back.

Quentin was a television and film natural, and the camera seemed to gobble him up, making him look younger and even more attractive with every new venture, and with this raised profile the paparazzi came scavenging and his career soared like that of the proverbial eagle.

As Quentin rocketed to the dizzy heights of success, Calvin decided to move on to pastures new.

The lights it seemed were too bright for him.

* * *

Quentin, now single and with lots of practice, perfected the art of the chat up, the approach, the conquest, and he was no different to any young male in pursuit of his natural goal, but in his case, it was men of the same sex, and the world frowned on it, despite outward assurances of acceptance.

He was always discreet, but whether standing still or leaning on a bar he was like a Venus flytrap.

His good looks had already helped with his earlier career as a bit part actor on stage and in television, but in the bars and clubs of New York he achieved even greater success, but romantically this time, and he quickly made up for the lost years.

At first, Quentin didn't earn a great living, but he received more than enough income to enjoy everything New York had to offer.

By early 1978 he had moved alone to his apartment in Queens, where he would live for the rest of his life.

His boyish charm, soft effeminate mannerisms, and quiet nature had made him irresistible to the denizens of the New York nightlife jungle.

This was especially true when he was introduced as an "actor."

It was the absolute best way to start any conversation with the wannabees who flocked to Greenwich Village in search of fame, fortune, and flesh.

"Hello, what's your name?"

"Quentin."

"Ooh, you are handsome, and what do you do for a living?"

"I'm an actor."

"Oh my, isn't that fabulous? Quentin's an unusual name, how do you spell that?"

"It's Q U E N T I N darling, just remember Q is for cute."

Quentin would then smile at his suitor.

The trap was set; the hunter had unwittingly become the hunted. It worked a treat.

Many a night he would be "picked" up by a stranger, leaving the world-famous Studio 54 to go home for a night of casual pleasure with some Freddie Mercury lookalike.

Quentin had a favourite saying that he would spout forth to his close friends after some conquest or other.

"The trap doesn't chase the mouse darlings, but it catches him all the same!"

They would then all guffaw and laugh together, whilst planning their next predatory assault on the best of the New York nightclubs.

Being gay in New York was as acceptable as being punk. It was just a genre. Next week it might be fashionable to be bisexual or bicurious, as it was now wryly described by those on "the scene".

These were the heady days of freedom, where tomorrow would never come, where alcohol, sex and drugs were as common and as natural as water, sea, and sky.

Quentin fared well off the back of his fame, making many a sexual conquest in the same way that heterosexual celluloid and stage heroes of the past had trodden that path before him.

Various partners came and went during those times of complete freedom, and Quentin never once felt the need to settle down, as the usual driving factor of fathering children was so obviously missing from his life.

As he reached the milestone of his thirty-fifth birthday in 1991, maybe he matured, but more likely it was the spectre of AIDS that changed his mindset.

The devil's disease was now beating down the doors of his friends and killing them one by one, and it suddenly made him wake up to reality and the risks he was taking in his hedonistic lifestyle.

Whatever it was, Walter let the barriers down and fell in love.

He met Erik, a tall, lithe, blue-eyed, blonde, Scandinavian fashion designer when he least expected.

It was purely by accident at a fundraiser, where the randomness of the single guest seating Gods had thrown them together. Within three months they were living together in Quentin's apartment in Queens.

A strong-looking, virile Viking apparition, Erik was two years older than Quentin and as partners go, he was the missing piece of his jigsaw, the soulmate he had always wanted.

There would be no more partners for either of them, for much to the disappointment of many a hunter, they would always remain together.

"Till death do us part!" was the private Sunday toast, while they consumed an expensive bottle of red Merlot on their day of rest, as was their habit.

After he arrived in New York City, and following a tough apprenticeship, Walter's career had quickly gone through the showbiz gears, and he was often the talk of the town with regular appearances on Broadway or in some Hollywood extravaganza.

Two Tony awards, various film parts, top billing in musical theatre, and scripts arriving almost daily, confirmed he was the flavour of every month, with an annual income that proved it. There was seemingly no end to the meteoric rise.

He had risen from anonymity to be one of the leading gay men in New York and beyond, with all the trappings of success that fame had brought. The bit-part players of his new universe, of the gay world, would call him a queen, a true leader of the queer ensemble. Quentin's gay American dream had become a reality.

If anyone who was anyone, planned a party or get-together of some description, and they wanted to attract attention, then they simply had to get Quentin to attend or one of the other queens such as Elton.

Having any of the queens in attendance at a fundraiser or a private party was a social endorsement to the host, a badge of authority, and an undeniable vote of confidence to the guest of honour.

When the magazine New Fashion, New York ran a four-page spread on Quentin, they spoke about his career, his life and friends, his charitable works, and the place where he lived in that city. Good old Queens, New York just like the Rolling Stones song.

The story was featured on the front of the magazine as an upsell and the title was rather clever, entertaining, and fetching.

"The King of New York."

It now seemed that Quentin had eclipsed Elton, the King of Queens. It was a grandiose title that would remain with him for the rest of his life.

AIDS had crept into the gay community with a whisper, but by the early nineties, it was beating a very loud drum throughout New York City, across the American continent and right around the world.

One night at a small AIDS charity fundraiser, Quentin was approached by two well-heeled gay investment bankers named Peter and Paul, who were a lot more than just well-connected, for they knew everyone worth knowing. There were the P I N and K in the pink dollar.

"Quentin, we are putting together an AIDS Foundation of our own. We have recruited all the good, the famous, the great in New York and beyond," said Peter.

"This is a Foundation that will take the fight against AIDS to a new level. It will be on a completely different scale from everything that has gone before. We have media connections, banking, industrial, commercial and showbiz friends and it is a sure-fire winner. It must be. All around us our dear friends are dying" continued Paul.

"How can I help?"

Paul coughed nervously.

"We would like you to be the figurehead, the President of the Foundation if you will kindly accept our offer. After all, you are "The King of New York," and we couldn't have a lesser mortal darling!"

Quentin was blown away, unusually silent, and completely lost for words. This was acceptance by the gay society that he was the top of the tree, the leader of the pack, the man about town.

"Can I think about it for a few days?"

Peter looked at Paul in surprise having assumed Quentin would jump at the offer.

"How about one week from today darling, Ok?"

"Ok with me, thank you for considering me and your kind invitation."

Pecking each other gently on the cheeks, they went their separate ways.

Quentin had much thinking to do, and he had to do it quickly.

When he got back home to Erik, he told him what had happened, and they both cried tears of joy for the endorsement, amid tears of fear for the dark shadow of AIDs that daily reared its ugly head in their gentle world.

Despite the excitement, it was early to bed, because Quentin had an important appointment at 10 am the following day, and to a serial night owl like him, this call to arms was in the middle of the night.

* * *

It was now late August, and the results would be in today. Quentin rose from bed, carried out his ablutions and left his apartment at 9 am on the dot.

Erik, clad in his favourite Disney dressing gown and fluffy Mickey Mouse slippers, made quite a statement for a fashion guru running a multi-million-dollar clothes business and made Quentin a strong black coffee before he waved him casually goodbye.

Quentin parked his three-year-old Corvette in the private car park of his doctor's surgery between 5th and 6th Avenue in Manhattan, where he had been a patient for what seemed like forever.

Exiting the car, he adjusted his cream linen suit so that it looked even more casual than it naturally was, taking the time to put his sunglasses on his forehead to look "extra cool," as he described that habit to Erik.

Sadly, the suit made him look more dishevelled than casual because, in the last three months, he had dropped ten pounds in weight.

Quentin knew how to attract attention. Years of experience had made him a very forward backroom boy.

He floated across the car park as if he was carried on the shoulders of the Gods themselves and pressed the buzzer at the private entrance of his personal physician.

"Who is it please?"

He summoned up all his acting experience to say in a vulnerable voice.

"It's Quentin, darling, do let me in, it's very hot out here!"

Taking the elevator to the 45th Floor he regrouped before exiting. Then he sauntered into the reception area as if he was the world's most famous actor, Sir Laurence Olivier, attending his first audition.

It was an entrance the two other patients in the waiting room would have paid to see. He pretended to mop his brow, looked at his audience for sympathy, and paused professionally to ramp up the suspense.

"It's so warm today, may I please ask you for a glass of iced water?"

The actor reigned supreme, and he was now firmly the centre of attention.

There was no aggression, no undercurrent of violence, no threat of unpredictability, yet Quentin had used his acting skills faultlessly to become the thing that mattered most to him, "the star of the show."

"Good morning, Mr Prendergast."

Darcy, the extremely professional receptionist played her part impeccably, for she had known Quentin for over ten years, and was used to the theatrical mannerisms of the Broadway star.

Turning to the water fountain, she dispensed an ice-cold drink and dramatically placed it in front of him.

"I do hope you are not going to faint Mr Prendergast!"

Quentin concluded a scene that had been played out on many occasions on his visits to "Jones, Seinfeld & Stewart, Medical Practitioners".

"Thank you Darcy darling, I don't think I will faint, at least until I get Dr Stewart's bill!"

This was followed by unsuppressed laughter from the temporary theatre crowd in front of him.

It was exactly 10.05 am and Quentin, having been sat in the car park for fifteen minutes, had as usual arrived "fashionably late" for his 10 am appointment.

"Once an actor always an actor," he mused to himself.

Darcy gathered herself together after the witty interruption.

"You can go right in Mr Prendergast; the doctor is waiting for you."

Quentin duly walked in to face his devil.

One week earlier he had been tested for AIDS and it had been his secret all week.

It was the only thing he had ever kept from Erik because he did not want to worry him, but it had been the little things that had started to niggle him, that had made him face up to the possibility that his worst fears may be true.

Moreover, it was why he had not immediately accepted Peter and Paul's kind invitation to head the AIDS charity because he was so concerned.

A meeting with a private New York doctor was expensive, but he had amassed more than enough wealth to cover those costs.

The results of the blood tests were a different matter.

He quickly learned that it was time to pay the ferryman, and he did not have any form of currency that would expunge his debt.

Quentin walked along to the door he knew so well, and stopped at the little brass sign that said "Doctor Charles Stewart M.D."

He knocked gently out of politeness.

"Come in."

A tall, thin, seasoned doctor, with a neat greying beard, urged Quentin to take a seat in the luxury chair across the desk opposite.

Charles was gay himself and had been recommended to Quentin many years ago by close friends as the "go-to" solution for all things medical for people in their circle.

Quentin liked Charles because he fired straight from the hip, Montana style. If something had to be said, then Charles would deliver the line.

Sometimes being fluffy and soft just didn't cut it.

As far as Quentin was concerned, medical matters were best dealt with in short, sharp sentences.

It was easier to understand what was said and it cost less, for time was money and Quentin never forgot those days long ago when he didn't have two dimes to rub together. If anyone understood the value of time and money it was him.

"Good morning, Quentin."

"Good morning, Charles, aren't you going to ask how I am?"

"I know how you are; I have your test results."

"Excellent, it's all going according to plan, what's the diagnosis?"

"Grim."

Quentin's palms began to sweat, as a surge of heat ran through his body, offset by a rapid pulse.

His worst fears began to surface.

"How grim is it?"

"As grim as it gets, you have tested positive for AIDS."

Quentin almost passed out but managed to regain his composure as the incoming dialogue signalled the start of the third and final fight of his life.

"Go on Charles."

"Quentin, the diagnosis is conclusive, and it is already far advanced, but you are not alone I'm afraid. AIDS is rampant and we know it's being passed to women as well. Within a couple of years, it will be the leading cause of death for all Americans aged 25 to 44 years of age."

Walter felt physically sick and chastised himself for burying his head in the sand for so long by ignoring the TV and news media bulletins forecasting the far-reaching effects of this gay plague.

"If only I had been more careful and used condoms, if only I had been less promiscuous, if only I'd met Erik years ago and settled down!" he thought silently to himself.

This diagnosis explained the weight loss and the sniffle he could just not shake off for the last four or five months.

Despite the anxiety, fear and trepidation, Quentin called on the acting skills he had learned when very young and suppressed this new horror, using humour to hide his fear.

"So it's a death sentence doc?"

"We all die in the end Walter, it's just timing. Quality wins over quantity every time! Maybe you need to think about that?"

"I never thought of it like that before. If it's only death I think I can live with that!"

The doctor smiled for he knew Quentin and his wry sense of humour of old.

"How long have I got?"

"That's the eternal question Quentin, we are still learning about this awful disease, but I would say six months to a year if you're lucky, possibly longer if you do as the doctors advise.

"I will be recommending the specialists you need."

Quentin felt like he had been hit by a truck.

"Does anyone else know I have it?"

"Certainly not, when I sent the tests into the laboratory, I used a pseudonym to keep your privacy. That's the difference between private and public medicine I guess."

"Thank heavens for that!"

"Furthermore Quentin, outside of this room not a soul knows that you have AIDS. Not even Darcy, even though you could trust her with your life."

The words were ironic, direct, and devastating.

"Thank you, Charles."

"It's very simple, it's your story to tell."

"I need to go and tell someone now."

"How much will the treatment cost?"

"Good news and bad news I guess!"

"The tests and consultations over the last week will be about $10,000 but because of my connections and our relationship, it will be anonymously covered by a little-known, low-profile AIDS charity made up of people like us, for people like us. They will not know your identity; they won't ask, and I won't be telling. We are like-minded souls and all in this together.

"Why sponsor me?"

"Because you have always given so freely of your time, talent and money, for the benefit of others, both before and after the arrival of AIDS."

"Thank you, but please send me the bill. I'll pay it regardless plus a few thousand on top. I ask you to discretely donate the surplus funds to that organisation. There will be people far less fortunate than me, and I can't take any money with me where I'm going!"

"Thank you, I hear you, Quentin. The cost of the ongoing treatment will be subject to how long you survive but based on experience it could easily be a half million dollars or more."

That doesn't upset me, the more I spend, the longer I've lived, so I'd be happy for it to be a million dollars. There are no pockets in a shroud!"

"Ok Quentin, we are done for now. I will make all the necessary arrangements. Please go and tell who you need to tell and come back here tomorrow at 10.00 am. I will have everything ready concerning your treatment and the points of contact needed.

"Once that treatment begins, the truth will slowly but surely leak out, so make sure you do everything you need to do while you have the privacy to do so."

He left the good doctor's office paler than when he went in, but there were no theatricals as he exited. There were decisions to make and a conversation to have.

Quentin wanted to tell Erik at once and to discuss the business matters afterwards.

Within an hour he had told the stunned Viking the sad news, and the estimated time he had left on this planet. They held each other with no words, only love passing between them in a scene that had been sadly acted out by many before them. They also knew that they would not be the last players to take part in this twisted game of love.

Quentin and Erik had been together for just over a year, and it had seemed like it would last forever but it was not to be.

There were two burning topics of business, that amongst other things, played on Quentin's mind.

After their emotions had subsided for a while, he looked to Erik for some advice.

"Should I take up the Presidency of Peter and Paul's AIDS Foundation?"

"I think it would be the right thing to do, but you must explain the circumstances first. They are discrete gentlemen, and you can be assured of complete privacy from those two."

It set Quentin's mind to think about the gravity of his situation.

"Do I want privacy, or do I prefer to let everyone know?" he thought, followed by "questions, questions, questions, they just keep coming!"

The discussion continued and now that Quentin was an AIDS sufferer, he agreed with Erik that he was well-placed to raise the profile of the charity.

Time was of the essence.

He would confirm his acceptance of Peter and Paul's offer that very afternoon, hoping they would still want him once he had let them know his devastating secret.

The second question was far more personal.

"What about my funeral?"

Erik shrugged his shoulders at this curveball.

"Where do you think I should be buried, I want a burial, not a cremation."

"When we are gone, we are gone. As you well know I am an atheist, so without wishing to upset you I must be honest, it doesn't matter to me at all, but it probably does to you.

"I suppose you should be buried somewhere special, maybe where you feel safe, particularly as you will be there for a while."

He managed a weak smile which partially relieved their joint stress for a few moments.

"Queens or Manhattan possibly? It's your choice."

Quentin's mind was a blur and he vowed to think it through carefully and decide in the next few days.

He was conscious of the unpredictability of his condition and terrified of a sudden unexpected downturn in his health.

A final resting place would be chosen post haste and before the week was out his lawyers would be instructed to add it as a codicil in his will.

Next, he looked for Peter's telephone number as he was "dying to tell him some news," and as the tasteless line in dialogue went through his thespian mind, he winced.

***

Quentin was a gentleman's gentleman, a handsome, quiet, impeccably mannered soul, who lacked the natural aggression and impoliteness of the indigenous native New Yorker. He was also a leading socialite in that fair city for many reasons.

Like many young, misfit, gay men, Quentin had come to New York in the mid-1970s to find himself, to discover people like him, to finally belong somewhere, and feel part of a society where the true companionship of likeminded souls, that was somehow lacking in his fearful, uncertain everyday existence, could be found.

He had arrived wide-eyed, defensive, shy, virginal, and clean. He looked as if he was God's gift to the throbbing jeans and nightlife of New York City, but the gentle new boy in town was no lamb to the slaughter, for he had an inner strength, born of life's early trials, that few could match.

However, he was not alone in that era. Every year thousands of gay men and women, just like chrysalises metamorphosing into butterflies, would suddenly and spontaneously sprout their wings, and fly off to the beating city hearts of the USA.

Youngsters of all creeds and colours living a physical, emotional, and sexual lie throughout American suburbia, would leave the disquiet of their sad and lonely miserable existence, to seek out others just like themselves. Their goal was not self-satisfaction, but to discover the purpose of it all, to find the joy, beauty, and love that every person on this planet deserved.

From the many thousands of wide-eyed, wannabe transients, entertainers and thespians, this abused, confused country boy had emerged as King, but now it was time to settle life's account with those he loved most.

* * *

Quentin asked himself the same question repeatedly as he had done every day for the last four weeks.

"How had it come to this?"

Here he stood in the Waldorf Astoria dressed up like a dog's dinner, in one of the world's finest hotels, at the biggest Gala Ball that New York society had ever thrown in support of AIDS charity.

He was to be the star speaker in front of over six hundred well-heeled guests, but his speech was not yet finalised.

Eight weeks to the day since his tragic news, Quentin was now a founder member and the first President of the New York City AIDS Foundation whose motto was "in the name of love".

This noble gathering of famous artists, thespians, politicians, industrialists, investment bankers and socialites had already within two months of its formation, been instrumental in pledging millions to support the victims of the modern plague called AIDS, and tonight would see a sizeable sum added to the war chest.

During the evening they would dine on the finest fayre, drink the best wines, and remember the fallen, such as the late, great, Freddie Mercury, Rock Hudson and others, all lost to the dreaded "gay man's disease".

The omnipotent Elton would be there to perform, thus guaranteeing a fabulously wealthy, generous crowd, who would each contribute thousands and thousands of dollars to the cause.

"I knew I could rely on Elton," Quentin whispered to himself.

The supporting act, much to the disappointment of their Japanese fans, cancelled a full stadium gig in Tokyo, to ensure they could be at this event.

Shelley and Quentin had a bond, and since the fateful day they had met in Central Park all those years ago, it was the only time that he had ever asked her for a favour. Rockaria would rock as requested.

Quentin, the talk show host, the stage actor, and the "must-have" party guest would bring it all together as fundraiser extraordinaire, and he knew that tonight he must give the speech and performance of his life.

* * *

He stood in the men's washroom taking a final opportunity to straighten his bow tie and adjust his pocket-handkerchief, his nerves getting the better of him as they always did before a big performance.

One more time, he looked in the mirror and thought about his lines, his entrance, his pauses, the things he would emphasise, and most importantly his conclusion.

Just twenty-five minutes later, after a gushing joint welcome toast to the assembled guests from both Peter and Paul, he was introduced live on national television to the dashing crowd as the inaugural President of the New York City AIDS Foundation.

"Ladies and gentlemen, to misquote the Beatles, let me introduce to you the man you've known for all these years, the one, the only, Quentin Prendergast, the King of New York!"

Wild clapping, cheers and celebration fuelled the airwaves, as the shiniest star in the room took his rightful place on centre stage.

Quentin stood up, looked deliberately at his watch and then slowly at almost every pair of eyes in the front row, in an opening that seemed to last a minute, but lasted just a few seconds, as the audience was professionally reduced to silence.

"I know what you are all thinking!"

Then he paused again for what seemed like an age until everyone focused on him and he had their full attention.

"What drama will unfold, which great joke will he tell, or what funny impression will Quentin do this evening?"

"Listen carefully to me my dears. He will never again do jokes or impressions, he will never host his chat show, and he will never star in a Hollywood film, or sing, dance, or act on the New York stage again.

"I buried him today; Quentin Prendergast is dead!" he shouted in a raised tone.

The crowd gasped, waiting for the punchline, or the wry smile, but he kept a stony silence and a hard glare.

Smiles on the faces of the cream of New York society grew weaker by the second, as guests looked at the countenance of others in the room, interrogating their compatriots' reaction to this strange statement, or at the floor whilst they gathered their thoughts and considered if the rumours might be true.

The showman shouted at the top of his voice, thus deliberately increasing the tension and drama.

"Quentin is dead because he was never born. He is a fabrication, an act, a lie!

"Quentin Prendergast was a name I invented, just like many of you have invented your names and history to escape your pasts and start anew.

"Less than half an hour ago I looked into the mirror in the washrooms, I stared into my soul and what is left of my future, and I quit acting forever.

Gasps of incredulity punctuated his opening sentences and a murmuring Mexican wave bounced around the room.

Quentin used his years of experience to let the audience recompose itself and then continued with his speech.

"The doctors tell me that one year from tonight I will be dead.

Shock, horror, and disbelief travelled like an uninvited electric shock through the entire gathering.

"The irony is that as President of this fine Foundation, I will be dead of AIDS. The very thing that we are here to fight!"

The startled crowd gasped as one, falling silent as the words hit home.

"Until then, what endures of the body and soul that is Quentin Prendergast has one purpose for the remainder of this life; to levy funds, to raise awareness, to assist in ridding the world of the plague that is affecting the gay community worldwide!"

Spontaneously the audience clapped loudly, which relieved the tension. It was as if a distant bugle from an unknown regiment had called them to arms. They stood in unison to cry, cheer, and gush in support of the heroic honesty of the condemned man.

Rivers of relief poured down Quentin's face as he laid his soul bare, and the audience leaned forward so that they did not miss one humble, heart-wrenching word.

"As President of the New York City AIDS Foundation, I feel that I should be invincible, and untouched by this biblical, modern-day scourge, that now affects people just like me and many of you.

"I feel that I should be a gay, virgin icon, remaining whole, uncontaminated, and clean, but I must tell you that I am mortal, that I have history, and that I am very real.

"I am not here to apologise for being gay, for my deeds, my thoughts, or my actions!

"Tonight, I am ashamed to say that I was going to put on the greatest act, nay, the bravest act of my whole career, by standing up here and pretending that all was well, and sticking to that party line, to be the apologist that I and we, have been all our lives, BUT NOT ANYMORE!"

The rising inflexion and emotion in his voice hit every man and woman between the eyes, the speaker striking his target as intended.

Six hundred guests rose to their feet, applauding, and wiping tears from their faces for what seemed like a full five minutes.

"I was planning to tell you that we would raise five million dollars in funds for "the cause" tonight and that in time we would find a cure.

"Willingly I was going to help in emptying your pockets so that on your way home in your fancy limousines you would feel good about yourselves.

"Let me tell you, good people, the apologies are over!

"The lies, mistruths, and misunderstandings are a thing of the past.

"It stops right here. There will be no more appeasement.

"This evening I approached the podium as Quentin Prendergast, actor, chat show host, film star, dancer, singer, and raconteur."

Quentin paused, pulled out the immaculate white silk handkerchief from his top pocket, and trembling, wiped away a flood of perspiration from his soaking wet brow.

The audience was mesmerised, including Peter and Paul, who despite their prior knowledge of Quentin's sad news, had not seen this coming. They held hands, unwittingly holding on for dear life, for three years later they would both follow in Quentin's well-trodden footsteps.

"Now it's time to tell you my story. Quentin is gone. You will never see him again!"

He paused and wiped yet more tears from his hot and reddened face, but now, just like those involuntary droplets of water, he was in full flow.

Audience members, both men and women, huddled together to jointly fight this awful new truth that had gate-crashed their conscious minds.

"Let me introduce myself to you.

"It is time we were true to ourselves. It's time we gay men and women were honest with the world.

"Honesty may indeed be the spark that lights the flame, which inspires the medical research inferno, which can prevent AIDs from wiping out the gay population of our universe!"

The words hit the target and once again the audience erupted, the increasing volume confirming he had everyone in the palms of his shaking hands, as it took over a minute for sufficient order to be regained, so he could continue with his ground-breaking delivery.

"My name is Walter Wyatt Palmer. I have decided that it's time the real Walter stood up and was counted!"

Audible gasps of further surprise were the reply from the room.

"Hello everybody!"

He paused, smiled, and then waved his hands in the air like an old-fashioned music hall minstrel.

A titter of laughter ran around the astonished dining room.

"I was born in Great Falls, Montana, a small cowboy town way out west.

"Yes, I'm a cowboy, although I've never been on a horse in my life.

"But let me tell you, I know BS when I smell it!

"My father and mother were both alcoholics. He was also a gambler and often violent and cruel to both me and my mother.

"Beatings were the things that punctuated our week. They were especially bad on weekends when his horses lost at the track.

The shocked crowd took in a deep breath as if to somehow help combat this appalling news.

"I started acting before I could walk, maybe before I could talk. I acted because I felt unworthy, and the truth is that all through my childhood and early teenage years, I never felt wanted."

Walter stared deep into the eyes of the celebrities in attendance, especially those at the tables closest to him.

"I am sure that many of you in the audience, if you think far enough back in time, truly understand what I am saying."

A few guests twitched in a reflex reaction that suggested they held a secret that was never to be told.

"All my life I have abhorred violence and fighting.

"I am, as most of you know, a pacifist, but the time for fighting has come.

"Walter, Elton, Peter, Paul, Shelley and Rockaria, and every one of you is going to fight AIDS and we will win, for together we are strong! We are winners! We are unbeatable!

"We will win because we will be honest, and be supportive of each other, and tell the world the truth about this invisible disease that is killing our friends and now me."

The TV crews were now concentrated on every word, as were the audience, the waiting staff, and all the dignitaries in attendance.

"In my case, my father beat me because I was a failure. I was different from the other boys.

"My only failing was that I was gay."

Supportive cheers came back from the audience now transfixed by this astonishing, unexpected verbal delivery.

Walter uncharacteristically beat his fist on the table.

"I never wanted to be gay!

"I never chose to be gay!

"I never asked anyone to do anything they did not want to do!"

He smacked the tabletop overly hard one more time with a thud, so much so that it hurt his left hand.

"Let me put it as simply as I can, and he stared right into the cameras.

"I am gay because I am gay. Nature has chosen this path for me, as I know it has for many of you in this room tonight and thousands of you across America.

"We have done nothing wrong!"

With that, he banged his already stinging palm on the table once more, and the wine glasses jumped half an inch in the air in agreement.

"Being gay is as natural to me as "boy meets girl" anywhere else in the good old USA or beyond. It's just a different set of genetic factors driving something that the straight population has forever been afraid of, and I weep for their lack of understanding!"

The New York gay community, as one, nodded their agreement.

"I blame our community for not being straight with them."

A wry smile crossed his face as he paused.

"No pun intended!"

The audience rocked with laughter, as for a brief second the showman in Walter had made a surprise uninvited reappearance.

"It is here we have the great hypocrisy. I am sure you will agree with me that the best actors, the greatest dancers, and the most entertaining showbiz people are always gays. We are artists, and our straight friends across this world enjoy every minute of our performances."

Looking directly at a camera that Walter had now identified as belonging to the national news channel he made a bold statement.

"On behalf of all the people in this world at risk of AIDS, I say to everyone on this mortal planet, please support us.

"Kindly realise that we are human just like you, with the same hopes and dreams, the same triumphs and disasters that you experience.

"Our one true punishment is that we cannot naturally have children, but that is God's will, and we accept it without question. We are nature's victims; we are not criminals!"

Walter stepped up through the theatrical vocal gears, and once again the whole gathering cheered until he begged them to be quiet.

"Please donate generously to the fight against AIDS, either in spirit or financially.

"Whether your contribution is ostentatious, flamboyant, or anonymous, on behalf of everyone concerned I thank you here and now.

"I left Great Falls because it was still coming to terms with my sexuality as indeed was I, and because my continued presence there was unfair to the people who had supported me and my individualism. I came to New York City to be with people like you, and I remained here long after Walter and the wonderful people of Great Falls had made their peace."

This was a crescendo speech, partly rehearsed, hugely ad-libbed, and now he opened his arms and chest wide.

"You are my people, my friends, my fellow gays, and I love you all! I love you all!"

Tears now flowed uncontrollably down Walter's cheeks, mirrored by many who watched him, locked on to his every breath, move and sound.

"I love this world and all the people in it, regardless of race, creed, colour, political, religious, or sexual persuasion. I say to you, that even if you cannot see it in your hearts to help us, then please look deep into your souls and be tolerant."

In under fifteen minutes, Walter had become the world's number-one gay icon, the heavyweight champion of that international community.

Before the hour was out, this magnificent speech would be broadcast in news bulletins worldwide, bringing the much-needed attention Walter had wanted to the AIDS cause.

"So now dear friends I must conclude. Do not run away from reality. Be honest with yourselves and everybody else. To thine own self be true!

"I ask you to donate generously this evening in the auction, and by post in the coming days and months.

"Quentin is gone but Walter will remain and let me tell you he will not be dead one year from tonight because I, we, will fight AIDS together, and we will educate the people of this world and make it a better place.

"Finally, I say to you, that as gays we may often look weak, but remember that beneath our exterior we have feelings, we are men and women too.

"DO NOT underestimate us."

He finally stood as tall, strong, and proud as his illness allowed, and banged his fist one more time to confirm that his conclusion followed.

"However long it takes, we will win!"

Walter hesitated, and then finished with the words that had once been said to him by a tough Irish traffic cop long ago.

"It is the size of the fight in the dog that counts, not the size of the dog in the fight!"

There was not a dry eye in the house as Peter and Paul helped the emotionally spent President of The New York City AIDS Foundation to sit down.

The crowd rose as one, and delivered a tumultuous thunderstorm of acceptance, recognition, and pure delight, knowing that they had witnessed one of the greatest speeches of all time.

In future, they would tell their friends that they were there on that night when the disease known as AIDS suddenly realised it had a serious fight on its hands.

It was fully fifteen minutes before good order could be restored and the final formalities of the evening politely executed, before the soundstage lit up and old friends entertained the audience.

Elton reached minds, hearts, souls, and wallets, with a deeply touching performance that would be talked about for years to come.

Rockaria, America's biggest rock band, fronted by a sassy little lady from Nebraska, played the gig of their life.

* * *

Walter was afraid of AIDS and terrified of dying, yet he had just given a better acting performance than Quentin ever had. He lamented a second career that would never come.

Newscasts around the world carried clips of the event, with a focus on Quentin's retirement and his admittance of having AIDs, but the real focus was on Walter, the new star that had arisen from Quentin's ashes.

Walter's emotional speech was shown coast to coast in an extended programme on CNN that evening because it was news of the biggest kind. The broadcast of the fight against AIDS was a guaranteed ratings winner.

Following his first and only speech as President, Walter retired as a performer as promised, but remained in post at the New York City AIDS Foundation, keeping in contact with close friends for as long as he was able.

By the time he was supposed to die one year later, over $50 million had been raised directly and indirectly from this one gala fundraising evening, and a new understanding of the gay community had filtered down into everyday society.

It seemed that the evangelical, fighting speech of Walter Wyatt Palmer had been a winner. The judges who would remain long after he was gone were certain of that.

* * *

The time sadly came for Walter to exit this world and he lost the third fight of his life on May 4th, 1995, with his soulmate, the mercifully AIDS-free "Erik the Viking," at his bedside to the end.

Whilst the hyenas of the world's paparazzi jockeyed for position on the pavement outside, a far gentler scene took place in a secluded ward in the east wing of a private New York City hospital.

Walter knew his final curtain call was imminent, and he gestured for his Viking to come near.

Erik took him softly by the hand.

As one they both mouthed the sentiment that they loved each other and a nurse on standby in the background began to shed tears.

Before leaving earth for his onward spiritual journey, Walter managed to say the final words he had planned some time ago before the illness had consumed him.

"Erik, here I am finally at the rainbow's end."

He struggled for breath but with all his strength and resilience he rallied one final time.

"Big Mick was right about the rainbow, I found it and I found you my beautiful Viking, you are my pot of gold."

Walter's eyes lost focus as if something else had now grabbed his attention and his body visually weakened and relaxed in the bed as he uttered his final Shakespearean theatrical exit.

"Hark he calls!"

His voice and mortal body faded away.

Walter was just short of his fortieth birthday.

The brightest star in the American sky was no more.

The King was dead.

*　*　*

The handwritten instructions were clear, with the burial place a surprise to the glitterati, but not to the good people way out west.

It was two years and six months after his outstanding speech before the tired, emaciated, worn out, and unrecognizable body of Walter was laid to rest in the West Great Falls town cemetery.

As the crow flies it was three miles from the gates of William Rodgers High School but a lifetime away from a downtrodden, miserable, neglected childhood.

Out of the darkness had come light, and that light had been a shining star, held in the greatest esteem by all who knew him.

Almost half a mile away on the poor side of the facility, in overgrown unmarked graves, were two unkempt, neglected, burial plots.

No one knew who lay there, no one ever visited, and certainly, no one cared. Things have a strange way of balancing themselves out in life and death.

His funeral was the closest Walter ever came to his mother's resting place.

Film stars, socialites and actors from Hollywood, New York and all points in between attended, for the funeral was the event of the decade, and they wouldn't have missed it for the world.

Amongst the mourners were many of the good people of Great Falls, including some of his "cheerleaders" and their families, now fully grown with children of their own.

Their families had never met Walter and only seen him through the medium of TV and film, but every time he appeared on their screens or in the newspapers, they had been reminded by the lady of the household that he was homegrown in Great Falls.

In a flamboyant ceremony where bright colours were the order of the day, and following Walter's instructions, the people gathered to say goodbye to the undisputed King of New York, the pacifist who had brought such joy into a troubled world.

Emma Carpenter formerly Wilson was invited by the Catholic priest to give a reading to the congregation.

She approached the lectern with great composure, but as she looked up at the assembled mourners, tears came to her eyes as her chest tightened and her palms and wrists became clammy with uninvited perspiration.

Emma carefully placed one sheet of paper in front of her and then paused for effect while she recomposed herself, as Walter had taught her in days gone by.

The reading would be the words from Walter's favourite poem, which he had successfully performed hundreds of times as a song on Broadway in his one man show.

A hush came over the congregation as Emma gathered herself together for this tribute to the boy who had walked her home from school aged five. The same boy who had eaten scones and doughnuts at her house and been her escort at the prom all those years ago. The same international superstar who had never forgotten the Wilsons or his Montana roots.

Emma stood tall and began to speak as she stared directly at the coffin of Montana's prodigal son, not once looking at the words she had written for she knew them by heart.

"Walter Wyatt Palmer, I love you, I hate you, I love you."

This demanded the attention of the whole congregation who now locked themselves on to every emotional utterance from the former prom queen.

"I love you for being my lifelong best friend.

"I hate you for leaving us too early, too young, too soon.

"I love you now, I loved you the day we first met, and I'll love you forever.

"People laughed at you when they called you the runt of the litter, they said you were weak, they bullied you and they made you cry, but the good people of Great Falls rallied round because they saw the goodness, the greatness in you and they were so right.

"You were sure different Walter, ain't that the truth. They laughed at you because you were not physically strong, but at great risk to yourself you once stood up for this sad old prom queen against the mighty school bully. You were my King before New York had ever heard of you!

"Walter Wyatt Palmer was born to be a star, to do remarkable things, to entertain, but sadly to never have children of his own.

"Oh how life has cheated Walter Wyatt Palmer and all of us, for the sight of seeing you play with your kids in Central Park would have been something to behold.

"My daddy once said that pound for pound you were the toughest guy in Great Falls, but daddy you were wrong!

"Against all the odds, against all the selfish prejudice in this world, you left your childhood home to find yourself, to discover new things but it didn't quite work out like that. New York discovered you first, and then so did the good old US of A and eventually the world got in on the act.

"You are the best pound for pound fighter we've ever seen for in the end you have single-handedly taken the fight to AIDS and slowly but surely, we are beginning to win small battles and eventually, just like you promised, we will win the war.

"Walter, you were unique, one of a kind. How lucky we were to have you, but now you have gone up to the angels, where you will surely be celebrated in heaven. They won't know what's hit them!

"Until we meet again, I say goodbye to you Walter, goodbye to the boy who would be king!"

There was not a dry eye in the house and even Father Murphy, the well-seasoned Catholic priest openly cried for the first time ever at a funeral.

Emma turned her teary gaze towards the weeping crowd and began the reading.

"Absent Friends"

As I wander down life's road, along it's winding bends
  I think of those who travel not, I think of absent friends

So I turn to memories made, in other times gone by
  I think of those I travelled with, I feel…… like I could cry

At first I fight away my tears, my mind is all a blur
  And then a smile lights up my face, as memories start to stir

The love and warmth you always gave, at last I understand
  I feel your love there is no grave, you're in the promised land

As I wander down life's road, along it's winding bends
  I think of those who travel not, I think of absent friends

And now I know we travel still, together all the way
  Absent friends we'll meet again, at God's behest some day

Emma read the words without missing a beat, as Walter's famous friends and the good people of Great Falls tried in vain to hold back the tears that fell freely to the church stone floor, like gentle rain from heaven above.

As she returned to her seat, she felt that a huge weight had been lifted from her shoulders and that her performance had somehow been assisted by her very own absent friend.

Her performance would have been worthy of Quentin Prendergast himself, delivered with respect, sincerity and unbridled passion for this had been a final declaration of love.

The priest continued with the solemn service and several of the Hollywood and Broadway A-listers in attendance gave wonderful personal eulogies in memory of the departed.

The towering Catholic church that stood on the corner of Main Street and Third Avenue witnessed a "first" as the priest ended the ceremony.

To the right of him stood the rock band Rockaria, fronted by the enigmatic Shelley from Nebraska, the darling of the international music media.

Right on cue the music started up as the band began to play Walter's favourite new song "Prodigal Son", a country rock crescendo anthem written for the occasion by Shelley about her best friend Walter, that would take the deceased out through the huge church doors and into the glorious Great Falls sunshine for the last time.

He had often said to his friends "only Shelley could have written that exit for me", when he thought of his life's early struggles in Montana, and against all the odds, his climb to fame in the New York entertainment jungle.

Nebraska's most famous rock star grabbed the microphone as her mind travelled back to a sunlit Central Park wooden bench where she once sat with an excited, wide eyed country boy who told her he was going to make it big in New York.

"Big?, who was he kidding, he was much bigger than that!" she thought to herself.

"Ladies and gentlemen. This is for Walter or Quentin or whatever you chose to call him.

"I love you Quentin, this one's for you cowboy!"

They laughed............................I said I'd be famous
  Laughed at me....but they're laughing no more
  They laughed...........................when I said I'd be king
  Laughed at me....but they're laughing no more

I hated to lose, just wanted to win, finding success, is never a sin
  Made it at last, against all odds, top of the heap, a gift from the Gods

Laughed at me, laughed at me, laughed at me, laughed at me

King of the hill.......................great things I have done
  Everyone loves me, coz I'm the number.........the number one
  Yes I am the number one, Yes I am the chosen one, Yes I am the Prodigal Son

Missing in action....when I needed you most,
  Snakes n' weasels, sniggering ghosts
  I struggled, I strived ....no one believed.....no one believed
  Now ex friends you knock on my door,
  Crocodile smiles ....score by score
  Look at me now...my time has come....my time has come

Laughed at me, laughed at me, laughed at me, laughed at me
  Laughed at me, laughed at me, laughed at me, laughed at me

Darkness fades...............................the winner takes all
  Everyone loves me, coz I'm the number.........the number one
  Yes I am the number one, Yes I am the chosen one, Yes I am the Prodigal Son

Laughed at me, laughed at me, laughed at me, laughed at me
  Laughed at me, laughed at me, laughed at me, the Prodigal Son!

By special request of his old schoolfriend Emma, the executrix of Walter's will, he was buried at the important end of the cemetery, next to a large white marble headstone of a man who had died some five years previously.

Emma remained at the graveside until everyone else had drifted away.

She carefully took two red roses from inside her coat pocket and threw one down onto the coffin of her lifelong best friend as tears flowed uncontrollably down her still-beautiful face.

Emma turned away and respectfully laid the remaining rose on the immaculately kept second grave.

Putting her fingers to her lips she kissed them, and then passed the kiss to the headstone, as she gently stroked it and thought of days gone by.

Hesitating for a moment, she softly touched the inscription and glanced at the loving words of endearment.

"Michael Wilson, father, husband, grandfather, a much-loved man of this town, respected by all who knew him."

Emma's moment was complete, and she whispered to herself.

"One day we'll all be together again, just like the old days," and with that final personal thought, the ceremony was over.

Walter would have been delighted to know that his mentor and guardian angel lay so close.

On his grave, the direct, honest, townspeople of Great Falls had commissioned a simple, true, and sincere inscription.

Walter "Quentin Prendergast" Wyatt Palmer

The King of New York

1956 - 1995

A Man's Man Who Soared with Eagles

* Both songs can be heard at www.odynson.co.uk

Chapter 7

A Good Suit

THE paper chariot was boldly decorated at its edges with unmistakeable red and blue diagonal stripes which immediately confirmed its origin.

The physically fading, yet mentally sharp old lady summoned up the courage to open the uninvited, unexpected envelope that had just landed unceremoniously on her doormat.

She gripped the paper knife with the Scarborough insignia and then used her least painful arthritic hand to carefully slice open the international messenger.

A trio of passengers fell out.

Two cheques and a letter bounced onto the table.

She panicked.

The first cheque was for £300 and the second for £50,000.

Both were made payable to the personal account of Clementine Hobson.

"It doesn't make any sense; it was all so long ago!"

The retired headmistress nervously adjusted her varifocal-lensed spectacles and examined the letter more closely; the handwriting was unmistakeable.

She panicked again.

* * *

Clementine Hobson had first panicked at ten-thirty that early daffodil-sprinkled March morning in 2019.

She was not expecting any letter; she liked her routine to be just that, a routine.

The postman was an hour late.

As she looked out of the window, he announced his arrival with the backfire of his engine as he thundered into view in a rusty red van, fumes streaming out of the back.

"Normality resumed," thought Clementine and relaxed.

Despite the brisk weather "Postman Pete" skipped around the small enclave of houses in his inappropriate tight-fitting shorts.

"He will be dead in six months if he doesn't learn to dress properly!"

Her beloved husband Desmond was casually watching a cricket replay of England's latest test match in Australia.

"It will soon be "Postman Paul" or "Postman Pat" the way he's carrying on!"

Desmond did not hear, for in his mind he was batting for the England cricket team in Melbourne, warmed by the summer evening sun and the sound of ball on willow.

The letter on top of the pile stood out like a sore thumb because the envelope was handwritten.

Not only that, but it also was an unusual shape, an American shape, and it said "airmail" on the front.

Clementine picked the letters off the doormat as "Postman Pete" galloped on around the windy, frosty close.

One of a dozen, substantial, four-bedroomed houses, they had lived in this delightful Yorkshire property for over thirty years.

The quality of letters received through your letterbox has a strict correlation with age. The older you get the less important you are.

These days Clementine only seemed to receive mailshots and supermarket offers, interspersed with utility company bills, and once per year the dreaded tax return, which according to her was a complete pain in the butt. She liked to call a spade a spade.

Desmond's concentration had been broken by the familiar bounce of the post and the vibration of letterbox metal on wood.

"Anything for me?" he asked.

Clementine was focused on the handwritten letter. The handwriting was unmistakable. There were also two brightly coloured mailshots, a free community magazine and a phone bill.

"No nothing special."

She filtered the post so that everything was put on the kitchen table, but the letter that caused the panic was held firmly in her grip. She was not letting go of that under any circumstances.

As she stared at the writing another bout of panic began to combine itself with excitement.

Pictures flashed through her brain of someone she had first met almost thirty years before.

"Why after all this time would he write to me?"

Clementine thought on.

"How on earth did he get my address and what is he doing in the USA?"

She remembered him when he was a boy and he had told her he had never been out of York.

Clementine had been retired for sixteen years and hadn't seen him since he left school in July 2000. It didn't make any sense, but it certainly gave her a buzz. There was only one way to find out what this was all about.

When you are retired so you make the most out of the post you receive, for it breaks up your day.

The seventy-six-year-old retired headmistress held the letter up to the light to try and see what was in it.

A bright Spring sun revealed a letter and some enclosures.

"How strange?"

This American communication needed closer inspection.

Clementine began to panic again.

"What if it isn't from who I think it is? It must be. Why would an American write a personal letter to Clementine Hobson of York? I don't know anyone in America!"

She had never even been out of Britain, and she always spent her summer holidays at Scarborough where she liked the sea air, the seaside fish n' chips, and the locals of that town who she called "the real people."

That destination brought back warm memories of when she was a little girl, for that's where her parents had taken her on holiday in much poorer times, just twice.

Clementine looked at the back of the envelope and saw it had been sent from California, via a town called San Bernadino, a place that she knew was in the heart of Silicon Valley.

The small handwritten sender label gave an address but did not identify any person. She was certain she knew the author. Only one person she had ever met had written like that.

As Desmond snored through the excitement, she turned the letter over and looked at the writing style on the front. The letters all ran backwards and the curls under the y's and g's meant that this letter was from the one and only Stephen Standfast Johnson.

"Why on earth would he write after all these years?"

Clementine began to think back to the first day she had met the angelic Standfast in September 1993.

He was certainly different.

Opening the letter Clementine saw the handwritten notepaper and two cheques which just added to the mystery.

Now there was no doubt that the sender was none other than the legendary Standfast.

She studied the two cheques before reading the letter and cackled to herself as memories of golden days flooded back.

The panic subsided to a more manageable state of anxiety.

Clementine had freely given the money all those years before, without burden or expectation, and this settlement of an old debt was a complete surprise.

She instinctively knew that she must cash the first cheque for the £300, as it would somehow mark the end of a journey for the two of them, and in her case a greater finality.

It had been sent as a mark of respect and she knew that it was important to do the right thing.

Clementine stared in disbelief at the value of the second cheque.

The sum of £50,000 was a vast amount of money. She did not know what to do with it, as she felt completely unencumbered by previous arrangements.

Carefully she put the second cheque into her brown leather purse and then into her handbag.

She was used to making decisions, but she could not do so in this case. To cash it for personal gain would be wrong, but to return it would be an insult, yet to tear it up would raise questions and so her procrastination began.

It would nag and worry her for months until the answer appeared as if it was heaven-sent, and she could finally match the cheque with a suitable destination.

* * *

Clementine hated red tape and had always been a nonconformist. That's why the kids all loved her. She spoke to them in their language. It was no secret that she was a chain smoker, liked a drink, or that she could swear like a trooper, and they all knew she could read them like a book.

The retired headmistress was herself from a city council estate which she always described to the children as "the Cotswolds area of York!"

Clementine was one of them, one of the real people, and everybody respected her without reservation for she was down-to-earth and genuine.

You could not put one over on Clementine. She had seen it all before because she had spent a lifetime in the teaching profession. There were rarely any new tricks for a seasoned campaigner like her to witness.

She was a council house General and back in the nineties, Clementine had been the headmistress of one of York's largest underprivileged schools in Battle, a run-down area of the city.

The kids loved her, the parents loved her, and she was held in awe by all and sundry, from the caretaker and cleaners to every member of staff. Everyone respected Clementine.

The kids called her the "Terminator" because she could stop anyone dead in their tracks with just one glance. It seemed she had a three-hundred-and-sixty-degree vision, and it was complemented by amazing hearing. She never missed a trick.

* * *

"Make sure you wear a good suit to the interview."

The words of experience that the mother of Clementine Stockwell spoke rang out loud and clear.

Then came the final advice.

"You never get a second chance to make a first impression."

The twenty-two-year-old postgraduate Clementine Stockwell did indeed wear a well-cut grey business suit and white blouse to that fateful meeting, neatly offset with highly polished black shoes.

It was for the post of English teacher at a brand-new school opening in September 1965, in Battle, York.

Her mother, as mothers usually are, was right.

Clementine certainly impressed the interview panel, and the job offer was hers alone.

It was also to be her last interview for she remained at Battle High School until her retirement aged 60 in July 2003.

She had arrived to accept her role one bright September morning, carried to her destiny on a scruffy, council-owned, faded orange, single-decker bus.

The number seventeen brought her excitedly from the central York bus station, along Castle Howard Way, and into Queen's Road where she alighted to begin a new career. In those long-gone days, no trainee teachers could afford to drive cars.

This first-ever teaching post followed the awarding of her teaching certificate the previous July from Durham University, and so began a journey that would last a lifetime.

Clementine was fiercely loyal, and she understood implicitly the underprivileged world that she had chosen.

She was a naturally gifted teacher with great patience and a wonderful organiser, who despite her later fierce reputation, was one of the kindest people you could ever meet.

Over the years every child and member of staff at Battle High School knew that if you had a problem you went to see Clementine, better known to staff and pupils alike as the "Terminator".

Clementine was the therapist, the counsellor, the agony aunt, and the oracle, who could always find a solution, for she was the one who put everything right.

The staff and children all called her by her nickname, but never to her face, and she loved it.

It was not a mark of disrespect; it was a badge of honour. This meant that she was accepted, trusted, and cherished.

On the day she retired on July 23rd, 2003, everyone cried including Clementine, and that just made things worse.

The assembly hall was jam-packed with teachers, ex-staff, and pupils past and present.

Amongst the friendly masses were tough boys, impossible girls, and difficult colleagues, but as one they gave her a standing ovation.

The boys in the senior form washed and waxed her car, the girls brought flowers and chocolates, and the Parent Teachers Association gave her a voucher for a two-night stay in her favourite Scarborough hotel to complete the event.

They didn't make them like Clementine anymore; the council house girl who rose to be Queen.

As Clementine left the stage, she thanked everyone once more.

"You make sure you all fulfil your promise and behave, or I might have to make a comeback!"

Weeping eyes together with damp tissues, handshakes, hugs and kisses marked the end of an era.

* * *

Monday, September 8th, 1963, was the first day of her teaching career at the brand-new Battle High School, built to replace the dilapidated, run-down namesake that had stood there for fifty-five years. She was just twenty-two years old.

Elsewhere in the city, in the better schools, they referred to the Battle council estate with its reputation for crime, violence, and poverty as "The Bronx" or "The Reservation."

The new school's write-up in the local press suggested academic excellence and it was one of two schools that acted as an educational facility for the children of the twenty thousand people who lived there.

In reality, it was a holding pen for teenagers until they were old enough to leave and find a job. It was certainly not a theatre of educational achievement.

The estate was split by the main road that went right through it from the centre of York to the Yorkshire Dales, and you either lived "on the other side of Battle" or "the other side of Battle". It was a confusing phrase to the outsider, and you had to live on one side of the main road or the other to understand it's significance.

Residents to the north lived in the Renton district but Battle High School was south of the main road. This was the Manton side of the sprawling, feisty housing estate, bordered by an ancient Roman villa, the gently meandering River Manse, ancient woodlands belonging to the Earl of Easthampton and a modern textile mill.

It was a tough environment, and Clementine was told on her first day as a probationer teacher that there were two types of people on the estate.

"Miss Stockwell," said Mr Barnett the headmaster of the school in their first meeting, "just remember there are two types of people in Manton, the quick and the dead."

Clementine looked back quizzically.

"I'm not sure what you mean, headmaster?"

"As you know I was the headmaster in the old school here and based on that experience I can tell you this. The quick ones have a chance, there is something that separates them from the herd, and if nurtured they can better themselves, but the dead ones will do their time here and leave with no qualifications just like many of those before them, to be the nothing of this world!"

Clementine was a young idealist and still wet behind the ears.

She thought every child was a good child and that they should all be given the right encouragement to better themselves.

"You mean they come here in form one and they are already labelled quick or dead?"

"Miss Stockwell, you didn't let me finish," he said assuming the moral high ground.

"This is a tough estate where people have low expectations.

"It has an awful reputation and there are good and bad people.

"We inherit their offspring and must make the best of it. Fewer financial resources are put into this school than in any other area of York, because politically it is traditionally deemed to be a waste of money.

"When the kids arrive here, they have about a year before we label them. It's black and white, the non-triers and the no-hopers become the dead. The rest of the pupils not so labelled, become the quick. These are the ones we can work with and try to get some education into their thick minds and souls.

"We cannot afford to waste resources on the dead as we simply don't have the money. It would be unfair to the quick ones."

Clementine was devastated.

"How an earth could a headmaster treat his pupils that way?"

He was an ogre. It was like something out of a Charles Dickens novel.

The new teacher thought about the school's name for a few moments.

"Battle? a misnomer, his attitude is the lowest of the low! Wormwood Scrubs had a better ring to it!" she considered in anguish.

***

Teaching was something that came naturally to Clementine. She had a way with her that immediately won the respect of both pupils and colleagues alike.

The new girl in town knew that there was a small element of truth in her headmaster's statement, but his attitude was certainly Dickensian. There were good people and bad people in Manton and sadly its reputation went before, but she decided to do her best regardless of the failing headmaster.

Clementine could not help thinking that it couldn't be that different from many other council estates, for she had been brought up on one herself.

Over the next few years, she dedicated herself to being the best teacher she could be. Her goal was to convert the dead to be quick before condemnation at the end of year one.

Teachers came and teachers went. Colleagues were promoted to other schools, and some moved up the seniority list in Battle High School, with Clementine being sucked along behind them.

By the end of the July 1971 term Mr Barnett, the seemingly Victorian headmaster was long gone.

The following September, Mr George Williams, a seasoned, progressive headmaster, was appointed to the school.

He had been successful in turning around Northgate High School, with its appalling reputation in the heart of the city, into an academic success.

Comprehensive schools for boys and girls were still a new phenomenon in the late sixties, and within just a couple of years, he had single-handedly changed the mindset of that difficult school, achieving outstanding academic and sporting success, with a new sixth form for senior pupils to boot.

George Williams had a track record to be proud of, and he had been sent to duplicate the result at Battle High School, which was perceived by the authorities as a "no hoper".

In recent years The York City Educational Authority had been taking much criticism for the lack of support and investment in deprived areas of the city, and so it was that George Williams had arrived at Battle High School in September at the start of a new decade.

He warmed to Clementine who was now known as Mrs Hobson following the marriage to her beloved Desmond the previous year. She was now under the mentorship of the hugely motivating influence of the new incumbent.

"Old George" as the staff called him, recognised a like-minded soul in Clementine. He saw her as an outstanding talent, and he nurtured it for all he was worth, and his work paid off as he knew it would.

By 1975, aged 32, Clementine was elevated to be the head of lower school in a vastly improved academic institution.

Eight years later in July 1983, in the week of her fortieth birthday and on George's recommendation, she had become the deputy headmistress of one of the city's largest and most improved comprehensive schools, her second home of Battle High School.

The school continued going from strength to strength and by early 1993 Clementine had become quite the accomplished manager and administrator.

She still taught the children, but with reduced teaching hours, and now paid particular attention to the quick and the dead of form one, organised the school timetable, and made sure she knew all the parents.

Clementine was a headmistress in waiting.

George Williams invited Clementine to his office in the February of that year. He asked her to pop in for a coffee at 10.30 am and suggested that she put a student in to look after her class for an hour or so.

Clementine was taken aback because there was no agenda for this casual get-together. George wanted to talk about something serious.

Mrs Hobson, the deputy headmistress, was not aware of any problems. The school was running like clockwork.

Arriving ten minutes early, Clementine tapped the door.

"Come in Clementine, please sit down there is something I would like to discuss."

The coffee with one sugar was already on the desk for he knew she would be on time.

George moved from his seat and closed the door. That was unusual for he had an open-door policy. It seemed George's door was always open but not on this particular morning.

"This could be important," thought Clementine.

"Mrs Hobson, I mean Clementine, I have something to tell you that is not for general release yet."

Clementine stared at him quizzically.

"In May I am sixty years old, and I shall retire in July of this year."

"Congratulations headmaster."

"Thank you, but cutting a long story short, this school has always been a most difficult challenge to run, and I don't think we would have achieved the success we have without you!"

Clementine blushed for the first time in years.

"Thank you, headmaster."

"When I announce my decision next week to the local education authority, I will be recommending that you take my place. You are the best qualified, the natural fit."

Clementine was speechless for she had never had time to think of being a headmistress. George was the leader. It was comfortable, she liked it.

"I want no objections, no self-doubt, for you know you have everyone's respect. The quick and even the dead love you. You know they call you the Terminator?" laughed George.

An hour later Clementine left the room wondering where all the years had gone. When she told Desmond that evening what had been proposed she pictured herself sitting in George's big leather captain's chair as headmistress of Battle High School.

"Now wouldn't that be something for a very ordinary council estate girl from the mean streets of Fenchurch on the other side of York!"

She smoked her last cigarette of the day, drank a glass of sherry in the comfort of her favourite armchair, and drifted off to sleep as the headmistress elect of Battle High School.

* * *

The best-laid plans of mice and men often go awry, and Clementine's world came crashing down just two months later in early April 1993, when she was handed a note from Mrs Carruthers, the headmaster's flustered secretary, who came to her classroom and called her outside.

Clementine went white as she read the hastily scribbled information, whilst the tearful messenger held a finger to her lips to reinforce the secrecy of the news.

Professionalism kicked in as she instructed her class to be taken over by her colleague next door, who now marshalled sixty pupils on his own.

She dashed across the school to the headmaster's office and there he lay dead on the floor, flanked by two senior male members of staff that the secretary had called to arms from the nearest classrooms, who stood erect like sentinels guarding the deceased body of a Roman Emperor.

A suspected heart attack had killed the man who had given everything for the sake of the children, just three months short of retirement.

"What a tragedy, what an unfair world!"

Tears of sadness ran down her face and onto the carpet of the late headmaster's domain.

The formalities were carried out, the body removed, and frantic calls made to the local education authority.

At 11.15 am Clementine was declared acting headmistress.

"Be careful what you wish for!" Clementine mumbled silently to herself.

It was April 27th, 1993. Clementine was forty-nine years old.

Mrs Hobson held the school together over the next five months, and there was no surprise for anyone when she was formally appointed to start as the official headmistress of the school in September 1993.

That is when, on the first day of term, Stephen Standfast Johnson entered Clementine's life.

* * *

Emotions ran high on her first day, but this did not prevent her from taking up her favourite position.

All the existing pupils knew she would be there, and out of respect for the new incumbent and old George, the older pupils made sure they behaved as they passed.

The Terminator took no prisoners.

Clementine liked to stand where the corridor of the junior block joined the foyer of the senior block, just outside the school assembly hall.

She could see every child as they walked by her; it was like shooting fish in a barrel.

"Do your tie-up, Jones," she barked.

"Carlton! have your trousers had a row with your shoes?" she laughed.

"Sally King, did I hear you say something about a fag lunchtime?" she cajoled.

"Yes Miss", "No Miss", and "No, Miss," came the answers. You didn't mess with the all-knowing, all-seeing Terminator.

Standfast was a misnomer because he came around the corner like a rocket. He was small but he was quick alright.

Unfortunately, on his first day, he had run right into the Terminator, chased by three new acquaintances.

The headmistress looked at him and a tortured face looked back. There was something wrong here. A mark on the side of his face suggested he had either been hit or fallen over. It was obvious that he wasn't a fighter in the physical sense, but she could see through those tortured eyes he was a survivor.

A Good Suit

The undernourished, mousy figure looked shocked as Clementine stared straight past him and bellowed at the three boys chasing him.

"You three, get in my office now and you too small fry," she said as she turned back to Standfast.

Three boys of mixed race marched in and stood in front of the Terminator's desk. The hunched-over Standfast tripped in behind and nervously stood apart from the other three.

Clementine let them sweat as she directed the free-flowing traffic in the corridor. As the hubbub reduced to a hum Clementine appeared in front of them and sat in the seat of authority, the captain's chair.

With great experience and an air of command, she examined the scene in front of her.

Four brand new form-one pupils looked anywhere but at her.

She asked the one question she had asked herself a thousand times.

"Are these destined to be quick or dead?"

Clementine felt the nerves transcend the room. The three bigger boys were friends from junior school. One was jet black, ebony in colour. The second was what they called in uneducated circles a half-caste, possibly the son of a black seaman father and a white mother. The third was a lighter shade again but not white Caucasian.

These kids were fit-looking, sporty boys, and used to fighting their way through life.

The headmistress did not doubt they came from poor backgrounds with low expectations, but that was ten-a-penny in Manton. Clementine knew this by the way they were dressed in scruffy shirts and trousers, and it was still the first day of term.

"What are your names?" she bellowed, keeping her eyes on the black lad, the obvious ringleader.

"Let's start with you," she said looking at the ebony child. Clementine knew that by taking him on first any resistance from the others both now and in the future would be futile.

"Always tackle the toughest one first," that's what George Williams had taught her through the years.

"Clinton" came the weak reply.
"Clinton what?" said Clementine, not losing eye contact for a second.
"Clinton Joseph."
Clementine's eyes flashed fire for she knew this family well.
"When you address me, boy, you finish the sentence with Miss or Headmistress, do you understand boy?"
"Yes sir," said Clinton.
His two friends smirked but it was for the last time.
"Yes Miss, you mean boy, and that goes for you lot as well!" she said, including the trembling Standfast in her all-points bulletin.
"Your name is?" she said to the half-caste lad.
"Eugene King, Miss," he said nervously.
"Now introduce yourself," she said to the one with the lightest skin colour.
"Manny Dorning, I mean Emanuel Dorning, Miss," he blurted out.
"Well in case you haven't realised, my name is Clementine Hobson, and I am your headmistress. Do you know what that means?"
"No Miss," they said with bowed heads.
"I'll tell you what it means, it means I'm the number one, the decision-maker, the big dog around here, and listen carefully Clinton, Eugene, and Emanuel, if you have any doubts about it ask your fathers when you get home tonight, because I know them all well and they are my friends."
The boys gulped as they realised the significance of her words. One foot out of line and their fathers would be told.
"Yes Miss," they said in chorus.
"While we are working on names and respect, I'll say one more thing.
"I will never remember the names Clinton, Eugene and Emanuel or is it "Manny"? I need a word picture to help me. In future, as you seem to be bosom pals, I will refer to you as the three amigos!"
The boys gasped. There was no doubt who was in charge here.
"You will be home an hour late tonight because you three are in detention. There is a lot of litter on the playing fields gathered over the

summer holidays. You can all spend an hour picking it up before you leave, understood?"

"Yes, Miss," they said, happy to get off so lightly but not quite understanding why.

Then Clementine added.

"I know you three have been chasing our friend here, and it looks like one of you has struck him. I don't care about the detail; I just want you to know that we do not accept bullying in this school in any shape or form. You may have taken a dislike to him because he's from a different primary school, or just because he is different to you, but let me tell you for the first and last time that I am the law here. No bullying. Understood?"

"Yes, Miss," said a trio of voices as they digested every word.

Clementine turned her attention to Standfast.

"Your name is?"

Standfast looked her straight in the eye.

"Stephen Standfast Johnson, Miss and no one hit me, Miss, I fell!"

Clementine almost burst out laughing at the name, but her reaction was tempered by his defence of the other three.

This was one of life's defining moments.

In that second, the name Stephen became redundant, for he would evermore be known as Standfast by staff and pupils alike.

"If you say so Standfast but remember I don't like bullies or liars."

The other three were amazed that Standfast had covered for them and assumed it was because of fear of retribution. They couldn't have been more right.

Standfast had enough problems in his life, including an ogre of a drunken stepfather and an alcoholic mother, notwithstanding his violent older stepbrother who years later would come to a sorry end whilst driving a stolen vehicle. It was life in the fast lane alright, the car was fuelled with petrol whilst the thief was fuelled with drink and drugs.

The haunted look in the young boy's eyes suggested he didn't need any more grief in his life, it was tough enough every day.

"Well," said Clementine "maybe I'm wrong but I cannot prove I'm right, so I am going to do something unusual. No detention for anyone this night, but do not rattle my cage again. Off with you all and get about your business," and with that, they were gone.

The three amigos accepted their new nickname without question as a badge of recognition. It was a championing of their friendship.

As they went off to find their first class, the three boys continued laughing and bonding with each other as Standfast kept a safe and respectable distance.

Arriving together, all four made their excuses to their Welsh maths teacher, the long-serving, long-suffering Mrs Ernestine Jankers-Bowen and so began their real education.

It wasn't long before the fragile Standfast showed signs of mathematical genius.

Whatever Standfast was taught he picked up straight away, and he would often answer questions as soon as they were written on the board.

This kid was exceptional, but it brought problems within the first month, as other less able pupils became jealous of the waif's exceptional understanding of the subject. The issue was reported directly to the headmistress, who had put herself in charge of the school's anti-bullying policy and enforced it with a rod of iron.

Mrs Jankers-Bowen had noticed that because of his outstanding ability the young maths genius was being bullied by some of the other boys. When she told Clementine her reaction was "not by the three amigos?" for everyone knew that's what she called the inseparable trio of Clinton, Eugene, and Manny.

"No, headmistress, not them, they just sit at the back of the class and keep a low profile in maths because they are struggling with the subject."

Mrs Jankers-Bowen explained the scenario.

"It's a bit more complicated because as you know the year one class is made up of the three feeder junior schools. Right now, there is much vying for social position, and that is how bullying in form one normally starts. It's meant to be a warning to others, so picking on the weaker ones is how the male league tables are decided."

"I know what to do Mrs Jankers-Bowen, I've seen all this before, old George Williams had a solution for it and that's what we will employ."

The following day when Standfast's class arrived for maths, Mrs Jankers-Bowen carried out the plan to perfection.

The three boys who had been hassling Standfast were put at the front of the class on one table so that they could be closely monitored. The three amigos and Standfast were put together in two more tables of two, right behind the bullies.

Standfast was put next to Clinton, the main man.

Within a month it had worked like a dream. Standfast helped the boys with their maths, explaining the ins and outs of the subject in a schoolboy language they could understand.

Immediately, their maths improved and all three moved up the class rankings, even receiving commendations for good work from Mrs Jankers-Bowen for the first time, and the three amigos felt good about themselves.

"Excellent work you three, you are the most improved students this month."

Unaccustomed praise now flowed regularly.

"Brilliant, it has been a pleasure to teach you, but you have to go a bit to catch Standfast as he is top of the class again."

The three amigos grinned at each other for they were now mathematical celebrities mentioned in the same sentence as the academic champion Standfast.

One Tuesday morning Standfast left class as usual and was suddenly pushed up against a wall by one of his classmates. As he tried to run away from the bully a second pupil slyly tapped his ankles, so he fell heavily to the floor, and then the third bully kicked him in the side of the face causing a heavy contusion.

It's ok being a bully if you are the top dog, but sooner or later all bullies get it wrong.

Life's lesson is that there is always someone tougher, fitter, more determined or prepared than you, and on this occasion, the bullies had made a serious misjudgement.

It was an elementary mistake to pick on Standfast, whose popularity via his mathematical allegiance to the three amigos was now entering orbit, compared to the exclusion he had previously known.

The girls screamed as Standfast was brutally assaulted with that boot and Clinton, as the leader of his troop was quickest to react.

They didn't see what was coming. Clinton struck first by thumping the first boy in the side of the head with a heavy black, clenched fist, and he dropped like a stone to the floor, screaming on impact.

Eugene and Manny were no slouches and where Clinton went, they followed. Without an invitation they raced up the corridor to back Clinton up, not that he needed it, for he was the genuine alpha male in the class and Clementine had been banking on it, even if she didn't know quite how it would eventually pan out.

Together, they took out the ankle-tapping bully, battering him against the wall and giving him more than a bruised ego in the process.

Clinton turned his attention to the third bully who just froze. This was the cowardly thug who had kicked Standfast in the head whilst he was on the floor. He had attacked their maths saviour.

"Big mistake," thought Clinton.

The girls screamed louder and Clinton, taking advantage of the bully's fear and hesitation delivered a fierce left hook to the ribcage, followed by a right hook straight to the face. There was, as is usual with a broken nose, blood everywhere, but Clinton was not taking prisoners.

Once again, he smashed a fist into the right eye socket, and the bully was no more as he fell to the ground. Clinton thought he heard him cry but it mattered little. It was over.

The bullies had learned it wasn't wise to bully the friend of a boy whose father was an English amateur boxing champion, as he might have taught his son a thing or two along the way.

The girls screamed again, and some cheered as teachers came from far and wide to stop the trouble but there was no trouble. The contest was over, the alpha league table decided.

All seven were taken to Clementine's office via the school nurse, who gave them all a check-up and permission to carry on with their business.

On looking at the sight that confronted her in the form of three damaged bullies, an immaculate three amigos and a slightly damaged Standfast, Clementine concluded to herself, "I think this problem may be solved!"

"What is the cause of this?" she bellowed at the top of her voice for effect.

Years of dealing with all types of children and staff had made her the school actress. She knew when to turn it on and turn it off.

"It was them, Miss, they started it," said Clinton.

The bullies said nothing, and their silence condemned them.

Clementine knew exactly what had happened because the emotional, excitable, and histrionic girls had already dished the dirt on the bullies, while they were being checked over and cleaned up by the school nurse. The headmistress had already done her homework.

"They're always bullying Standfast because they are jealous. He's good at maths, and they pushed him against the wall and tripped him up Miss, and then one of them kicked him in the head for nothing" followed by "and Miss, the amigos were just helping Standfast, they didn't start it, Miss!" That was all the confirmation that Clementine needed.

Clementine turned to Clinton. "OK, why did the three amigos set about hitting our three silent friends?" she enquired.

Clinton's answer was short, sweet, and delightful, after which he said no more because no more was needed as far as Clementine was concerned.

"Miss, they were bullying our friend," he said.

This broke Standfast's concentration and instead of staring at the wall in front of him, he looked incredulously at Clinton.

"Did he say friend?" he thought.

Clementine continued, "and who is your friend?" she asked.

"Standfast Miss, we sit together in maths."

As Clementine listened intently to the account he gave, she had a tear in her eye. She told herself it was for her old mentor George Williams, but she couldn't convince herself.

"Right, you three bullies will have detention for one hour after school with me for a week. Do not be late or else. At playtimes, you will pick up litter on the field. Do not go missing and again do not be late. If you do, I will make you sing a solo on stage at this year's Christmas Concert in front of the whole school, including the girls. I feel sure you do not want me to contact your parents, so you know what you must do. There will be no bullies in this school. Is everything understood?"

"Yes, Miss!"

Clementine now addressed them all, giving the bullies light relief for a moment and launched into her favourite sermon.

"One more thing, education is a journey. Learn your lesson today and work hard while you are in this school, so your eventual destination in life is a thing of joy. You alone can make your chosen future happen. Do you understand boys?"

"Yes Miss," the seven replied.

"Unless you work hard and set yourself goals you will forever live in a sea of uncertainty, at the mercy of everything life throws at you."

She turned to the three bullies who now stood in disgrace.

"In this school, there are two types of people who we call the quick and the dead, and if you miss your chance you'll end up as one of the dead. Do you know what it will say on your gravestone boys?"

"No Miss" they answered with bowed heads.

"It will simply say "destination unknown" and no-one will ever remember who you were.

"You are dismissed," she said, after imparting the phrase and lesson for which she was probably most famous.

Wandering back down the corridor to class, the bullies all thought the prospect of detention and litter picking, as opposed to the threat of contacting their parents or singing a solo in front of the girls, was a good result.

All three decided that they would never be bullies again in that school, and they stuck to the promised task for the Terminator and the three amigos were ever-present.

Education is the key. The Terminator had terminated but some things are incurable.

As they left the office they were unwittingly headed for educational oblivion and the dead zone, for the road was set and not even Clementine's intervention would redeem the future for those woeful three. Years later they would be consigned to a life of petty crime and drugs fuelled by their family's historic lack of self-respect, ignorance, and excess.

Never again would Standfast be bullied in Battle High School. He would thrive under the protectorate of the three amigos, but now they were the four amigos. Inseparable friends bound together in warfare, for all time.

The tightly knitted group had expanded to three darker lads and an undernourished white boy. Skin colour meant nothing here, there were no barriers, for they were joined at the hip.

They were Battlers in more ways than one and would always remain so, even when they eventually moved along life's path to new adult horizons.

Clinton was now established as the physical alpha male and Standfast as the academic alpha male. It would prove to be a winning combination.

Clementine's life had become intertwined with these four amigos from that day forth, and she supported them through all their scrapes and hiccups, as she always did with her favourite boys and girls, even if she continually suggested there was no such thing as favouritism.

**

As a member of the four amigos, Standfast now had a place in the school hierarchy, but at home, he was a misfit.

His mother Angela had lost her first husband James when the boy was just two. He had been in the Royal Navy and was sadly killed in a military accident off Gibraltar.

Standfast had been James's middle name also. There had been a long naval tradition in the family and somewhere in the annals of history, one of his ancestors was named Standfast. Legend had it that he had been a heroic figure standing toe to toe with Admiral Nelson at the Battle of Trafalgar.

Life without a husband was tough on the "reservation" in Manton, and Angela had quickly and foolishly remarried an abusive amateur rugby player and bricklayer.

As he aged and was no longer able to play, he would spend longer and longer in the clubhouse drinking cider and dragging Angela along for the ride.

There was no doubt in the eyes of the authorities that Standfast was neglected, and that little money existed for the basics, let alone luxuries.

As Standfast grew up, his stepfather gave him little clips around the ear with his palm, which later became thumps and punches. He would often have bruising to his torso which is why he didn't like stripping off for physical education in school.

Standfast couldn't hide it forever, and when he started being late for school and missing whole days off, the staff alerted Clementine to the potential problem. Of the thousands of pupils that she had taught Standfast had helped her to break her own rule, which was not to have favourites. It was impossible, he was her all-time favourite.

Standfast was the son that she never had. He was tough, resilient, honest, and trustworthy. She just wanted to hug him and show him some love, so that he knew he was safe, secure, and wanted.

***

Remarkably, with Clementine's encouragement the four amigos all stayed on to the sixth form to further their education.

A Good Suit

When Clinton got into trouble for fighting on the local council estate it was Clementine who spoke at the Magistrate's Court. She explained that Clinton was defending himself against three drunken men who were abusing an old man and his wife outside a supermarket. He had intervened to help the elderly couple. It was plain self-defence. Clinton's case was dismissed.

When Clinton won the honour of boxing for England as a schoolboy against Scotland, the supportive headmistress and her husband went to see him win his bout at the Northwood Sports Centre in York.

Clementine insisted he bought himself a good suit for the subsequent presentation at City Hall.

Clinton's father was immensely proud; worked extra hours for a month and bought the smartest outfit he could find for his son, from the best shop he knew, Carrington's of York.

Using the sewing skills that she had been taught in needlework class at Battle High School some thirty years before, Clinton's mother proudly sewed on the embroidered badge that he had been awarded from the English Schoolboy Boxing Association.

At eighteen he became a professional boxer for six years, which he did in tandem with a position as a trainee youth counsellor for York City Council. On retiring from boxing, he progressed quickly through the ranks to become a much-respected social worker in the more difficult areas of the city.

Clementine was the matriarch who gave Eugene great advice when he thought his girlfriend was pregnant and told no one except her. It was a false alarm and her coolness ensured he stayed on to the sixth form and achieved his qualifications. He had been terrified at the thought of being a father at just seventeen years old and considered leaving and taking a dead-end job.

When Eugene decided to apply for a career in the army after he finished the sixth form, he was not surprised to hear Clementine say "and make sure you have a good suit" for the interview. His mother took on board the headmistress's advice and bought him a fashionable off-the-peg charcoal suit and all accessories from her Littlewood's clothing catalogue, with thirty-eight weeks to pay.

It was Clementine's reference that enabled Eugene to join the army.

On leaving the army after six years of impeccable service, Eugene trained as a school teacher. Once more it was Clementine's indirect intervention and recommendation that saw him appointed to the post of geography teacher at Battle High School, where he would serve his whole career, just like his headmistress before him.

Manny, inspired by the sight of Clinton in his new outfit, had applied for the position of trainee manager at the Carrington's of York store because he loved the great style of that upper-class establishment.

He especially liked Clinton's new suit which had been bought there at great expense. Naturally, Clementine insisted Manny also procured himself a good suit for the interview along with a new white shirt and a smart tie for the occasion.

Her advice was accepted, but money was tight in his parent's household, so he borrowed Eugene's full soldier interview regalia, but insisted on wearing his socks and underpants. Once again, Clementine's reference ensured he was employed from the September he left school.

Within ten years, Manny, the third of the amigos was proud to say he was a departmental manager of fashion at York's most famous emporium.

* * *

Standfast did not have a suit, but he had won a bursary to stay on at school.

He learned of the scholarship in his last month of form five and readily admitted to everyone that if it wasn't for the funding he had been awarded, he would be out working and no longer in school.

She knew that Standfast was under pressure from his mother to leave and get a job. His exam results at the end of form five were truly outstanding, with ten straight A's being recorded in the national exams for the first time in school history.

When Clementine had personally visited and told his mother how bright he was, it was only then that she waivered about her decision to make him leave.

The headmistress took the opportunity to tell her that Standfast had been awarded a scholarship at the princely sum of ten pounds per week to stay on and study.

This was enough to take the financial pressure off Standfast's mother, and he was duly allowed to study chemistry, pure mathematics, and physics at A level for another two years.

The scholarship was the first-ever awarded at Battle High School and it turned out that it was from an anonymous donor.

Clementine later confessed to Desmond that she was the unknown factor in the mystery.

"We won't miss the money and in the long run it will be worth far more to Standfast!"

Desmond raised one eyebrow in fake protest, knowing that resistance was futile.

"I've got another confession to make Desmond, I've given Standfast a role in the dining hall or should I say I have invented the role of pupil supervisor. All he must do is tick off the names of the children who attend and hand the sheet to my secretary at the end of lunch. It takes about fifteen minutes and is completely unnecessary."

Desmond chirped in, "so why did you create the job?"

"Because with the role Standfast gets a free lunch every day; it works so fluently and goes completely unnoticed."

"What goes unnoticed?"

"It brings no attention to the free school meal he receives, and it guarantees he is eating properly. The social worker who visits his mother occasionally, says money is non-existent and the boy is never fed properly."

"I thought he already had free school meals?" asked Desmond.

"Yes, but this allows him to be first in the dining hall before the other pupils, so he can plate up a meal, put it in some Tupperware boxes I gave him, and take it home for his mother so she gets fed as well later that day."

"You are an angel," said Desmond, giving Clementine a spontaneous hug.

Clementine cried because she knew her husband was a gem.

It was a fine line, a balancing act that Clementine engaged in to ensure Standfast reached his full potential in school.

She made sure the authorities were carefully and discreetly involved when appropriate, as she did not want to break the fragile trust that existed, but it was a tough time for pupil and headmistress alike.

Clementine confided to Desmond.

"Some days it's like watching a car crash and I can't do anything about it."

Maybe the pressure from social services did the trick, but Standfast's mother and the abusive stepfather split up as the boy approached the end of his first year in the sixth form, just before entering that all-important final year where examination results would be critical.

As he entered his senior year, Clementine raised the bar for this most gifted of pupils and organised extra tuition for him in all subjects from her excellent staff.

They all knew Standfast was exceptional and delighted in harvesting his enthusiasm to take him to higher levels of knowledge.

Every day he applied himself by studying for an extra hour or two after school had ended, and then Clementine dropped him home personally in the car she referred to as the headmistress's Rolls Royce.

This was a clapped-out champagne-coloured Austin Allegro that did less than thirty miles to the gallon, but Clementine loved it because there was a consul to put her cigarettes and lighter in, and her handbag fitted in the glovebox.

Standfast also convinced himself it was a top-of-the-range marque because his mother and stepfather had never owned a car. It was the only vehicle he had ever travelled in, except for the occasional bus journey.

A Good Suit

***

By October of the final year in the sixth form, it was obvious, as it had always been, that Standfast was something academically special.

Clementine decided that whatever it took, he must be encouraged to go on to university and every member of staff thought him well capable of going all the way to Cambridge or Oxford if he worked hard enough.

Standfast duly applied for a place at Brasenose College, Oxford.

Despite competing against the very best mathematicians in his age group from all over the world and sitting a seriously difficult entrance exam at a local venue, the promising student reported that all had gone well.

The result was sent to the school and a fortnight later Clementine proudly read that Standfast had passed with flying colours. She now knew for certain that this was his big chance.

At lunchtime, Clementine released him from his dining hall duty by sending a note to his class but personally collared him as he exited his last lesson of the morning.

"Get some lunch Standfast and come to my office because I have some news for you from Oxford University!" she said quietly, as she played down her natural emotion and excitement.

Fifteen minutes later she told him the good news.

As he had passed the initial exam he would soon be invited for an interview at Oxford. They then ate together "like in the great hall at Brasenose College," Clementine quipped.

Following the feast, she filled his head with tales of academia and great hope for the future, which inspired him.

***

The next Friday morning Standfast came into school and rushed to Clementine's office holding a letter in his hand.

"Miss, I have to go to Brasenose College, Oxford next month for an interview and I've never even been out of York!"

"Calm down and let me have a look at that letter."

On inspecting it closely, it confirmed he had been called for an interview at 9 am on Thursday 12th February.

"Right, my boy," said Clementine "the first thing you need is a good suit!" she said, taking command of the situation.

"You and I are off shopping this afternoon!"

"But Miss, I don't have any money!"

"We'll talk about that on the way; be outside my office at 1 pm because we are going into Carrington's of York!"

Clementine duly photocopied the letter and did not see Standfast again until she opened her office door at 12.45 pm and saw him already standing as instructed, waiting for the shopping trip.

On the way into York, Clementine was incredibly diplomatic because she knew Standfast was very sensitive about his home life, the vulnerability of his mother, and their distinct lack of money.

"Now Standfast, I am going to do a deal with you which will involve me investing £200 in your future."

"£200 Miss, that's a fortune, what deal?"

"Well, you need a good suit, a pair of shoes, socks, underwear, a white shirt, and a good tie to set it all off. Oh, and a smart warm coat as the icing on the cake, so you look the part! Just for starters, I have given us a budget of £200, which is the total level of my investment in you."

"But investments have to be paid back and I don't have any money!"

"It's a long-term investment and it's my decision, so subject closed, ok?"

"Yes, Miss," he replied in a well-trained reflex reaction.

"You don't have to pay me anything back until you are a millionaire, at which time, I would like my £200 to be returned plus let's say another £100 in interest for the risk factor. That should be in another thirty years or so for taking a chance on you. What do you think about that?"

"That would be fabulous Miss, but I won't ever let you down. There is no risk, but I must stay overnight in Oxford and how am I going to get there?" asked an increasingly perturbed Standfast as he accepted the contract along with the growing responsibilities of burgeoning adulthood.

"You will travel by train with me, and we will both stay in Oxford overnight. I will escort you to and from Brasenose College myself, and don't worry because the school will be swallowing the bill for that," she said, telling an unaccustomed white lie.

"Wow, Miss, so we are both going to Oxford; you're the best!" and he smiled brighter than she had ever seen him smile before.

"Miss, if I ever become a millionaire, I'll pay you the £300 including the interest and a £50,000 bonus," he grinned.

"I don't want a bonus Standfast," she said as her eyes indiscreetly welled up.

"Just the £300 and the knowledge that you have succeeded in life will do," she said, enjoying the moment whilst paradoxically writing off her initial £200 and the cost of the Oxford adventure.

"It's a deal Miss, and when I make my first million, I'll pay you first," and the bargain between the naïve, underprivileged schoolboy and the long-served headmistress was struck and forever sealed.

The history books would confirm that in the Summer of 2000, Standfast returned the finest set of senior school exam results that Battle High School ever produced.

He left that theatre of unexpected academic dreams with good wishes from all the staff, especially Clementine who gave him an irresistible, embarrassing hug, to become an undergraduate at Brasenose College, Oxford in the following September.

Some years later he posted to the school a copy of his graduation photograph which was proudly put up in the main reception area, as a beacon of hope for all the underprivileged children of that poor housing estate, where it would remain until the school either fell or burned down.

As the years rolled by, time confirmed that Clementine had performed her role over and above the call of duty, as occasional news bulletins from the social network announced that Standfast had successfully spirited himself away to new friends and experiences, and no doubt she thought, to greater successes in London and maybe beyond.

* * *

One Friday lunchtime in May 2019, two months after receiving the mysterious letter and almost sixteen years after she had retired, Clementine and her husband Desmond were enjoying a beer and a cigarette whilst sitting outside one of York's swankiest city-centre pubs in the brewery quarter.

All the old drinkers, cribbage, skittles, and darts players were long gone. This redeveloped conglomeration of old pubs was now haunted by the nouveau riche at night, but in the daytime by retired teachers, policemen, and civil servants who had pensions that could fund them to socialise there, whilst the unemployed and those on benefits drank in the cheaper establishments dotted around the edges of the eclectic urban sprawl.

On this Friday afternoon, Clementine was consuming life for all it was worth through Benson and Hedges Virginia Slims cigarettes and strong Belgian lager.

Unfortunately, they were also consuming her. The doctor had clearly said that within two years of this leisurely afternoon, the years of hard living would catch up with her if she didn't stop drinking and smoking, but Clementine elected to meet death head-on in the same way she had conducted her life.

She knew she had lung cancer, the deep heavy cough gave it away, but she figured that if she was lucky, she might get through to next Summer. Little did she know that within four months she would be dead and gone, but Clementine would go out in style regardless.

The retired headmistress had not been sitting there long when other random guests joined the table, which created a full-on party atmosphere.

In York, Fridays were known as POETS Day which meant "Push Off Early Tomorrow's Saturday". The numbers of retired civil servants were quickly being joined by the half-day crowd of office workers who could not wait to start their weekend.

A Good Suit

Out of the blue, Clementine received a tap on the shoulder and looked around to see three instantly recognisable figures stood looming above her.

"How things have changed!" she thought. She remembered the first day she had seen and towered over all three of them.

Even in 2019, some people on the table veered back at the sight of three York men of obvious non-white ethnicity approaching a lady in her seventies. These were hard, fit-looking men. You could see it in their eyes. They were journeymen.

"Well, if it's not the three amigos," she cackled.

"I haven't seen you for years!"

"Hello Miss! how are you?" they beamed like an angelic schoolboy choir.

One of the random guests on Clementine's table grimaced. She was a snobbish, plump lady, with too much makeup that made her look fatter than she already was.

"You cannot call them the three amigos, it's racist!" the tipsy woman howled.

The three amigos replied in unison.

"She can call us what she likes missus; she's the Terminator, she's our headmistress!"

In an instant, the snob had been cut to ribbons and not a punch had been thrown. It had been a classic three amigos pincer movement.

The overweight, overbearing woman, never spoke another word, but finished her drink quickly, leaving a copious amount in the glass. She then signalled to her husband it was time to go, and they left as soon as they possibly could.

"I hope we didn't upset her Miss!" remarked Eugene.

"Maybe you taught her a lesson boys, she probably thinks too much or watches too much TV! What she doesn't understand is that the four of us are one and the same, from the same tribe. We are Battlers through and through, joined together by our common experience. It's about respect; not about colour or money".

"Quite right Miss, good for you," replied Manny.

The young men joined Clementine at the table, and she insisted on buying them all a drink.

"Three Coca-Colas?" she asked again, "you don't even drink, you are tough guys!"

Not realising the irony of her words Clementine added.

"I'd die if I didn't have a drink every day!

"What are you up to these days?"

"Miss, you'll never believe this," said Clinton taking the lead as usual.

"Since I finished boxing, I've qualified as a proper community social worker and I work in Manton, Northwood and Battle, and it's fantastic Miss!"

Eugene butted in.

"I'm an ex-soldier Miss, and now I'm a geography teacher in our old school but you might know that, because some of the staff were there when you were, and you probably see them from time to time."

"I'd heard about that," said Clementine, knowing that Eugene had always loved his favourite subject of geography. That was why with her encouragement he had joined the army to see the world when he left school, but she didn't mention the leg up she had given him for his interview with her old colleagues.

"What about you Manny, where has life taken you?"

"Well, thanks to you Miss I am the deputy general manager just around the corner in Carrington's of York, the posh shop where I got my first job years ago," he said, handing Clementine his equally posh business card for inspection and ratification.

"I'm impressed," said Clementine "but what are you three doing together in town today drinking Coca-Cola!" she asked authoritatively, for in her mind they were still her pupils.

"We have to go to the bank Miss," Clinton said.

"You won't believe this Miss, but we have formed a limited company to run a new part-time community centre attached to Battle High School, and we must open a bank account.

"The centre is for girls and boys. There will be all sorts going on Miss: boxing, dancing, needlework, bricklaying, plumbing, fashion, and everything in between. We'll teach them to be good kids just like you taught us, Miss!"

For an hour they talked of the "good old days" with Clementine's mind drifting back to the best time of her life when she taught the quick and the dead.

Looking at the three amigos for what she privately believed was probably the last time, she had a sick feeling in the pit of her stomach.

"Nothing is permanent," she thought.

After unrestrained, unmasked tearful goodbyes Clementine made her way home with Desmond at 2.30 pm on the bus, just in time to miss the start of the evening traffic.

Like all retired teachers she could not help being as pleased as punch that they had remembered her.

Passing the New Theatre on Churchill Way, the thespian centre of York, Clementine's mind flicked between reminiscing and her final conundrum.

"My life may be ending but I know for certain I took three dead people, gave them life, and quickened them up enough to be successful. They are good men; they are respectful, and they will take my place when I'm gone. Education works!" she mused and then the solution to her nagging problem came to her.

She thought of the letter she had received from Standfast a couple of months earlier, and she smiled proudly when she silently recounted how a personal cheque from him for £300 was also enclosed.

It was just as he had promised in a private contract long ago, which she had reluctantly and proudly cashed because she felt it would be an insult to do otherwise.

Her thoughts now turned to the contents of the letter in which Standfast had filled the gaps of the last nineteen years, telling of his first-class honour's degree from Oxford University, his career success in London, of being head-hunted to the USA, of his American wife and two children, and his position as the Chief Executive Officer of his own Californian software company with a capitalisation of $45 million dollars.

She had laughed and cried when she saw Terminator Software Inc. had been listed on the New York Stock Exchange and that Standfast was now a multi-millionaire even if it was in dollars.

As they travelled on the bus through the Tangmere shopping district she turned to Desmond.

"Quick, we need to get off now!"

Without further explanation, she stood up from her seat and to Desmond's surprise made to leave.

He followed as he knew he should, all the while bitterly complaining that this was not their stop and asking "why?", but to no avail, as Clementine strode purposefully down the crooked stairs, alighted from the bus, and walked across the road to the nearest Barclays Bank.

She pulled her purse out of her handbag and from there she took out a folded cheque for £50,000 made out to her personally from the CEO of an American software house, which she promptly paid into her bank account and the conundrum was solved, at least for the time being.

* * *

In the congregation sat four men, three darker than the other, who stood out like D'Artagnan and the three musketeers. On their right-hand lapels, they all wore an enamel badge of office that had been given to them by the deceased during their schooldays.

The vicar looked at the front right-hand seats and from the insignia, he identified two prefects, a deputy head boy, and a head boy in front of him.

They occupied the seats next to Clementine's husband Desmond, at his request, for he knew them all well from his wife's stories, and as her favourites, he felt they were most representative of everything she had stood for in life.

If you didn't know better you would have thought they were part of Clementine's family, which in many ways they were in every sense, for she had never had children of her own.

They also stood out because you could not help noticing that they were all immaculately dressed. Each wore a crisp white shirt and perfectly shiny black shoes.

Instead of a mournful black tie, the amigos all wore their original school tie from Battle High School, the infamous maroon and amber stripe.

They never missed one word of the service, taking in every sentence, and singing each word of every song.

Years before they had skulked their way immaturely through morning assemblies but now, they stood up proud and true, as they had been taught.

They would never let Clementine down at a time like this. It was goodbye and it was going to be done properly, in Battle style.

The service was given to one hundred and fifty mourners assembled in the Heslington Crematorium on a small low-rise overlooking the city.

Despite the inclement weather, another four hundred and fifty people watched on the television screen outside and listened as the service was broadcast to the thronging crowd.

Clinton, the former head boy at Battle High School had been asked to represent the community and stepped forward to give a reading.

"Yea though I walk through the valley of the shadow of", and tears began to stream down his face. This tough man, this ex-boxer, cried in front of a packed house and everyone, as one, cried with him.

They cried from respect, they cried for the joy that Clementine had been, and they wept because they had loved her.

This support enabled Clinton to complete the task and return to his seat and his three friends patted him on his shoulder, each giving him a silent nod of respect, having carried out this most difficult of personal tasks.

Short Stories with A Twist

The vicar concluded the sombre service and the four unlikely friends stepped forward and picked up the coffin, just like they had practised together a day earlier.

They removed it carefully, under the supervision of the funeral director, and with a futile attempt to not shed tears, they placed it on the crematorium plinth that would in a few moments send Clementine to a greater calling.

Near the casket on full display, they placed two items that the ex-girl pupils of the school had laid on top of the coffin earlier. These would remain for inspection by the mourners long after the moving ceremony had ended.

Firstly, a bouquet of beautiful flowers was arranged to say, "Best Teacher Ever," which brought tears to the eyes of everyone who read the simple proclamation.

Next to it, they positioned the second item, a simple handmade wooden cross, about twelve inches high with a two-by-three-inch engraved metal plate on the front, made by the school pupils in woodwork and metalwork classes.

There were two lines of text.

Firstly, was engraved "Clementine Hobson". Underneath it said, "Destination Certain" and then there was a space and a cheeky arrow pointing upwards.

Clementine would have laughed like hell, getting full volume from her smoker's cough had she been alive to see it.

Unbeknown to the thronging masses of ex-pupils, staff, friends and family, Clementine's last will and testament had promised a bequest of £50,000 to a brand-new company formed just months earlier.

Amongst the mourners, the three directors of a certain community service organisation, were oblivious to the donation they would receive, as they continued to wipe tears from their eyes as the ceremony concluded.

Desmond had insisted she had been dressed for the occasion by the funeral director in her standard grey business suit, which was offset by an expensive clean white blouse, and never worn patent leather shoes, as she had requested.

Looking proudly at the four amigos, Desmond could not help noticing that through their left lapel buttonholes were slotted four identical white roses worn as the last mark of respect for their dearly departed headmistress, a fervent supporter and promoter of all things Yorkshire.

Finally, there was one other visual factor that made them stand out from the crowd, that Clementine would have noticed in an instant, but she was no longer able to admire, but it confirmed her work on this earth was done.

All four stepped back and bowed respectfully to their headmistress one last time. They fought back tears as they returned to their seats.

There was absolute silence both inside and outside the crematorium. You could hear a pin drop.

The vicar pressed the hidden button below the lectern and a low humming noise broke the silence. The red curtains gently swung into action and eased silently around the oblong frame to envelope the coffin. A few moments later, unseen by the mourners, it had sunk into the fiery pit below and Clementine was physically no more, but her influence would be with the congregation for as long as they lived.

The community worker, geography teacher, department store deputy manager, and the mousy maths genius, all educated at Battle High School had one thing in common which would have made Clementine incredibly proud.

They all wore a good suit.

Chapter 8

THE GRADUATE

"He's leaving tomorrow, my baby boy is leaving home! Where did all the years go? Do you think we did enough?"

"Enough for what?"

"Enough for him to survive in the big wide world? I mean, he's only eighteen, is he grown up enough to go to university?"

"All baby boys must grow up in the end. He's our son, isn't he? Anyway, Rhodri Davies is a six-foot tall, fifteen stone Welsh rugby player so I think he'll be ok, and if he's lucky, he'll end up just like his father!"

"I knew you would say that! You mean just like you, just like Peter Pan, the boy who never grew up!"

"You married me, didn't you?"

* * *

The alarm sounded at 7.00 am but there was no need for it, because they had both been awake for at least an hour. Worry, nerves, and trepidation, have a way of unsettling the mind, and interfering with your body clock.

"Who is in the shower first?" asked Antonia through half-opened misty eyes.

"You go first," replied Dylan, as he staggered stiffly from the marital bed.

"I'll go and put the kettle on and get the breakfast ready, we'll need something before we set off."

"Ok, I'll have a quick shower and wake him up, it's a big day for Rhodri and I want to make sure he's packed everything."

In the distance came an unexpected, frustrated reply.

"I'm already awake and I packed everything yesterday!"

Today was the day, the watershed, the striking out on your own day when Rhodri would finally be the last sibling of the Davies family to make his way to university.

Dylan and Antonia smirked silently and glanced at each other with a knowing look.

They had just experienced the invisible conversation that only parents who have brought up children can have. They had said as one.

"I knew he'd have an answer and I didn't even know he was awake!" but not a word passed their lips.

By the time Antonia had arrived downstairs to the ageing, battered, cream-coloured, shaker kitchen, two teas and one coffee were sat on the dining room table, complemented by a rack of fun free brown toast, best butter, and blackcurrant jam.

"You must have real butter with "good for you" bread!" she suggested.

Dylan remained at the stove cooking the condemned man's meal of four rashers of smoked bacon, two sausages, no eggs or beans, lashings of tomato sauce and for some reason which the parents never quite understood, and Rhodri couldn't explain, a lump of Feta cheese on the side.

All of this was flanked by two doorsteps of crusty white bread; for teenagers believe they are invincible, and the phrase healthy living is a milestone yet unreached and unheard.

The freshly showered Rhodri, having used at least a quarter of a tank of water, swanned in half-dressed, trailing a wafted scent that suggested he had either just left a cheap brothel or misfired his underarm spray.

"Keep your opinions to yourself," said Dylan under his breath, "today is not the day to have a row."

"Everything packed?"

Antonia gave Dylan the "don't wind him up look" whilst Rhodri rolled his eyes.

The Graduate

The curt communication was evidence of the tension in the air.

Rhodri had packed his bags but unknown to him so had his mother, cleverly adding little things she thought he would surely need, like nail scissors, plasters, a picture of him holding some trophy or other, and a packet of tissues which were secreted in between layers of shorts and sports clothing.

The only things she didn't put in were a couple of conkers, an elastic band, and a piece of string, although she had considered the elastic band.

Breakfast was consumed, the dishes put in the dishwasher and the car packed under the predetermined rules set by Antonia the night before.

"No arguing in the morning!"

Dylan and Rhodri obeyed the instruction to the letter with knowing winks as they exchanged father-son banter whilst completing the task at hand.

"Are we ready to go; is everything packed?" asked Antonia, echoing the words of mothers and fathers throughout the land on that early, brisk, September morning.

Dylan checked that his car keys were in his pocket.

"All good!"

Rhodri salivated at the thought of finally going to university, whilst a little bit saddened at leaving the safe and loving hearth that he had known for these last eighteen years.

"All good!"

Antonia felt a lump in her throat as she crossed the threshold. Her last baby was leaving the nest today. She was entitled to be sad, but no one would see it. She was going to be strong.

Dylan glanced around the kitchen as he locked up, with entirely different thoughts than Antonia.

"At last, I can get the kitchen decorated with those two hulks having flown the nest," he chuckled to himself.

The sad parents and the excited ex-schoolboy boarded the shiny silver Lexus car on their drive and Dylan started the engine in earnest.

"Got your phone, Rhodri?"

A bored "Yup" was the reply.

"Got your charger and your earphones?" asked his mother.

Silence ensued, followed by sudden movement and the sound of the back car door opening.

"Where's the house keys?" grinned Rhodri.

"I left the earphones on the end of the bed in a safe place!"

Everyone laughed and the morning tension was finally broken.

The budding student whirled into the house and two minutes later the security alarm was on, the engine started, and Rhodri finally packed and en route to the University of Southampton, where he was planning to study economics, unlike his father who had majored in law thirty years before him.

"Which way are we going?" asked Antonia.

"Newport, the Severn Bridge, Bristol, Swindon, turn right at Newbury and Southampton here we come," said Dylan enthusiastically.

* * *

Despite the good weather the journey from Cardiff to the picturesque southern county of Hampshire took nearly three hours.

Heavy traffic suggested all was well with the nation, and business appeared to be booming, as large vehicles weaved incessantly between lanes on extremely busy roads.

Dylan privately noted how "mother and child are doing well," after eighteen years together, as they jointly identified and counted the number of cars so obviously packed with student's belongings, navigating similar journeys to their own.

This was a new day, a new dawn, and for every empty chick's bed that evening, there would be a wide-eyed university fresher trying out a new mattress in some new town or city.

"It is," said Dylan silently to himself, "part of the cycle of life. It's all about growing up, being mature and meeting life head-on."

As they pulled into the halls of residence at Montefiore House in Swaythling, Southampton a shiver ran down Dylan's spine as he viewed the places he had frequented when he was a student there over three decades before.

He noticed much had changed since his undergraduate days, and as he parked the car Dylan excitedly addressed Antonia and Rhodri.

"If they blindfolded and parachuted me into this place, I could tell you where I am. It's like a scented tattoo on my brain."

Mother and second son grinned at each other, half expecting Dylan to start his next sentence with "during the war" like grandad used to, but Dylan at forty-eight years old was far too young to have ever seen any action like that.

Dylan noticed obvious changes in traffic flows and parking space layouts but expertly navigated his way into the last space at Chez Rhodri, the home of their baby boy for the next year.

"Astonishingly well done!" laughed Antonia, "considering you couldn't afford a car when you were a student here!"

They exited the vehicle and as he tried to work out his bearings, Rhodri started to show signs of nerves for the first time. Antonia picked up on the inconclusive vibe and began to fret.

"When I was here, we used to," are the only words Dylan expelled before Antonia snapped, "well you are not here now! Rhodri, where are we supposed to go to get your keys?"

Stress it seemed was viral.

"Once a mother hen, always a mother hen," Dylan said to himself, low enough not to be heard for fear of swift and instant reprisal.

Sent to Coventry in disgrace for a few moments Dylan wondered if Rhodri, as their baby boy, would ever be allowed to leave the nest, despite the distance now being forged between them.

Rhodri dug out the seventh-generation, crumpled, photocopied map he had received some weeks earlier in his fresher's information pack, where a smudged asterisk marked the administration office.

Dylan noticed this and grinned, realising that he could have told them where it was two minutes ago, but he kept an astute and wise silence.

Out of the door of a building named "C" block walked a confident-looking blonde girl holding a similar-looking map to the one held by the confused Rhodri.

"Hello," she said, oblivious to Dylan and Antonia as her eyes locked on to the rugged, rugby-playing, half-shaven, cool-looking, Welsh progeny that was Antonia's baby.

Rhodri looked up and warmed to her smile, open countenance, and obvious female charms. He was dumbstruck, as was his father.

Thoughts and memories, like rapid gunfire, shot through Dylan's excited brain as so many past student adventures came to mind.

He could not help noticing that the brassiere under the new girl's skimpy T-shirt appeared to be a size too small and that her denim skirt had shrunken at least one size whilst in the wash.

His wife glared at him and dared him to make any comment.

Using over twenty years of married experience he chose a peaceful solution, quietly regrouped, and then took Rhodri's bags and belongings silently out of the back of the car.

The new girl prophetically spoke to Rhodri and said, "are you going my way? as she flashed her own Montefiore treasure map.

"I know where it is, I was there earlier. They gave me the wrong key!

"My name is Annabelle, I'm from Coventry," she said in a soft Midlands accent as she linked arms with Rhodri and led him away.

Dylan smiled, "I know it well, what a coincidence, I've just come back from Coventry," he mused.

Antonia and Dylan looked at each other with a smile of accomplishment, and a proud look of confidence for the future crossed both of their beaming faces.

Rhodri, now looking two inches taller, strutted away with young Annabelle on his arm, more confident with every step as he strolled into adulthood.

"I'm Rhodri, have you ever been to Wales?"

* * *

The Graduate

Two hours later Rhodri was unpacked, albeit most of it had been done by his mother who automatically assumed command of goods inwards as expected.

It was the last rite in a ritual that all mothers experience who send children away to higher education.

The handing-over ceremony was taking place with all three attendees ignoring the elephant in the room and avoiding the sad, but joyful subject of the youngest child leaving home.

Rhodri, while his mother fussed around his creased-up packing, inadvertently met his new flatmates as they went about their business in this new accommodation.

Toby, Abby, Clarissa, and Harry introduced themselves to him in turn.

"Five down, two to go!" said Toby and they all continued with the business of the hour.

"Still seven to a self-catering flat," said Dylan "but when I was here it was strictly boys and girls in separate accommodation."

"Like when dinosaurs ruled the earth!" Rhodri quipped as he smiled at his mother.

"Please don't encourage him!" begged Antonia to Rhodri.

"Let's finish this so we can get off home and let you get on."

Amongst the new residents, kitchen conversations began in earnest, as they crossed paths looking for fridge and cupboard space.

Antonia remarked on how civilized and orderly the kitchen looked.

Dylan thought to himself, "I'll give it 24 hours maximum; it won't look like this for long once the chimpanzees are off the leash and on the lash!"

The haphazard, informal, embryonic meetings of the new incumbents were interspersed with fleeting glances of other parents carrying in boxes, clothes, and books. All of them it seemed, under the strictest orders not to speak to anyone at the risk of embarrassing their charge.

Rhodri, all fear, nerves, and trepidation now gone, encouraged his parents to disappear, as he said he had much to do, having just read his exciting fresher's week itinerary, that he had found under the door, on entering his boudoir come study.

He suddenly announced that he had been invited to a fresher's beer festival that evening and by sheer coincidence, he went on to say he had arranged to meet Annabelle from Coventry.

"Would you believe it? The sly old fox!" remarked Dylan.

Mum and Dad, together with Rhodri, had their last belly laugh together before the cycle of progress moved on.

As they drove away, they both shed a silent tear for their not-so-little boy.

Dylan thought of the 1970s TV biopic "Roots" about the birth and life's journey of a prodigal son.

"Kunta Kinte, is no more, but Mr Rhodri Davies is now being manufactured at the University of Southampton," pronounced a tearful and proud father as they started the engine of a much-lightened vehicle.

"I hope he doesn't get homesick," said Antonia nervously.

Dylan looked in a mental rear-view mirror to somewhere in his distant memory and then in the car rear-view mirror to correlate the facts.

He then saw the waving Rhodri turn away and greet Annabelle as if they had known each other forever.

"Somehow," said Dylan, "I think he will be ok! Did I ever tell you about the time?" and passed Antonia a tissue to dry her eyes before continuing with a story she had heard a hundred times before.

* * *

Antonia daydreamed as they made their way back up the M3 towards Newbury, while her baby chick Rhodri set out on his new path to becoming a fully-fledged adult.

As she closed her eyes it all went floating past.

Firstly, the twenty-hour maternity labour pains. "If he was the first, he would have been the last!" she always said to Dylan, but she would do it all again tomorrow.

She fondly remembered the chuckling baby, his first day at school, and all the other mothers she met at the infant's reception class, who she was still friendly with after all these years.

Together they shared one of life's great bonds and no get-together was ever complete until stories of infants' school were trotted out between sips of prosecco and dry white wine.

Antonia thought of the day he put on his two sizes too big pre-cub's beaver outfit, handed down from his older brother Dafydd, and how Dylan convinced him he would grow into it.

He was such an easy child, he loved hand-me-down trousers because they were so soft and comfortable, but more importantly, they were from Dafydd, who he worshipped.

Only once had she ever really seen him upset. A smile crossed her lips when she reminisced about the time when he had been chosen for the infant's school play. He wanted the part of Joseph just like his brother two years before, but he was given a supporting actor role as the innkeeper. He was not happy about being overlooked and he let them know in his special way.

He brought the house down when the little boy chosen to play Joseph arrived with his pregnant Mary and knocked on the inn keeper's door. Rhodri opened it and Joseph spoke his line right on cue.

"Is there any room at the inn?"

The innkeeper was word-perfect when he replied "No," but he never offered an alternative as the script demanded.

It was a standoff in front of three hundred parents, grandparents, and members of staff.

Rhodri just stared at Joseph for an uncomfortable ten seconds and the play's director Mrs Griffiths began to cringe.

The boy chosen to play Joseph was one smart cookie, which is why he was given the part, and he now tried to limit the damage. He took up the cudgel.

"Well, is there any room in the stable?" he politely enquired, and Mrs Griffiths looked momentarily relieved, but it didn't last for long.

Rhodri stared back at him.

"No!" came the stern reply and he closed the door firmly shut.

End of subject, end of a whole religion.

They were rocking with laughter in the aisles. Mrs Griffiths intervened to save the day and Rhodri had a very weak telling off.

It was a hilarious moment and never to be forgotten.

That was the only time Rhodri ever really did anything wrong. He and his brother never threw punches at each other and rarely argued. They were great together.

Antonia followed the natural flow of her thoughts. Saturday football and Sunday rugby filled her mind as they travelled between Reading and Bristol. The matches, the tours, the lumps and bumps and the hospital visits came flooding back.

"All part of growing up," she mused to herself.

She remembered what Dylan always said, "He's got your temperament, that's why he is so popular, the mothers love him, the boys respect him, and the girls swoon and he isn't fifteen yet!

"I don't know what that boy's got," said Dylan one Sunday afternoon, after seeing yet another group of besotted teenage girls ogling Rhodri, whilst pretending not to be interested in rugby.

"Whatever it is, I wish I could bottle and sell it. We'd make a fortune!"

Antonia thought to herself that Annabelle had somehow picked up the scent and she smiled again.

Dylan noticed the glint in her eye.

"What are you laughing at?"

"Just the old days and Rhodri growing up. Will you ever grow up?"

"Absolutely not," said Dylan, "Peter Pan will be here for a long while yet!"

They both laughed their way across the Severn Bridge into the final stretch of a lonely journey home.

The last thirty miles were the most emotional, as the realization hit them both that the little boy who had given them so much fun, would now be giving hours of entertainment, good humour, and friendship to strangers instead.

"I hope they appreciate what they've got in our little boy at Southampton!"

Dylan thought back to the glint he saw in Antonia's eye, which naturally led to a vision of Rhodri's new friend Annabelle.

"I think so!" he said.

The silence was broken by a text message alert.

Who is it from?"

"Rhodri,"

She tried to unlock the device that her sons referred to as a "brick."

"What's wrong?"

Five seconds passed and Antonia smiled.

"Can we send Taffy to him?"

"Taffy is going nowhere!" He stays with us. Anyway, you can't put Taffy in the post. It's too risky. What if he gets lost? He might be a teddy bear to the rest of the world, but to our family, he's real, just like Rhodri, Dafydd and Scruffy."

"Well Scruffy did eventually go with Dafydd to Nottingham Uni; Dafydd called him "his secret aftershave" which I never quite understood."

Her husband smiled, sometimes his darling wife could be so lovely, so innocent.

Dylan would never say it, but he was reluctant to let that last teddy bear go because he was the link to their youngest son and marked the end of an era. Taffy, the world's most over-loved bear, was as much a comfort to Antonia and Dylan as he had been to Rhodri.

"Why does a gigantic, rugby-playing Welsh neanderthal want a teddy bear anyway?" asked Dylan, already knowing the answer.

"All the boys have them, even the sporty guys. He said in the text it's a great way to meet girls and get them talking when they visit his room. Aaaahh! Now I know why Dafydd was so keen for Scruffy to go with him to Nottingham!"

Dylan smirked.

"Talking, is it? Ok, ask him how he's getting on without us, and tell him we'll do a drive-by and discretely drop Taffy off in a couple of weeks, and then maybe take our abandoned baby out for a large steak if he's interested, and possibly Annabelle also."

Antonia dutifully fired the message back and it seemed to bounce back with new words immediately. "Taffy ok, steak ok, two weeks ok, Annabelle? Two weeks is a long time in university!"

Dylan and Antonia cried with laughter as she read the message aloud.

As they pulled the Lexus up onto their drive just under three hours later, she reread the final message out loud and they burst out laughing again.

In those split seconds they had another invisible parental conversation. "Our boy is growing up!"

The next three years flew by in a whirl of academia and social exploration and the threesome was rarely apart. Rhodri, Annabelle and Taffy, the legendary Welsh teddy bear were an item.

His delighted parents couldn't have been prouder of their little boy when he graduated from the University of Southampton with a very respectful 2:1 degree in economics.

He announced that like his mother before him, he wanted to be a teacher rather than pursue a career that he hated, as his father had done almost thirty years before. His parents were delighted for they had always impressed upon him that happiness was a far greater reward than chasing money for money's sake where every working hour was despised.

At graduation Antonia's beautiful smile made her look like a crocodile on steroids, while Dylan looked every inch the proud father.

"That's my boy, take a look at my boy!" he kept saying until eventually, Antonia interrupted.

She winked at Annabelle who had gone with them to Rhodri's graduation ceremony.

"I think if you check you'll find he is our boy. Well, he's mine anyway, it's a wise man that knows his own father!"

The following day they had been invited to see Annabelle receive her French degree and finally meet her parents.

The blonde teenager who had handpicked Rhodri in fresher's week was long gone, and in her place was an even more beautiful, confident young lady.

Dylan couldn't help noticing how her clothes seemed to be a much better fit than at their first jaw-dropping meeting three years previously.

A stunning smile, athletic figure, and enthusiastic personality made her the pick of the paddock, yet she was the one who had done the picking.

When the parents were introduced to each other they stood back and realized why their child's partner was so outstanding.

Both young adults were the product of clean, professional, healthy people, with impeccable manners and social standards.

The ceremony went off without a hitch and the party of six later went to the White Swan, better known in local circles as the "Mucky Duck", for an early evening meal and celebration party.

Within minutes relaxed conversations ensued and it felt like they had all known each other forever. The two mothers talked endlessly of everything and nothing, from nappies to mortarboards, while the two husbands spoke of sport, sport, sport, and rugby.

The young lovers laughed in all the right places, holding hands throughout, whilst exchanging knowing glances and smiles of hope for a certain future together. All too soon it was over, as genuine, heartfelt invites to Coventry and Cardiff were exchanged.

"It feels like we have known them for a lifetime," said Antonia as they went back to their hotel, "and the kids are so mature; didn't they both do fab yesterday and today?"

"Will you ever grow up?" asked Antonia.

"I sincerely hope not," said Dylan, and they headed for a nightcap at the bar of the Polygon Hotel.

The following day on the way back to Cardiff in yet another new Lexus, but black instead of silver this time, they discussed Rhodri's future.

Rhodri had confirmed at the graduation ceremony that he would be applying to Cardiff University to take a teacher training course.

His mother and father were both delighted, and two days later, after a whistle-stop visit to Coventry, Rhodri was home, and it seemed like he had never been away, except for his obvious new maturity.

Dafydd visited for four days from Nottingham where he was now working as a newly qualified lawyer, and for the first time since Christmas, the family spent three wonderful days together, exchanging banter, laughing, playing board games, and just enjoying each other's company.

On the last evening, after a great meal out at a local restaurant and a shared bottle of wine on their return home, Dylan motioned to speak.

"Did I ever tell you about the time?" and then the other three looked at each other in dismay as Dafydd said with an exaggerated rolling up of his sleeve, "is that the time?" and they all went to bed laughing like drains.

On Sunday, Dafydd returned to his job in Nottingham and his specialism of company law, which he had confessed to his father that he was slowly "overdosing on," whilst Rhodri began drawing up plans for his future, and which schools he might like to teach in.

His chosen subject would be business studies, which was a natural fit for an economics graduate.

Dylan returned to his daily task of never growing up, while Mum continued with her job as head of year and maths teacher supreme at a local comprehensive.

It also turned out that Rhodri had something else to tell them.

The following weekend he announced that Annabelle was planning to do teacher training, specialising in languages, and would also be applying to Cardiff University.

Dylan and Antonia looked at each other.

"Another brick in the wall," they said, but there was no sound.

Life's wheels continued to turn and before the commencement of the new term, Annabelle turned up as planned in Cardiff in August, to become the latest member of the Davies household.

It proved to be a wonderful decision, for with zero resistance she moved in with Rhodri and his parents, and the two women found sisters they had never had.

Rhodri and Dylan continued to act the goat, which would often lead to one of the females saying to the other, "one day they will be adults!" and everyone would laugh.

As the year progressed the interview season arrived. This was a critical time when your school and your future would be decided. It could influence your life for many years to come and the whole family knew that the quality of the school appointment was critical.

Antonia and Annabelle travelled into Cardiff and bought a complete new wardrobe of interview clothes from John Lewis, courtesy of an expensive personal shopper appointment, previously arranged by the senior of the two.

Rhodri's mother paid for everything and would not hear a word of Annabelle paying anything.

"Pay me back out of your first pay packet" she barked, as they sipped tea and coffee in a celebration break at Starbucks, and there was no witness for the defence.

The prospective young business studies teacher also acquired a smart new wardrobe, but he had help from Dylan and both women in his life.

Rhodri heeded his father's advice when he said that the shoes are the foundation of the interview.

"All interviewers look at your shoes; they are always noticed. As I keep saying, don't wear your normal footwear, buy something decent!" he emphasised.

"What you need is a sharp-looking pair of leather uppers and soles from a more traditional shop. Brogues would be ideal, or even better, a nice pair of slip-on loafers because they allow the trouser leg to fall better than a shoe with laces!"

Dylan did not rise to the bait of the young bull, who feeling his feet, challenged the older one with some verbal jousting.

"It's a job interview, not a dance or a fashion show!"

The views of young and older men are usually miles apart, but some basic elements remain true. Dylan had tried to steer a sensible, mature line in his advice, which for Peter Pan was a great achievement.

Rhodri's favourite joke while growing up would be to wait until his father was dressed up in a dinner suit or similar and then while pulling on the waistband of his low-slung hipsters say to Dylan, "What chest size are those pants dad?"

He would then look at his older brother, mother, or both and laugh uncontrollably for the next ten minutes, no matter how many times he said it.

Dylan had thrown enough mud for some to stick, and a chord had been struck.

One evening, arriving home later than expected with Annabelle on his arm he proudly announced to his parents, "I've bought a pair of shoes, two pairs in fact; for my teacher interviews."

His parents were at once taken aback. Again, they glanced at each other and without so much as a flinch of a lip said, "he has grown up."

"Let's see them," said Antonia excitedly.

Rhodri opened the bag and produced two high-quality pairs of shoes.

The first was a brown lace-up pair of brogues and the other a very smart pair of shiny black slip-on loafers, just as suggested by Dylan days before.

"Hugely impressed, I'm hugely impressed!" said Dylan repeating himself for effect.

* * *

All the ducks were lined up and everything was now set for the interview season.

In no time at all Annabelle was invited to join the staff at West Cardiff High School, one of the city's finest, the following September.

In the business studies recruitment drive, things were slower getting going, so Rhodri decided to break in his two new pairs of shoes by wearing them now and then to school, against solid parental advice.

"Worn shoes means dirty shoes, and dirty shoes means cleaning shoes!" advised Dylan.

After two weeks of shoe training, the four of them were having dinner one evening when Mum innocently enquired.

"How are the new shoes going?"

"Aaargh! One small problem, the seam has come away on one of the black shoes, it's split."

Dylan quickly interjected with some misplaced, poorly timed humour.

"You haven't been playing football in the yard, have you?" and chuckled out loud while an exasperated Rhodri just stared at him.

Antonia glowered and the comedy hour was over.

"Show me," said his mother as if he was ten years old.

Rhodri retrieved the damaged black shoes from under the stairs and sure enough, the right shoe had a split seam.

"It's just poor quality, it's certainly not Rhodri's fault," said Dylan.

"He's only worn them three times," he concluded.

"Twice actually," said Rhodri correcting his father.

"You've got another interview next week," lamented his Mum.

"You'll have to take them back!"

"How much did they cost?" asked Dylan.

"£90 for each pair," replied Rhodri.

"Well, they can jolly well have them back," continued his dad.

"I've already taken them back once and they wouldn't change them," said Rhodri.

The hairs on Dylan's neck stood up and Mum ground her teeth.

"They wouldn't change them because I couldn't find the receipt."

His father then took up the moral compass and proceeded to metaphorically beat all of them over the head with it. He wasn't a career lawyer for nothing.

Quoting the Sale of Goods Act and anything else he could remember, most of it from his student days, as he was now a divorce solicitor, he told Rhodri that a bank account statement would do the trick.

"It's an audit trail, a proof of the transaction."

Antonia, Annabelle, and Rhodri endured the onslaught for fifteen minutes until Dylan started repeating himself.

The matter was closed when Rhodri agreed to take the shoes back to the shop and to do as his dad suggested with the bank statement on the coming weekend.

Leaving the table, the prospective teacher climbed back under the hallway stairs, pulled out a shiny Clarkes Shoes shopping bag and unceremoniously deposited the black pair therein.

The bag and offending articles were then placed in the hallway near the front door, as some sort of pledge to Dylan that they were ready to be returned, as promised, in a few days.

Normality resumed and the rest of the evening drifted on as they all calmly went about their business.

In the morning Annabelle, Antonia and Rhodri had left the house by 7.30 am to ensure the wheels of Welsh education kept spinning for, as Dylan was often told, without those three, the world would be damned.

Dylan had an appointment to attend a local court for a preliminary divorce hearing on this day, so he dressed up like a dog's dinner.

"You never get a second chance to make a first impression!" he always told Rhodri.

"These elderly judges are a bit old-fashioned, and in my experience, they respect you and assume you know what you are talking about if you look the part."

A black pin-striped suit, black socks and an expensive new red and silver striped tie were complemented by a shiny silk pocket handkerchief and a clean-shaven appearance.

If you didn't know him, you would be a fool to think this man was not important.

The business of the morning was concluded in record time to Dylan's advantage, just as he planned, and by 11.00 am he was done, with an hour to spare in his timetable.

Infused with confidence and good thoughts, he put his briefcase in the boot of his latest Lexus and walked purposefully out of the law court car park.

His mind was now relieved of legal torture, where there are more words than pictures, and he realised that Rhodri's nemesis, the Clarkes Shoe Shop was but a few hundred yards away.

An impulsive decision, totally out of Dylan's character and against all his legal training was made on the spot.

"It's time to "grow up at last" and impress the family!"

In the past, it was Antonia who had always dealt with these things. Dylan could stand in a crowded courtroom verbally jousting and waffling for hours on end, but he disliked arguing with shop personnel. It was an oddity that had been with him since he was a young boy, and his wife just accepted it.

It was his way, but today he was going to show them all. Now was the hour, and cometh the hour, cometh the man. It was time to prove himself in battle.

"Maybe Peter Pan is about to leave the building forever?" he suggested to himself as he quietly made his way to the front door of Clarkes Shoes.

Dylan stood outside the shoe shop and stared in through the window, quickly working out who the players were in the scene that would shortly take place.

He saw three customers, two of whom were together and one alone, a young shop girl who didn't appear to be very interested in shoes, and a middle-aged lady who stood by the till, with hawk-like eyes, obvious years of experience, too much makeup and a large set of keys in her hand.

"Enter stage right," thought Dylan and with that, he carefully and gracefully entered quietly through the glass front door.

The serenity of the stage was shattered as the opening door set off a chime at the back of the shop, and all five players in the room glanced up in a casual attempt to check out the new actor.

Dylan closed the door, looked slowly around the theatre of war, and then stared at the lady with the keys. He said nothing at all, but kept eye contact for two or three seconds too long, until she looked away, thus gaining the upper hand.

From where he stood, he said in a loud deliberate voice.

"Who are you?"

His immaculate appearance combined with his confident air put all cast members on the back foot.

Weakly she answered.

"I'm the manageress."

"Excellent," said Dylan, walking forward towards her, not for one minute averting his gaze.

"Just the person I'm looking for!"

The shop manageress was beyond nervous.

Dylan later said he felt she would have given him the contents of the till if he had asked for them.

All the other players in the shop were now static, equally nervous, trying to work out what it was they were seeing.

Dylan, after a suitable silence, continued confidently in a deep, educated, practised, authoritative voice.

"I wonder if you can assist me, please?"

The manageress felt slightly relieved.

"I hope this is friendly fire," she thought.

"I'll do my best," she said in a nervous Welsh valleys accent.

"My son bought two pairs of rather expensive leather shoes here a couple of weeks ago."

The manageress nodded.

"He's only worn them a couple of times and the black pair, all £90 worth, has split along the seam. The young man is a trainee teacher, he doesn't have much money, and he certainly doesn't kick a ball about in the yard anymore!"

The manageress managed a weak grin as her best reply.

"He brought the shoes back last week, but he was refused a refund because he didn't have a receipt," added Dylan, as the audience looked on.

"However," he continued, changing the pitch of his voice for effect, "he has the bank statement proving the transaction which he would be happy to share with you."

The manageress wondered where this conversation was going, as did the other silent, attentive bit-part players.

"Now if he was to bring those shoes back here, together with his bank statement, I feel sure you would be able to change them for him or give him a refund, don't you?" he said, putting words in her mouth.

The manageress now saw her chance at closure and would have agreed to anything to remove this discomfort from her shop.

"Yes sir, that would be ok sir, it wouldn't be a problem," she said earnestly.

Dylan concluded.

"For clarification then, we agree that he can bring his shoes and bank statement into the shop, and you will do the necessary?"

"Yes, that would be fine," she said apologetically.

With that, Dylan spun on his right heel.

"Thank you ladies, thank you all," and he left his temporary stage as proud as punch.

* * *

That evening over a light supper he regaled all with his wonderful tale, describing in detail his quick win in court, which gave him the free time to exact a brave deed on behalf of the family.

He explained how he did not care anymore about taking things back to shops.

"That strange fetish is a thing of the past," he stated firmly and meaningfully.

His wife and prospective daughter-in-law were in stitches as he relived his adventure which had ended with his classic victory. They both felt that it was yet another story that would be introduced in years to come with, "did I ever tell you about the time?"

Dylan continued, "Peter Pan has finally grown up and flown away, and from now on you will have to accept me as I am!"

He raised a glass of wine and toasted all present.

Finally, as Dylan concluded his speech, he turned to his impassive son and said in that playful way that had endeared him to Rhodri's mother all those years ago.

"You see Rhodri, it's like I always told you, we must all grow up sometime! You can go into Clarkes Shoes at any time you choose, and they will give you a new pair of shiny black shoes or a refund, and as you are family, there's no charge for my legal assistance!"

With that, the lawyer closed the case for the prosecution.

There was silence for a few seconds as Dylan and the girls looked to Rhodri for a response.

Rhodri looked at the two women he loved most in his life and smiled, then maturely and squarely into his father's eyes.

"I didn't buy the shoes in that shop!"

Peter Pan flew back in through the window, assumed his natural position as head of the household, and they all laughed until they cried.

Chapter 9

WHITE KNIGHT

Where is that knight in shining armour when you need him most? She arrived at Reading University as a bright, promising, wholesome first-year student, and for the first time in her life, every vice was suddenly within her grasp.

Her parents had taught her right from wrong, but her new friends had no respect for older people, or themselves for that matter, and none for the shy, innocent girl they would drag down to their low standards and beyond.

It would be a traumatic journey from success to excess, to despair, self-isolation, and dark thoughts.

Only she could halt the fall into oblivion.

That was the problem.

She couldn't stop herself.

For salvation, she needed a guardian angel, but the horizon was empty.

* * *

Their clocks both went off at 6.30 am Greenwich Mean Time, but as the crow flies, they were separated by three busy, congested, London miles.

The contrasting ideals, morals, and beliefs of the seventy-three years young Colonel Peregrine Farquar Thomson, and the twenty-three years old Jennifer Lawrence were planets apart.

A retired Colonel, Peregrine was a lifelong professional soldier, a veteran of the Falklands and Gulf Wars, with extensive service in Afghanistan.

It seemed to his friends at "Lancers", his private club in the Mayfair, that he had served in almost every theatre of war of the last fifty years.

A widower, he sported a well-groomed moustache that suggested "military type," and lived comfortably and discreetly in his Chelsea apartment.

Peregrine could best be described as a debonair, accomplished, disciplined man, having spent much of his adult life as an officer in the British army.

The Colonel was polite, courteous, friendly, and always accommodating in keeping with his life's education, achievement, and experience.

"I'm blown if this is retirement," he would say tongue in cheek to his cohorts.

"Here I sit, heading for eighty, still fighting the second world war this afternoon, and working five mornings a week; beats doing nothing though!"

Next, he would take his turn at buying a round of rather expensive drinks to lubricate the throats of his retired military chums, whilst they refought old battles and conflicts.

He didn't need money. His pension was more than enough, but he felt duty-bound to contribute to society, especially to the victims of the horrors of war, of which he rarely spoke unless it was out of necessity to another time-served soldier.

From Monday to Friday, he represented The Army Veterans PTSD Charity based in Marble Arch, London. His specialism was counselling soldiers who were experiencing real post-traumatic stress disorder, as they attempted to weave their way back into normal life on "Civvie Street".

War, injury, and fear had been the tools of his professional trade, yet his astonishingly polite, comforting, and knowing bedside manner, was a delight to all who sought his help.

Peregrine was seriously connected in society, and he could point many a struggling victim in the right direction, supporting his decision with readily available funds he had personally raised for the charity.

The Colonel was one of life's good guys.

***

At the sound of the bell, Peregrine was out of bed without hesitation, as if a distant bugle had called him to the parade ground.

Fifteen minutes later, as standard in the time he allotted himself, he had completed his ablutions, showered, shaved, dressed and was ready to greet the day.

He ignored the aches and pains of a lifetime's passage, as he looked in the mirror and saw an uncomplaining, arthritic ex-soldier, surely entering life's final furlong, who in his opinion still had a lot to offer.

The soldier in him, that had never left the decaying body and mind, stood erect as he saluted himself in the full-length bedroom mirror.

"I'm not dead, there's life in the old dog yet!" he said silently,

Peregrine was a fair man, a decent man, and one of life's contributors, who felt he should give something back to those less fortunate than himself, and so he engaged in voluntary work for four hours each morning, Monday to Friday without fail.

Every weekday he assisted the charity as a non-executive director and ambassador, working in both roles to enhance the reputation of the organisation.

He called on the power of the old boy network to generate charitable aid in times of great personal need, the very oxygen of life for so many long-suffering ex-soldiers.

Following his voluntary contribution to the charity, he would next seek his daily medicine of gin and tonic at the club and discuss the week's cricket, or next week's, depending on England's fixture list. This was interspersed with the odd revisited military campaign of yesteryear.

These long-standing relationships were of great value in London business life. In his role as ambassador, he would call heavily on the strength of old friendships to raise and distribute funds from large corporate financial, government and local authority sources.

Immaculate in a Harrods suit and old school or regimental tie, Peregrine was born to the task.

An Eton School, Cambridge University or Guards tie opened doors that others could never imagine.

Many a trauma victim riddled with suicidal depression, could thank Peregrine for the vigour with which he carried out his role, and the millions of pounds he had raised by cajoling, palm pressing and requesting monies for his army comrades of all ranks, colours, and creeds.

He would very carefully choose his outfit of the day for these fundraising meetings, but it was to his choice of tie that he gave the most attention.

The right shade or the perfect combination of stripes could still silently and easily open many powerful doors in England in the twenty-first century.

As a fully paid-up member, he cherished his well-worn tie with light blue stripes on a dark blue background which advertised his membership in the Old Etonian Society. He lamented that probably only twenty per cent of people who wore it these days did so by right, having paid their financial and academic dues, but society had changed since he was a boy.

His Cambridge University tie, that cradle of learning where he had acquired a first in Psychology followed by a PhD in Applied Psychology, was possibly his favourite.

It reminded him of those golden years at Trinity College, spent with the cream of his peers. When he put on that tie, he always reminisced of a bygone age in a theatre of excellence that remained timeless after almost a thousand years.

The light blue of Cambridge University was Oxford University's nemesis, and he wore it with pride.

His third social weapon was his Guards tie, manufactured by Vanners and Fennell. It was a striped affair of equal maroon and navy which signalled to the right people on the appropriate occasion, that he was a time-served military man, which earned automatic respect in relevant society.

* * *

On this day he was to play both ambassador and fundraiser.

Peregrine chose his Eton tie with a purpose, for at 9.00 am sharp he had a meeting at Pinner Financial Investments in the heart of the city at Threadneedle Street. It was a foregone conclusion that it would be successful, for the old schoolboy network had already declared and passed him the result. The brief get-together was simply to catch up, talk about old times, update each other on the cricket and put a stamp of approval on the deal.

John Pinner, the old Etonian who headed the company, would gain massive publicity for his £50,000 charitable donation and serious tax advantages at the same time, whilst Peregrine would divert another huge cash sum to the needy.

The good Colonel arrived at his appointment fifteen minutes early as was his tendency.

He took a seat in the waiting room opposite a young lady who for the next few minutes stared at the floor, the ceiling or anywhere else but at him, in a kind of self-flagellating, brooding manner.

As he sat, he said "good morning," but although hearing his greeting, her ill-mannered response was to pretend she hadn't noticed, choosing instead to snub him, whilst looking down with a black foreboding focus.

Taking advantage of this absence of eye contact the Colonel studied his fellow visitor, quickly identifying her as a nervous-looking, boyishly handsome young lady in her early twenties.

He couldn't help but notice her ugly, shapeless, crude haircut and he found it difficult not to stare. His honest impression was that this cranial disaster had been conducted not by a qualified hairdresser but by someone with a shotgun. It was repulsive but he regrouped and chastised himself for his unkindness.

Then he focused on the rest of her wardrobe. The standout items were a pair of unkempt Doctor Marten's boots and a woollen dress that looked as if it had been rudely plucked from a charity shop that neither matched the venue nor fitted her slender, athletic body.

Assuming that she was there for an interview, he at once concluded that her physical presentation would certainly not impress the interrogation panel that would greet her in about fifteen minutes.

The retired Colonel was called through to his appointment by the receptionist exactly on time, with John Pinner's secretary greeting him personally, before leading the way to the office of the company chairman. As he followed her, he faintly heard the conversation behind him.

"Jennie Lawrence or is it, Jennifer Lawrence?" rang out as she was called for her interview, followed by a curt reply from the sullen young lady that won her no friends.

As he disappeared along the corridor, rather like the rabbit down the hole in Alice in Wonderland, something began niggling him greatly, so much so, that he found it difficult to concentrate during his short meeting.

He had seen it before, he knew the look, he could feel the atmosphere, taste it like he could taste the sulphur of gunpowder even if he was blindfolded, and it troubled him.

In the hinterland of the office spaces, the morose young woman in the woollen dress had snapped, "it's Jennie Lawrence," and without further ado and a complete lack of niceties, she was ushered through to her appointment.

The position of trainee financial analyst and the decent starting salary was not so much what she wanted; it was what she desperately needed.

* * *

Several hours earlier across the city, at the same time as the Colonel, Jennie Lawrence's alarm had woken her from a deep sleep in an unmade bed, where she slept huddled to one side because the free half was festooned in scruffy unwashed clothes and half-read magazines.

"Tarzan" the tortoiseshell stray cat she had adopted, so at least something would love her, opened one lazy eye, and wondered what the unusual fuss was about, before scratching himself, rolling over and deciding to sleep on to a more civilised time.

Her waking thoughts were of procrastination and avoidance.

Eventually, she dragged herself from her messy mattress prison out of necessity, had a one-minute shower just after 7.00 am, and was aware she was already running thirty minutes behind schedule.

Money was becoming scarce, and she needed the job. The interview was on the other side of London and Jennie knew that allowing for the unscripted events that plague city travel, she must allow at least an hour and a half for the journey.

Next, she fed the cat because she knew that if she didn't do so, it would die. The cat loved her, but it had no real choice. Jennie was a master, slave, nurse, companion, unreliable litter tray emptier, and keeper. She was also desperate to get the job at Pinners which offered a great salary, a bright future and possibly a way out.

She quickly completed her flash-over make-up and wardrobe choice, which left her feeling woeful but somehow deliberately inept.

"Why do my parents always make me feel so inadequate?" she screamed out loud, but no one heard, as she referred to an exasperated, heated conversation with both mum and dad on the phone the previous evening, where they had told her to "buck her ideas up."

The joyless daughter had responded by trying to act normal, but she wasn't normal. Everything was going wrong, and she just couldn't prevent it. Jennie just couldn't help herself from fanning the flames of distress.

Approximately five feet away in the full-length mirror lay the focus of her consternation.

The underweight, pasty-looking, aggressive, young lady, who had taken flight to London in a misguided quest for salvation from what she perceived as overbearing parents in Lincoln, stared back at her.

The real reason for her demise was closer to home. It was self-anger.

Her return after graduation to her parent's home in Spalding, that delightful small Lincolnshire market town, had been a comedown in more ways than one from the heady temptations of the University of Reading, where every hobby, every pastime, and every temptation was at less than arm's length.

The gentle, angelic teenager with delightful friends, so much promise, but also so much pressure on her shoulders, who had left almost five years before to surely win a first-class honours degree in finance and accountancy was no more.

There was certainly no return of the prodigal daughter to joyful parents. The vision of loveliness that had gone away had vanished, and in her place was a surly, noncompliant, bitter soul.

She rarely left the house, except to work, and during the two years at home, she took a series of low-paid jobs.

Lateness, resistance to authority and a poor attitude, meant that she lasted but a short time as a waitress, barmaid, club flyer distributor and whatever else she turned her hand to, all the while avoiding those who had known her in a previous life.

The once hugely popular golden girl would not contact any of her friends less the sins and spectres of the past rear their ugly heads on social media, a flame which once lit could virally spread its way to her parent's unsuspecting, clueless front door.

Her shame and avoidance of people and places gained Jennie no relief from the pressure, as the fear of being found out only got worse, and her strange, hermit-like poor behaviour became increasingly unbearable for her wonderful mother and father.

For two years Jennie simply hid away lamenting the errors of her ways, and the naivety of youth and freedom, until she could stand it no more. She had to run away and hide.

Inevitably the vortex of self-destruction began to spiral out of control and the Spalding retreat proved to be temporary.

When the arguments and rows about "being normal and going out and meeting your friends," could no longer be tolerated, something had to give.

Jennie decided to hide in London where she could fade to grey, and no past ghost would recognise her. There she could be free to start again and to take refuge in her head, where she would let no one in.

Early one afternoon, she slipped quietly away, hurting the people who loved her most, without so much as a smile or a goodbye, just a brief handwritten note saying she would call from time to time.

* * *

Her arrival at Reading University had been the biggest shock of her life.

When she first arrived from her small, slow-moving town, it took her two weeks to adjust to the freedom and the eye-opening ill-discipline of her random flatmates.

Before a month had elapsed, Jennifer had changed her name to Jennie, knowing that her parents hated that label, as she cocked a snook at the very scaffolding of her formative years.

Marian started it, the thoroughly modern, heavily tattooed, sexually liberated, weird-dressing, boundary-pushing Londoner in the opposite room.

One night halfway through the first term, she insisted that they all drink shots of vodka at a flatmate's party. Jennie, not realising the strength of those potent miniatures, drank on pace with the professionals in the midst.

Marian and her friend Josie, a loud, overweight girl from Brighton, specialised in low morals and virtue, whose sole aim in life seemed to be to drag others down to their poor standards.

Jennie quickly managed to get herself wildly drunk in no time. They all giggled as she got louder and unintentionally funnier. For the first time in her life, she felt grown-up, free, happy, and devoid of responsibility and she liked it.

Popularity it seemed was the biggest drug of all.

As the evening wore on cannabis came out, that friendliest of drugs that relax the brain and reduce the morals, which for all the free spirit it gives, it takes away in equal measure with addiction, mental illness, and depression.

The quiet country girl, on cloud nine with her new friendships, and not wishing to look as if she didn't fit in, was egged on by her flatmates and she smoked her first cannabis spliff, against her best wishes and her parent's biggest fears.

That was how it all began. By the end of the Christmas term, she had become a regular smoker and let her hair down at weekends, sleeping with a boy for the first time before that first term had ended, whose name she could not remember.

Contact with home grew less and less as her middle-class, thoughtful, and supportive parents assumed she was looking after herself and studying hard.

"Don't worry?" said her mum to her dad, "if she's too busy to call, it's because she's enjoying herself, so we have to grow up as well sometime; she can't be our little girl forever!"

* * *

At the end of the first year, cannabis had become her friend, her social comfort blanket. Jennie smoked it every night, and sometimes in the daytime too if it suited her.

"I can give this up any time," she thought, whilst smoking a large joint at an impromptu gathering one evening, conning herself into the false sense of security that millions had visited upon themselves before Jennie was so much as a glint in her father's eye.

Her drug of choice began taking her to new horizons and with Marian and Josie leading the way, their party reputation snowballed. There was hardly any boundary Jennie did not explore, and by the end of the second year, the list of casual lovers had grown long and unimportant.

As an extremely bright girl, she still did well despite the missed tutorials and lectures, because Sally Hawkins, a friendly Geordie and one of three non-smokers in the original flat was taking the same course at university.

Geordie Sally was Jennie's saviour, for she allowed the increasingly erratic Jennie to copy her notes.

The three years were a whirl of cannabis smoking, heavy music, and sex, and that was how the whole thing started.

There is a clearly understood difference between right and wrong, between black and white, that is burnished in our minds when we are young. That is where guilt emanates from; it is when we cross from one side to the other and we instantly know we don't belong.

In the final term of her last year, after a night of wild celebration and too many drugs, Jennie, feeling quite liberated, took her experiments to new heights, ending up in bed with three members of the university rugby team.

The following morning the hazy memory of guilt as she realised what she had done, was only surpassed by the extreme shock of being sent pictures and videos on social media of her decadent sex and cannabis antics, which had been taken by the boys on mobile phones during her willing, chaotic engagement.

She froze and felt sick and ashamed, as the digital evidence was now out there for the world to view, and for the first time in her university life, she was confronted with the reality of her shameful ways. Worse still, she had no control over the digital frenzy that followed among her fellow students.

Jennie perceived everyone was now laughing and sniggering at her behind her back. Quickly she went into a meltdown and became a virtual recluse, hiding away from reality and only leaving her bolt hole to sit exams, scolding herself for the stupidity she had shown.

As the drink and drugs wore off and sanity returned, Jennie realised how far behind with coursework she had fallen and tried in vain to catch up, miraculously attaining a high grade of 2:1 in her degree before that fatal homecoming.

The day her final exam was complete she had silently slivered back to Spalding, saying goodbye to not a soul, leaving her trail of self-destruction behind her, but terrified that one day it might come again to haunt her, for she knew the internet was a powerful medium.

* * *

On leaving her parents in Spalding and arriving in London, she spent the first night in a cheap hotel in Paddington, where she flicked the television channels for hours whilst planning her future.

The following lunchtime she managed to find a small bedsit, using the unspent money she had earned sporadically over the last couple of years.

She immediately looked for interviews in well-paid jobs, and as it seemed these came with a long-drawn-out interview process, she took work as a barmaid for three months, at a rundown Soho pub called The Three Crowns.

Any estate agent worth his salt would describe it as "full of character," whilst any potential buyer would describe it as "tired."

Old, compulsive, addictive habits die hard, and with anonymity secured, and against her better judgement, Jennie began to fall into one of her old ways, because it was the one thing that eased the pain and made her feel good about herself.

Jennie began smoking occasionally spliffs, but on an increasingly regular basis to fit in with the bohemian, eclectic society into whose lap she had fallen. She just couldn't help herself.

The smoking helped her to get rid of the black thoughts, the guilt, the self-imposed exile from her parents, the lost friends and sexual shame, and the lack of self-respect and dignity that had brought her to this sorry place.

This second wave of drug-taking wasn't a lack of willpower, it was an ill-measured, hypnotic, magnetic behaviour. Once more a bout of self-destruction took over, in all its cancerous form, working against the logic that marginally remained in that bright, intelligent, well-educated, impeccably brought-up mind.

Jennie had been a vivacious teenager, but the university experience had changed her for the worse. She was still a naturally pretty girl with a very attractive slim figure, but now she specialised in dressing as ugly as possible. Each day she wore scruffy, passion-killer outfits, designed to keep the opposite sex at a distance.

The mismatched colours, the aggressive boots and attitude, were a force field thoughtfully put together to say, "leave me alone," or "do not come any nearer!"

One of her cannabis-smoking, easy-living barmaid friends at the pub was a tall, gawky-looking lesbian called Maxine, who like Jennie wore equally bizarre sets of clothes, to let men know that they were shopping at the wrong store.

Subconsciously, Maxine saw through Jennie's camouflage and recognised the air of repellence and hatred of men. As hard as she tried, she couldn't work out what lay behind it, yet she still fancied her co-worker, because she was a "little hottie" as she often told her.

One day on seeing Jennie behind the bar in a pair of baggy black, shapeless trousers, worn-out trainers, and a drab top that she wouldn't wear to clean the car with, Maxine quipped.

"I like to dress skilfully darling, but that outfit is something else, you are dressing killfully!" before continuing with, "no guy or gal will even look at you in that garb," pressing a mental button to see if Jennie might be persuaded to declare which side she was batting for, but it backfired spectacularly.

"I dress for me, not for anyone else!" snapped Jennie.

"Are you afraid someone is going to get their hands on your goody bag?" quizzed Maxine, as the sexual connotation and lesbian promotion continued.

"You've got to attract them in the first place to turn them away!" leered Maxine as she put her hands under her boobs and pushed them upwards.

Jennie remained in a self-angered black mood for the rest of the shift, and then went straight home, drank a six-pack of lager, and smoked a spliff that was too large, all the while knowing that she shouldn't, and fell asleep in her clothes until the alarm went off at 6.30 am.

The journey to the interview at Pinners had begun, hopefully to a new start and an escape from the horrors of her very own self-made, self-imposed destruction.

***

Picking up one of the shoes she had just kicked off at the wall in a fit of rage, she grabbed it and projected it violently at the image staring at her in the hallway mirror and the glass cracked diagonally.

As the footwear bounced back towards her, tiny shards of glass answered her by glinting from the carpet as they landed.

Not satisfied with the first result, she rallied again, throwing the matching left shoe which hit home right in the exposed crack, and the glass splintered into hundreds of pieces, falling like summer rain to the floor.

It was no surprise to Jennie, after the involuntary morning tantrum, that she arrived at the tube station fifteen minutes late, but it was a real shock to travel seamlessly and fluently across London and arrive at Pinners fifteen minutes early.

At Pinners Financial Investments, Jennie's interview did not go well from the outset.

Her curt, rude tone did not register any positive ticks. The three senior managers asked her questions about her academic career and her social life, thus putting her immediately on the back foot.

To get the withdrawn Jennie to engage, one of the interviewers asked her a mental maths question.

"What is 27 x 37?" said the blonde haired, middle-aged, impeccably presented chairwoman of the panel.

Jennie hesitated, "1001" she snapped, subconsciously knowing it was 999 but she just couldn't help contesting their authority and winding them up, even though her future depended on it.

"I think you've forgotten one of your three R's," said the increasingly perturbed question-mistress.

"The three R's aren't what they used to be in your day," Jennie rudely replied, "these days they mean reading, writing and reaching for your calculator, so we don't have to do mental maths," and smirked, thus ending any chance of employment.

The interview was cut short, with a cordial exchange and an obvious and unanimous, "don't ring us, we'll ring you," from the full panel of three who, with no more time to waste, sent her on her way.

At about the same time, the good Colonel exited John Pinner's office, with a cheque in his pocket from a successful meeting, and ebulliently made his way back to reception.

As he walked down the corridor and on opening a glass door in front of him, he was aware of rather hurried footsteps behind him. Looking around he saw the flummoxed, reddened, angry and dark countenance of the girl he had seen in reception, the face that had troubled him for the last half an hour.

He hesitated and held the door open wide for the young lady.

"Don't open the door because I'm a lady!" she snapped.

"I didn't hold open the door because you are a lady, I held it open because I am a gentleman!"

Peregrine smiled to himself whilst Jennie grimaced at his reaction and her old friend, self-anger, kicked in.

Suddenly it was all too much, and the smouldering volcano of the last two years erupted.

This was the critical moment when chances are taken or lost, as Jennie burst uncontrollably into floods of tears, spending rivers of pent-up emotion that the Colonel recognised, and then he knew what had been troubling him.

Depression.

Jennie had realised the moment she left the interview room the job was lost, which justified the self-doubt she had experienced before she went in.

She had known since she left university two years ago and been sacked from that succession of jobs that things weren't right, but who could she speak to about it in a serene small town like Spalding or a foreign, fast-paced city like London, where people would rather look at the floor than at people's faces.

Nobody understood her self-destruction, the compulsion to self-harm mentally and physically, the fact that she couldn't help the way she acted, how she felt hopeless all the time, that she felt lost, that she ashamedly experienced suicidal tendencies and wanted to cry all the time, but luckily for her, the good old Colonel did.

He firmly took responsibility and control, and assuredly helped the fully compliant, desperate, and distraught Jennie to a chair, becalming her like a long-lost grandfather.

"I know, I know, I know," he said softly. Slowly and surely the young lady, with the savage self-styled haircut began to travel in her mind to a long-overdue place of safety, comfort, and reassurance.

After a full five minutes, when all of Jennie's tears had been spent, and all of Peregrine's tissues had been used, he spoke gently to the distressed young woman.

"Here is my card and my specialism is counselling, a very specialist kind of counselling. I recognise people in this life who are not at peace with themselves, and I saw it in you this morning. You, young lady, are a troubled soul but I think that this moment is the start of the journey back. You've reached the bottom and it only gets better from here. We don't judge, we simply help."

Jennie took the card and stared at it without saying a word, for an overly long further three minutes.

Her heart rate and emotions returned to a sense of normality, as Peregrine with a comforting hand around her shoulder, moved not a muscle, the rude woollen dress and the Eton tie matched perfectly together in this moment of real need and giving, as two worlds collided.

She looked at the name of the organisation and she read his impressive, unmatched credentials.

Suddenly she felt that she was no longer alone in this world, no longer isolated in her battle against all-comers and that a champion had been sent to save the day.

Jennie looked at him kindly, an aged, worn figure of experience, who offered salvation and for the first time in a very long while, she smiled a bright, happy, girly smile of relief and promise for the future.

"My name is Jennifer," she whispered.

***

Epilogue

Clinical depression kidnaps the soul.

It is a cruel, destructive, and terrible affliction that creeps up on you when least expect, affecting both individuals and families, and if unchecked it can damage lives forever.

Especially when you don't know you have it.

At the first sign of depression seek help, for somewhere out there in the darkness, your knight in shining armour is expecting you.

Chapter 10

I Wish I Could Fly

S HE was big alright, just like they said, the largest of ladies calmly lying there naked and beautiful in all her glory and magnificence, beckoning the next customer, available and receptive to all who wanted her, but at a price.

This lady was both mistress and master; imposing, in charge, in waiting, as if daring someone to challenge her authority, but no such challenge would come, for she was the last of her kind, the Queen of all she surveyed.

* * *

The well-respected lawyer stood up to speak to the conference in his role as the new Chairman of the Schumacher Disability Association.

"I have been an idiot and you can quote me on that!"

"Let me take this opportunity to apologise to all the disabled people here today and throughout the UK and beyond, for I have been a fool in my lifetime, an ignorant selfish fool who could have used his able-bodied prowess and higher education to help so many.

"Sadly, I did not, for I was blinded by my own physical and mental abilities which I took for granted.

"Now, at last, I hope I can put that right.

"In the last year, this charity has raised over £1 million for disabled men and women in the UK alone, and huge amounts more in the USA. It would never have happened in the UK if it wasn't for a chance meeting I had with a little guy from South Carolina, with a big heart, our President and founder sat right next to me today, Mr Gary Schumacher.

Applause filled every corner of the international conference at the Birmingham NEC.

"Unwittingly he changed my whole mindset and set me free from the bondage of an unfulfilled life, for only now do I realise the importance of my fellow man, regardless of their physical ability, and maybe my purpose here on earth.

"Prejudice is a curse which at times afflicts us all. When something is different, we feel threatened, and our logic becomes flawed.

"The solution is to educate ourselves and open our minds to the possibilities we may have missed.

"As you will shortly find out, my journey into the world and restriction of disability began in 2019, but it's now 2023 and the world has finally awoken to the fact that disabled people are human just like the rest of us.

"It's taken me these last four years to grow up and on the recommendation of my American friend, I am delighted to accept the Chair of this fine organisation.

"You may well ask yourselves; if I was so immature then why on earth would he choose me, a successful, career-driven, able-bodied British lawyer? I shall tell you shortly, but first, let me ask you all a question.

"It is often said that to understand something we need to "walk a mile in another man's shoes."

Please ask yourself, how can you do that, if he is in a wheelchair?

Let me tell you a story!"

* * *

In the strict pecking order, according to cost and loyalty, Sam and Jayne were some of the last to receive their invitation, as they followed the others up a zigzagging temporary corridor made of casual plastic and steel, all the while climbing higher.

On the last corner a female Filipino security guard, wearing an orange vest, walkie-talkie in hand, smiled graciously before acknowledging their presence.

"Welcome," she said, followed by, "this way," as she pointed to the right, before looking beyond them to see who would appear next.

Passing the guard, they both knew that the sound of voices followed by the sight of smart uniforms and welcoming smiles heralded their arrival at their world-class transient destination, which would be a luxurious home for the next fortnight.

The metal wall that now emerged in front of them, had a large rectangle with soft rounded corners, expertly and neatly cut away, very much like the top of a sardine can without the metaphorical connection.

More smiles were freely given to the two embarking passengers by the immaculate reception committee.

Jayne, pausing for effect, raised her hand in the air, before turning excitedly to Sam.

"You know, I'm a Queen Mary girl!"

"Welcome back, ma'am," said the next security guard as he swiped the identity card Jayne had been given not twenty minutes earlier at check-in.

"How do you know I've been on here before?"

"Because this is Cunard ma'am," beamed the guard and they both laughed.

A warm feeling exuded from the reception committee of officers and crew, who greeted them like old friends.

Indeed, they immediately recognised some faces, even though it was twelve months since they had made a similar fourteen-day honeymoon return trip from Southampton to New York.

This year their itinerary was a little bolder than before.

It had been chosen by Jayne who thought the place name of one destination sounded sexy, for she had always wanted to visit that country.

They would sail from Queen Mary 2's home port of Southampton to Lerwick, in the remote Shetland Islands off Scotland, then on to sexy Reykjavík in Iceland, before going on to Halifax in Canada.

Finally, they would sail to New York from where they would fly back to the United Kingdom two weeks later.

It was immediately evident that a Cunard voyage was a special one, a five-star experience where you were cossetted, served, entertained, and looked after by a "house of many nations," who the company treated as one big family.

Jayne was overcome with emotion at her return to the world's only true ocean-going liner.

"I won't be flying to the USA again, because in future I'll be sailing on the Queen Mary 2, there and back!"

Sam smiled.

"Is it because you like this ship, or because you can take a dozen pairs of shoes and as many clothes as you like?"

"I wouldn't like to say, but I think I'd travel on here with just a pencil case for luggage, this is my favourite ship in the whole world!"

The inner sanctum of the Mary was as equally classical and striking as the elegant, iconic lines of the exterior, where the large red funnel acted as a warning to others that her architectural beauty and sleek persona, announced that not only was she the flagship of the legendary Cunard line, but that she was also the world's most famous cruise liner.

Sam was fascinated by the look and feel of the ship.

"Did you know it was built in France and launched in 2003, so we missed the first dozen years, shame eh?

"It's got forty per cent more steel than any other ship afloat, that's why it crosses the wild Atlantic so much better than anything else, it sits deeper in the water and has a thicker hull, so the band can just play on through those Titanic moments!"

"Don't say that! I only retired from flying the Atlantic five minutes ago, don't frighten me and make me retire from cruising as well.

"How many passengers does it take?"

They made their way towards their cabin, knowing that their luggage, unknown to Sam, sixteen pairs of shoes included, would either be there before them, as they arrived, or shortly afterwards in typical Cunard fashion.

"Two thousand six hundred and ninety-five passengers and up to twenty-four animals, mostly dogs and the occasional cat, since a refit a couple of years back."

"Those modern ships, you know the ones that the snooty lady in the hotel last night described as "Butlins-on-Sea;" don't they carry about twice as many people?"

"Nearly five thousand, I think, with bigger ones to come, but each ship is aimed at different markets with varying tastes and interests. It works, I guess."

They arrived on deck four via stairway C and both marvelled as they looked at and remembered the incredible length of the ship's corridors.

"I'd forgotten how long these were," said Jayne pretending to pant for breath.

"The ship is three hundred and forty-five metres in length, and we've got a lot of dancing and walking to do to keep the weight off from eating and drinking!"

They were fast approaching room 4178, allocated at their request, because of its great location and proximity to the Queen's ballroom, which as dancing was their passion, was very handy.

Both were in the habit of describing this lowest-grade cabin as "the honeymoon suite," after a memorable two weeks the previous July.

"For heaven's sake, you are becoming a cruising trainspotter, I don't want to hear another fact about this ship for two weeks, but here's another question, what time are we going for cocktails?"

With that, they were in their room.

They were followed by a Cunard steward bringing their luggage from a cart that had arrived at the same time as them.

He looked pleased to be rid of the heavy bags and probably wondered why anyone would need so much baggage, but like Sam, he probably only owned three or four pairs of shoes, trainers and sneakers included.

In the blink of an eye the heavy portage was deposited, a "thank you" imparted, and the courier was on his way to the next shoe mountain.

"All these guests paying thousands of pounds for a trip on the Mary, they don't get it, do they?" said Sam.

"Get what?" quizzed Jayne.

"Well, they don't get the fact that firstly, there is so much to do that you are never in your room, and secondly, it doesn't matter how much you pay for your cabin, they all look the same with the lights out!"

She laughed and then interjected. "Oh look, brilliant, we are on first dining just as requested, and here is a bottle of champagne to welcome us back!"

"Sounds good to me, shall we go explore?"

"Not before we unpack, and you can help me this time. You never help!"

"I tell you what, let's swap roles, you go and explore the ship and I'll unpack it all."

"You must be joking, now put that large case on the bed so I can get started please, then get me some coat hangers from the wardrobe."

* * *

Once they had unpacked, they spent the afternoon wandering the ship, reacquainting themselves with the priceless works of art, the restaurants, the ballroom, the nooks and crannies, and the King's Court buffet on deck seven, where they would often go for a cup of tea to kill half an hour between activities, or for a splendid late-night supper which they had promised themselves they would not eat.

They stopped at this favourite haunt where Sam made two cups of tea and bagged window seats looking out over the dock and then spent time watching excited new passengers join the ship.

I Wish I Could Fly

Walking the corridors and stairwells they delighted in pointing out to each other the many pictures of Hollywood stars of yesteryear.

Spencer Tracy, Clark Gable, Marilyn Monroe and what seemed like a cast of thousands looked back from the hallowed miles of walls, for these were the famous people who had all travelled on the original Queen Mary to and from Europe in days long gone when regular commuting across the Atlantic by air was a thing of the future.

Occasionally they would encounter new guests, almost salivating as they stared wide-eyed at the opulence of their temporary home, already eagerly anticipating the meeting of new friends, and the adventures yet to be experienced.

Having found themselves on the third deck, they decided to walk through the shops, temporarily closed as they always were when a ship was in port, just to see what would be on offer in the coming days.

Following the winding corridor that ran both sides of the ship, they ambled towards the back end which the captain always referred to as the stern, but Jayne called the blunt end, where they could see the Britannia restaurant in which they would dine that evening.

"Remember darling, we must be at the table first, I don't want to find myself sat with my back to the room for the next fortnight!"

"I agree, even if it is a man thing," said Jayne, "it's always better to face down the room, so you can see what's happening, rather than having your back to hundreds of people."

About two hundred feet from the restaurant, they passed the hugely impressive, faux copper-like friezes on the corridor walls, that the ship's designers had incorporated in a Greco-Roman art style. These included sports scenes and famous events.

This was a favourite place to take pictures for all the guests and ship's photographers, but one frieze held the "ship's secret" that every child knew of, including Sam, who had never quite grown up, but of which most adults were oblivious.

Etched into the frieze at about four feet high or more notably, at a kid's eye height, was a cartoon character. It was about one and a half inches square on the giant artwork, and even when you knew it was there, it was difficult to find, especially if you hadn't seen it for a year.

"There it is!"

Jayne pointed it out to Sam, who had been looking completely in the wrong place to find his cartoon hero.

She paused and touched Homer Simpson on the nose. He was depicted watching his television, and the little guy moved not a muscle, for he was ingrained and trapped there by the artist, motionless for all time. Sam copied her in a childlike fashion before they continued the exploration of the Queen Mary 2.

Next, they took in the Planetarium, the only one at sea that featured stunning 3D lifelike tours of the galaxy, and later took time to study the impressive silver Samuel Cunard Trophy above the casino.

It had been personally presented to Samuel Cunard by his home townsfolk of Halifax, Nova Scotia, to celebrate the arrival of the first Cunard transatlantic ship in 1840, a voyage which began the cruise line industry.

Marvelling at the intricate work of the silversmith on the fabulous trophy, Jayne read the dedication underneath which stated that if Samuel Cunard, a denizen of Halifax, had accepted all the dinner invitations he received on the arrival of that first ship, he could have dined out every night for over five years on the trot, without a break.

"Old Sam didn't know what he started but what a guy, I love him!"

Jayne turned to her husband, her very own Sam, a commercial lawyer who at the age of thirty-two had a booming business of his own.

He was also examining the silverware and reading the sentiment below.

"Looks like I got the wrong Sam!" she said.

They both laughed.

"You are over a century and a half too late my dear, so I'll just have to do!"

As passengers who had sailed before, Sam and Jayne kept a close eye on the time, lest they get carried away and forget the most important meeting of the day, although it was hardly likely you could either miss or avoid it.

"The muster is at four o'clock, so we need to get back to the room as its 3.40 pm already," said the ever-diligent Jayne.

They returned to their cabin where they found their steward had tidied everything up shipshape and Bristol fashion in their short absence.

Kate the Filipino room stewardess, who had vigilantly been watching for their return, knocked on the door and most humbly introduced herself to them both.

"If there is anything you need, please ask or even telephone and I will help. It means a lot to make you happy. Have a good day."

With that gentle welcome, she left to assume her predetermined position under maritime law at a ship's muster station for the lifeboat drill was compulsory to all new embarking guests.

Sam and Jayne waited for the call to action by way of the long, loud, ship-wide whistle. This signalled they should go to their pre-determined muster station, one of many designated within the vessel.

They headed for station B situated in the Queen's Grill, the retreat of the top-paying guests on this cruise. Residents therein had paid ten times the price of Sam and Jayne's fare.

"Take a good look Sam; it's the last time we'll be in here on this voyage!"

Just after 4.00 pm, with just a few stragglers being guided into the room by the amazingly attentive staff, the captain began the same speech he gave on every passenger embarkation day.

The senior officer spoke of the necessary safety rules and regulations required to operate the cruise in good order and wished everyone a wonderful holiday.

At the end of the presentation, guests were compulsorily invited to try on their lifejackets, which they had all brought with them from their rooms as instructed. Sam and Jayne found it a breeze, but the usual stragglers were helped by the staff to carry out this simplest of procedures correctly.

One or two were found to be in attendance at the wrong station and some had to be woken up at the end of the captain's short speech, but most were on the ball and completed the task to the letter, before being released to waddle back to their rooms where, God willing, they would return their lifejackets to the dark recesses of their wardrobes, never to be seen again on their chosen voyage.

"We're not doing the sail away at 5.00 pm are we?" asked Jayne, knowing full well there would not be time, but just wanting some female reassurance.

"I don't think so" came the quick reply from Sam, "we need to get dressed so I suggest we let all the newbies, amateur photographers and videographers have all the space they need up there," he quipped, as he pointed upwards to an unseen vantage point several decks above.

"Anyway, we've seen it before, and we can watch it in the room when they show it on our cabin TV in the morning."

"Good point," said Jayne as they slowly descended the stairway to the stateroom that they had departed just thirty minutes before.

By the time the two had returned to their "hobbit hole", as Sam called it, thoughts had moved to freshening up and dressing for dinner at 6.00 pm sharp.

"What are we wearing tonight?" asked Jayne.

"It's casual tonight, so I'm wearing my green short sleeve shirt and my blazer with a pocket handkerchief to set it off; just enough to make a first impression on our new friends at dinner, but not enough to frighten anyone into thinking they are at a fashion show."

"What am I going to wear?" she asked, knowing exactly what she would wear all the time.

"Shoes I guess," he said, glancing at the vast array of expensive footwear on her side of the wardrobe, which somehow had also decided to take over most of his half.

"Don't be funny, I'm going to wear my green blouse and black trousers, that'll be good, it will look like we are together!" she said, accepting Sam's verbal joust and matching his sardonic wit.

"It's 5.15 pm, so if we hurry, we'll just have time for a quick aperitif in the Chart Room," added Jayne.

"If that's the case I'll be ready two minutes ago."

Sam duly made himself presentable, combed his hair and announced. "I'm ready!"

"And me!" his darling wife replied and with that, they left the room.

As they strolled arm in arm from the cabin, they heard a little voice.

"How are you sir?"

"Very well Kate, thanks, but more importantly, how are you?"

"I'm very good sir."

"No one ever asks how you are, do they, Kate?"

"Sometimes sir, have a nice night sir."

The two guests made their way to the infamous Chart Room Bar near the Queen's Ballroom, which could tell many a tale, for a white wine spritzer for Jayne, and a pina colada for Sam.

* * *

A pina colada was the only cocktail Sam ever drank, and only as his first drink of the evening before dinner on a cruise ship.

The drinks were ordered, smiles exchanged, and fellow guests acknowledged.

A trio of professional Ukrainian female musicians, dressed in glowing, flowing, sky-blue evening dresses, played beautiful classical music in the background.

It washed across the room like an ocean wave over a warm, welcoming, white sandy beach at sunrise.

"Drink up, it's 5.50 pm, time to go and meet our dinner companions for the week."

Sam downed the rest of his drink and like a pair of meerkats disappearing into a den, they made their apologies to the bar staff, with a promise to return later. They nodded at the two violinists and the cello player, and by the time they exited the bar, their warm stools had been occupied by the next two cruise and music lovers.

The Britannia Restaurant was their next stop, and they strolled arm in arm at a leisurely pace, admiring everything the ship had to offer, glancing in the now open shops with Jayne promising to Sam that she would visit them all tomorrow, whether he came with her or not.

As they passed the Greco-Roman friezes, Sam couldn't help himself touching Homer on the head for luck, whilst Jayne mockingly chastised him for interrupting the path of an overweight American couple, who looked like they wouldn't need a meal for at least the next three months.

Before they left their cabin Sam had carefully slipped the dining invitation card into his inside jacket pocket. They were obliged to carry this with them on the first evening for the attention of the maître d'hôtel in the Britannia Restaurant, to prove they were in the correct venue and to identify at which table they would be sat for the duration of the two-week voyage.

It said, "Table 267, Lower Britannia".

As they approached the restaurant three queues of people had already formed. One set of double doors was in the centre, and these were flanked by single entryways to the right and left of the ship, where hordes of waiters stood ready to guide hungry new guests to their table.

At 6 pm and not a moment before, the doors flew open in all three orifices and the hands of guests were sprayed with an anti-bacterial lotion used regularly on cruise ships to repel any hint of a virus, which could render a ship quarantined for weeks in some foreign port should an outbreak of a loathsome disease occur.

The maître d'hôtel welcomed the couple to the restaurant, expertly passing the card they gave him onto a waiter, with instructions to take them to their table in a fast-filling, increasingly busy dining room, as hungry guests began conversations with strangers at their allotted tables.

Table 267 was set for eight people just as requested, but Jayne and Sam were surprised to find that it already had six guests sitting in residence, who had been further up the queue and quicker off the mark on this first evening.

"Wow, I thought we were the early birds, this should be interesting," said Sam.

The previous year they had spent their honeymoon on board gazing at each other over a table for two, even though they had been together for ten years, but decided that although they loved each other madly, a big part of the holiday was meeting other people.

Sam and Jayne described themselves as "people, people," so they had opted for something different this time.

They had discussed the table arrangements for months before deciding a table for four was risky because they could get stuck "with some right turkeys".

Sam felt a table for six was another potential disaster, as there might be a family of four or two other couples, and they could arbitrarily be frozen out, thus defeating the object of joining others.

Furthermore, a table of ten was also a "no go", for they had observed last year that these large-sized tables seemed too overburdened and big to work socially, as people broke into subgroups, with some guests being unwittingly excluded from social interaction.

"Well, it leaves us by default with a table of eight, even if we get the odd turkey there is almost bound to be someone interesting to talk with. Let's go for the eight, shall we?"

"I agree," said Jayne.

She completed the internet form and pressed submit and it was done.

That is how they knew that all being well, it would be a table of eight on this voyage.

As Sam and Jayne approached their designated table that first evening, they were greeted by three separate pairs of strangers who looked up to inspect the final two arrivals at the table.

All six echoed the chant of "good evening," and "how are you enjoying your cruise so far?"

Two seats were available next to each other.

To the left was a man in a wheelchair, who resembled Stephen Hawking in looks. His obvious lack of motor neurone skills suggested a serious physical restriction and malfunction. Sam could not help noticing he was dribbling slightly from the right side of his mouth.

When he had said "good evening," it was lucid enough, but it came out as a mumble through clenched teeth, and you had to concentrate to understand.

He later introduced himself as Gary Schumacher and next to him sat his fully able-bodied twin brother Barry.

They both originated from the eighth state of the union, nicknamed after the indigenous tree, "the Palmetto state", for they had both been born to serious old money in South Carolina.

Once a year, come what may, even though they were now separated by employment and geography, they took a holiday together to remember the old times when life was pure fun, without the responsibilities of work or the attrition of a slow marching incurable disease, when brothers competed, laughed, and cried together.

To the right of the other available seat, and half facing them was a clean-looking, well-dressed, middle-aged lady from Derbyshire in England, with a wonderfully engaging smile, who sat next to her husband.

He later turned out to be an advertising salesman with a great range of shaggy dog stories and jokes to keep the evenings going.

The third couple was a smiley duo from the USA and as the week wore on it seemed they both had something to smile about. He was rich and she was beautiful.

Sam was a genius at getting tables of strangers bonding together. He used the oldest trick in the book. He simply asked people about themselves, because he knew it would be their favourite topic and most confident subject.

"I love that American lapel badge, now let me guess where you are from," he said to the couple opposite, and before long, the gentleman he had just addressed, delighted at being included, had told the whole table how his ancestors had sailed on the Mayflower from Plymouth in "Ingerland" with the Pilgrim fathers, followed by unlikely tales of his Irish family ancestry.

By the time dinner was over, he would have coaxed out of all the guests the details of family members, hobbies, pets, favourite films, cruises they had taken before, and a hundred other things with the consummate skill of a verbal surgeon.

Conversation flowed easily and in a balanced fashion when Sam sat at a dinner table, with everyone taking their turn at the microphone.

Gary and his brother Barry were born and raised in the famed "Gone with the Wind" country of the Deep South and their residence in the Queen's Grill hinted at their family wealth. There was a twist here, for instead of dining each evening in the exclusive Grill restaurant they had chosen to eat with the great unwashed.

When Sam enquired about this anomaly Barry confessed it was because the Britannia restaurant was a much bigger room and he felt more comfortable there with guests who behaved more naturally.

He went on to say he suffered from claustrophobia when in smaller spaces, especially if he was trapped with unwelcome, nouveau riche company. This was often the case in the heady heights of the modern first-class area of the ship, where new money tried to impress old money.

In essence, Barry said "no class meant no class" wherever those lucky suckers went on the ship, and he didn't want to hear it!

Both brothers attended the University of Atlanta where Gary studied accounting and finance and Barry majored in law.

Degenerative disability meant that Gary did not usually stray far. He still lived in Georgetown, where he had been born into a classical plantation house dynasty.

Sugar cane had long since been replaced by rolling fields of sweet grass and racehorses.

Gary was an enigma, running a multi-million-dollar storage business, living in a specially adapted home and "training" quarter horses, which was his passion, despite his obvious serious disability.

Barry had upped sticks and moved to Capitol Hill, Washington, about fifteen years before, where he vigorously pursued a career as a political lobbyist. His ambition was to one day be a South Carolina Senator.

Sam, in his cheesy way, would always refer to the two very likeable brothers as Arnie and Barnie when he and Jayne were alone, as he could never remember names very well.

He had a habit of tagging people with his very own made-up, memorable solutions to the problem.

It wasn't a criticism of Gary and Barry; it was simply Sam's lack of ability to put names to faces.

Sam suggested to Jayne that he should sit next to Gary because of the very evident disability which he feared could be off-putting at dinner, but she shrugged this off in an instant.

"No, I'll sit there!" Jayne insisted.

He subsequently felt ashamed of himself as his wife took the lead, and he humbly took the last seat next to her, on best behaviour for at least five minutes.

Sam quickly learned that the smiling lady from Derby was named Michelle, or "Camera Woman" as he would call her when he mentioned her to Jayne.

This tag came from her penchant for photographing every single food course served at the dining table each evening, before sending them on cue to her friends on social media around the world.

"These meals are a work of art, I have to photograph them for posterity, I couldn't spoil them by eating them otherwise!"

Michelle's husband was Stephen, and he seemed to be a quiet sort, but he was a bit of a dark horse and had a great personality.

It turned out that when he was a young travelling salesman selling advertising, staying away on weeknights in lonely hotels and guest houses up and down the country, he had decided to choose between drinking himself slowly to death with strangers or learning something new.

He turned his hand to magic, spending hours practising, and each night at the dinner table, to the amazement of the waiting staff and fellow guests, he did many tricks that kept everyone enthralled and entertained, and naturally attained the nickname "Magic Man" from Sam.

The remaining couple were a husband and wife from Texas.

He was a doctor named Joshua, a handsome, polite, and good-natured Californian man, who was employed at a hospital in a small town near the Mexican border, where he spent his working hours dealing with gunshot wounds and overdoses. Sam referred to him tongue in cheek as "Dr Death".

Joshua told the ensemble without boast one evening that their cabin came complete with a "butler", at the behest of his wife who wouldn't cruise without one. In reality, with some subtle questioning from the lawyer the "butler" turned out to be their room steward. All rooms came with a room steward just like Kate. The phrase the good doctor had used was what Sam called an "Americanism"!

Money seemed to be no object and Joshua's young wife was always dressed up to the nines, with immaculate make-up, show-stopping casual daywear, offset by an hourglass figure, and designer ballgowns that ensured all the other ladies could only compete for second place in the fashion stakes.

She had the enchanting name of Cherokee, an expensive wardrobe, long legs, a flashing smile, nails that had never emptied a dishwasher, and the air of someone, who despite her loveliness, had a very interesting back story that would never be told. Sam respectfully named her "The American Princess".

Later that evening Jayne bumped into Michelle in the lady's washroom, who was very obviously feeling the effects of the first night's overdose of white wine at dinner, which loosened her tongue for a second or two.

"Cherokee is beautiful, isn't she? but high maintenance, I guess. I wonder if she did an apprenticeship in a Coyote Ugly Bar back in the States?"

The statement was implicit. Jayne did not bite and changed the subject to that old favourite "the weather".

"It won't matter two weeks from now and it is none of anyone else's business," Jayne thought.

The ship sailed boldly on over the next three nights to reach the first port, whilst the table guests laughed and bonded together on increasingly relaxed evenings. The table was a social success, and everyone had worked hard in their way to make it so.

***

Out of a light sea mist, the small picturesque, castled town of Lerwick in the Shetland Islands soon loomed.

Sam went up on deck alone as the ship arrived offshore and looked through the pair of small binoculars he had brought from his room. He surveyed the horizon and took mental notes of their first destination so he could report to his wife on his return to the "honeymoon suite".

It was a gloomy, cloudy, Scottish, late July day, and he described the vista dramatically to Jayne on his return to the cabin.

"It stands like an outcast on a barren rocky outcrop to the north of the United Kingdom as if it were a condemned prisoner waiting for the last rites."

"Thanks a bunch, shall we ask for a refund?"

"I just don't want to get your hopes up, the weather is not great this morning and we have to tender ashore on the lifeboats, as the Mary is too big to get close enough to park or whatever it does in port."

"We've got all day, and we are on holiday, so we'll just have to take our chances, I'll be ready in five minutes," which meant at least fifteen.

"Do I need a coat?"

Sam feigned biting his fist, suggested she may need a light anorak and quietly got ready.

"I'm getting good at this marriage game!" he said to himself.

Forty-five minutes later, having been given a number on their arrival in the eight-hundred-seat theatre, where all the passengers going ashore had been instructed to meet, they were safe aboard one of the lifeboats which were being used to take guests to the quayside.

I Wish I Could Fly

As the bright orange, unsinkable rescue craft reached the docks, the sun came out and backlit the ancient sturdy castle that stood guard over the town, like an old nanny safeguarding her favourite charge.

The old stonework of the buildings, the traditional pubs, and the small businesses, combined with the waft of the freshest fish and chips you could ever taste, was enough to convince Jayne that Sam would never be a copywriter for a travel agency.

His early morning description could not be farther from the truth. This hidden gem was a delight, despite the intermittent, fine misty Scottish rain that haunted such a pleasant day.

Within an hour Jayne and Sam had marched up the hill, past the local council offices and places of official business of the island, hidden safely away from the tourists' prying eyes, to the delightful granite castle which had ruled from a lofty height over the bay since 1607.

Relaxing and enjoying the fine scenery and vantage point for an hour or two, Sam and Jayne took the obligatory holiday snaps which they did not upload digitally to any place at all, for they were old-fashioned like that.

As they reached the heavily cobblestoned streets on their return below Jayne let out a cry.

"Look, there's Gary on his own!"

Sure enough, Gary sat hunched over in his usual failing way, with a sort of grimace on his face, parked outside the front entrance of Boots the Chemist, and his brother was nowhere to be seen.

Jayne gravitated towards him.

"Everything ok Gary?"

"Waal, not really!"

Jayne looked suitably puzzled.

"I know where he is, he's left me here and gone up to the county hall or library or whatever they have here, so he can get on the internet properly and talk to his colleagues back home. The ship's wi-fi is too slow for him."

"Are you ok, can we push you somewhere?"

"I could really use the bathroom, but he'll be along in a minute, he just forgets time when he gets on the web, he'll be along in a minute for sure," said Gary as he tried vainly to cross his legs together to assist the control of an inflated bladder.

"You go on, he always does this, he's been gone over an hour, and he'll be back any second."

Jayne and Sam walked off as instructed along the cobbled street, looking at all the individual shops that offered unique handmade gifts, sweets, and woollen clothing.

"It's like Christmas in July, you don't see stuff like this anymore, it's all Amazon, all Chinese these days."

It didn't take them long to cover the half a mile to the end of the street and back, which ran at a higher elevation, parallel to, and some two hundred yards to the rear of the main harbour frontage.

Within forty-five minutes, under the onset of yet more drizzle, they were back outside Boots the Chemist and stood at the side of the increasingly uncomfortable Gary.

"Are you ok?" said Jayne.

Once again Gary lamented the absence of his brother.

"He'll be here in a moment for sure," he said as the rain continued to land on his unprotected head and wheelchair, whilst he was marooned there amongst the cobblestones.

"It's at times like this that being disabled is a curse. I can't walk fifty yards. What it must be like to be able-bodied like you, …………..oh I wish I could fly!"

As the words hit home Sam felt a lump in his throat, and he realised how lucky he had been in this world, as a physically fit man who thrived in all aspects of his life. This was an unexpected, humbling experience, that was heartfelt by the young lawyer.

At that precise moment, Joshua and Cherokee walked up to say hello and immediately recognised that Gary was in some distress by the contorted face, confused words, and obvious pain.

Jayne and Cherokee took over.

I Wish I Could Fly

"You'll have to do something, you'll have to find him a bathroom, the man's desperate!"

Sam responded whilst Joshua obfuscated, possibly wondering if his doctor's medical insurance covered him practising his art so many thousands of miles from home, but while he dithered, it was the lawyer who took the lead, even though he had never pushed a wheelchair in his life.

Gary's new carer took the reins of the wheelchair and then Sam remembered the words of William Shakespeare that he had scripted in the play Macbeth.

"If it were done, tis well it were done quickly!"

Grabbing the arms of the wheelchair firmly, he then rushed Gary six hundred yards over an obstacle course of cobblestones to the place of salvation, and with each rise and fall of the wheelchair, the desperate passenger squealed out loud in discomfort and pain.

Arriving at the toilet and restroom block under Sam's stewardship, skilfully signposted "Toilets" and "Washrooms" in both cruise languages by the local Scottish council, a lady attendant helped Gary into the bathroom, where he carried out his ablutions without assistance, let alone the help of the Californian doctor who was found wanting in his hour of need.

Sam took time out to think about the situation.

"How humbling it is to push a man's wheelchair; how do these people manage? I have taken so much for granted, but never again!"

In just a couple of minutes, a new Gary emerged grinning like a Cheshire cat, the relief on his face palpable.

Sam proudly assumed his preordained position behind the wheelchair, and Gary was whisked in a much more comfortable fashion back up the cobbled stones to his starting point on the grid, where Jayne and Cherokee stood waiting in case Barry turned up and wondered as to the whereabouts of his sibling.

As the five reunited and smiles went around the group, Barry came down the lane to greet them.

"What's been happening?"

Gary replied in a deep, unforgiving South Carolina accent with short, sharp, unflattering tones that his nearby heroes and heroines did not understand, but were clearly understood by Barry, who was so obviously not only on his best behaviour for the rest of the day but also on the back foot.

The rain worsened and they all decided to retreat to the comfort and safety of the resplendent Queen Mary 2.

On arriving back down the hill at the dock, just opposite the washroom area, two lines were waiting to get onto the tenders to be ferried back aboard.

The line on the left numbered about two hundred people in total with a wait time of approximately thirty minutes, but to the right, the disabled line was enjoying immediate relief, something Gary could only dream about half an hour ago.

"Come with us," said Gary to all of them as Barry took control at the helm of the wheelchair.

"I know we are family now, but I don't think we can wangle it so five people push a wheelchair down the fast lane, do you?" said Jayne.

"Waal, not really!"

The trip ashore, the bonding, and the unforgettable memories of Lerwick were complete. Exactly one-half hour after Gary and Barry had left for the ship, the four additional friends sailed back over clear water in the now sunny skies to their ocean home.

Later that evening Sam recounted the day's events once more to Jayne.

"Joshua may be good at attending victims of drug-induced warfare and overdoses, but he is not a guy you would want around when you need a push in a wheelchair. He just followed me and Gary while checking his emails.

"All I heard was "Clip clop, clip clop," as I heaved and dragged Gary like I was driving a racing car over the cobblestones, down the hill to the tourist restrooms. He yelped as each cobble imparted a shot of lightning to his bladder and Joshua just made up the numbers.

"You know something, I was so wrong about Gary," continued Sam.

I Wish I Could Fly

"Why is that?"

"What a guy, he's fantastic, I assumed when I first saw the disabled figure of a man in that wheelchair that somehow his brain was disabled too! What an idiot I've been."

"We learn something every day!"

Jayne thought for a moment she had witnessed an involuntary sniffle as they set out to the Chart Room for their aperitifs.

* * *

It was a two-week trip across to New York via Lerwick, Iceland and Halifax and during that time, table 267 became firm friends, sharing hopes, dreams and experiences born of a common zest of life.

Over the remaining eleven days, whenever Barry did his vanishing act and disappeared into the digital fourth dimension, the extremely sociable Sam and Jayne adopted Gary as one of their own.

The only time they were not at his side was during their visit to the blue lagoon, that geothermal theatre of God's excellence in sexy Iceland, which served as a private and personal experience underlining their commitment to each other a year earlier.

In Halifax, Sam wheeled Gary everywhere, checking out where the washrooms were as they arrived on the dock, just in case.

Gary's attempt at Karaoke in the Red Dog Saloon ashore at lunchtime would live with them forever. He was a star alright, but he would never be top of the musical charts.

Wherever they went Jayne would sit next to Gary and proudly introduce him as her "American boyfriend" to all she met, describing Sam as his driver, for he thrived on pushing his best wheelchair-bound buddy up and down the long corridors of the Mary towards pinheads of bright light at the other end.

One night before dinner Sam was quite philosophical.

"You know darling, I am truly humbled, to think I didn't want you to sit next to Gary lest you be embarrassed by him or catch something. I just don't know what I was thinking. He's so much fun!"

"Judge not lest ye be judged!"

Gary, with unexpected friendships and personal assistants, now thrived in the perfectly safe environment of the cruise ship.

He attended every daily quiz in the Golden Lion pub on the third deck, with both Sam and Jayne in tow, and occasionally Barry, when he wasn't on the internet.

One day he had everyone in stitches when he addressed the assembled crowd.

"Waal, I go to a quiz in our local bar back home every Friday and I tell you, it's a rough joint. The first time I went there the quizmaster's first question was "who are you looking at?"

His fellow quiz fans were beside themselves with laughter.

Jayne took him to water painting classes and in no time, he was at it again. The group of budding artists were asked to paint a copy of the world's most famous painting, The Mona Lisa.

Gary's effort was not something to boast about and easily set the lowest bar in terms of quality.

His very serious French painting instructor inspected his masterpiece and turned his nose up.

"I thought you said, Moaning Lisa! She was my first wife and with every brushstroke, I kept thinking of the alimony I'm still paying her!"

Once again, the crowd was crying with laughter, except for the Parisian artist in residence who missed the joke.

His last assault on the craft, hobby and pastime world was an unlikely one.

Once more, he went with Jayne to flower arranging. It was a high-class affair costing just over fifty dollars to join, and places were rare and exclusive.

She had been waiting for it to be discreetly advertised all week, and as soon as she saw the notice, she added her name and Gary's also, at his insistence.

Jayne, with a little help from the instructors, proved to be a natural, while Gary, with contorted fingers limited in dexterity, struggled to make anything of beauty, even with the best of assistance, yet he surprised everyone with his positive reaction for he was far from downbeat.

"It's a lesson to me I guess, I'm going to get rid of the flowers in the front garden at home, and put in some concrete seeds instead, even I should be able to manage them!"

His humour in the face of adversity, all the while knowing that things would only ever physically get worse, was inspirational to all, and aided by Sam and Jayne he made many friends along the way.

* * *

On the last but one night, the ship's company held the world-famous Cunard Black and White Ball where everyone dressed up in tuxedos and evening dresses.

The men all looked the same, like handsome penguins who had all been through the same shower, the only noticeable difference being the colourful bowties and pocket handkerchiefs on display, as cock birds competed for attention.

In the beauty and elegance competition, with the exclusion of Cherokee who was a class above, the women jousted in a far more ostentatious way, gilded in their finest jewellery, and lightly fragranced with their favourite, expensive perfumes.

On this, the penultimate evening, before the ball could get underway, they all met for the traditional "farewell meal".

This was a strange cruising misnomer, for the final night would be the following evening, but that would be a very casual affair with finery all packed away by socially exhausted, soon-to-depart guests.

The evening was a true extravaganza. The chef's culinary delight of choice, beef wellington, was followed by the traditional parade of the ship's executive chefs, who carried "baked Alaska" around the dining room, whilst everyone waved serviettes and cheered.

In the restaurant they had come to know so well, there was not a table within a hundred feet of them that did not know who they were, for their fame had spread on a gentle, soft, joyous, happy wave throughout the dining room.

Gary, with his southern charm, and infectious personality, was undoubtedly the brightest star, making everyone feel a little bit better about themselves, just for knowing him.

At dinner that evening, Sam, the dinner table chairman, noticed his new best friend Gary was a little bit left out of things, and as this was technically their last hurrah, he wanted to make sure he was fully included.

Just after the main course, whilst waiting for the waiter to take the dessert order Sam asked Gary a question.

"Heh Gary, so what do people do back down there in South Carolina for entertainment?"

"Waal" Gary responded, and at that point, it happened, the pause.

Not from Gary, but from the whole room.

For some unfathomable reason, everyone, as sometimes happens, ended their conversations, thus making Gary's words louder and more important. They were the only audible noise in the restaurant and every single man, woman, and waiter eavesdropped intently.

"Waal, what do we like to do back there in South Carolina?"

He then repeated it as if for the benefit of anyone in the listening crowd who may have missed the title of his speech the first time.

"Waal, what do we like to do back there in South Carolina?"

The room closed in a little, but Gary hadn't noticed, whilst everyone else on the table had, as they focused in on the disabled social giant, the absolute epicentre of attention.

"Waal Sam, I tell you what we like to do back there in South Carolina," he stated quite clearly, followed by a discernible pause, as the crowd anticipated his reply.

"We like to shag."

Sam almost choked on his wine, while Jayne's face was a picture.

The room of fellow guests, stretching out in concentric circles around the centrepiece of entertainment heard every word. They sat with

I Wish I Could Fly

mouths opened wide as they looked at this polite, well-mannered, southern gentleman who had just announced to the world, that shagging was one of his favourite pastimes.

Gary picked up on the vibe.

"Do you know what shagging is?" enquired Gary.

Jayne cringed, for she knew Sam could be a devil when roused.

"I'm from Wales, let me assure you I've got a fair idea!" he said comically, as Gary picked up on the attention he was now receiving.

"We like to do it on the beach!" said Gary.

The people at the table behind were crying with laughter, shock, and amazement, whilst Sam kept a straight face.

"Do it on the beach?" repeated Sam.

"Yes, it's the State dance!"

The dining room rocked with laughter, and everyone applauded.

Sam stood up and addressed the whole assembly.

"Ladies and gentlemen let's hear it for Gary!" and once more they clapped with some guests rising to their feet to give him a standing ovation.

Everyone who had experienced the company of this son of South Carolina reached for their handkerchief. It was a full minute before good order was restored and the waiters could go about their business.

The small, contorted, disabled man in the rickety wheelchair, from whom life was ebbing slowly and cruelly away, had been prised out of the shadow of his able-bodied brother to a place of bright sunlight.

At that moment Gary was the tallest, happiest, strongest man in the room, with his joy being measured by a smile as wide as the Mississippi river itself.

In total respect, and now openly wiping tears from his eyes, Sam turned to his friend Gary.

"Hey big guy, you are as free as a bird, spread your golden wings and fly away!"

Jayne cried.

About the Author

Kevan Eveleigh is an author living in Wales in the United Kingdom.

He is available by request to speak at book clubs, writing groups, and society meetings.

If you would like to comment on one of his stories or simply engage with the author then please contact him as follows:

E: info@kevaneveleigh.co.uk

W: www.kevaneveleigh.co.uk

Printed in Great Britain
by Amazon

cf9f63b1-a948-4c4e-b98f-56eb9e90cb34R01